MYSTICS ON THE MOUNTAIN

Riders of Dark Dragons Book I

C.K. RIEKE

Books by C.K. Rieke

Riders of Dark Dragons I: Mystics on the Mountain
Riders of Dark Dragons II: The Majestic Wilds
Riders of Dark Dragons III: Mages of the Arcane
Riders of Dark Dragons IV: The Fallen and the Flames
Riders of Dark Dragons V: War of the Mystics

The Dragon Sands I: Assassin Born
The Dragon Sands II: Revenge Song
The Dragon Sands III: Serpentine Risen
The Dragon Sands IV: War Dragons
The Dragon Sands V: War's End

The Path of Zaan I: The Road to Light
The Path of Zaan II: The Crooked Knight
The Path of Zaan III: The Devil King

By Sword and Sea: A Novella

Copyright

This novel was published by Crimson Cro Publishing
Copyright © 2020 Hierarchy LLC

All Rights Reserved.

Cover by Chris Rieke.

All characters and events in this book are fictitious.
Printed in the United States of America. No part of this book may be used or reproduced in any manner whatsoever without written permission except in the case of brief quotations embodied in critical articles or reviews.
This book is a work of fiction. Names, characters, businesses, organizations, places, events and incidents either are the product of the author's imagination or are used fictitiously. Any resemblance to actual persons, living or dead, events, or locales is entirely coincidental.

Please don't pirate this book.

Sign up to join the Reader's Group
at CKRieke.com

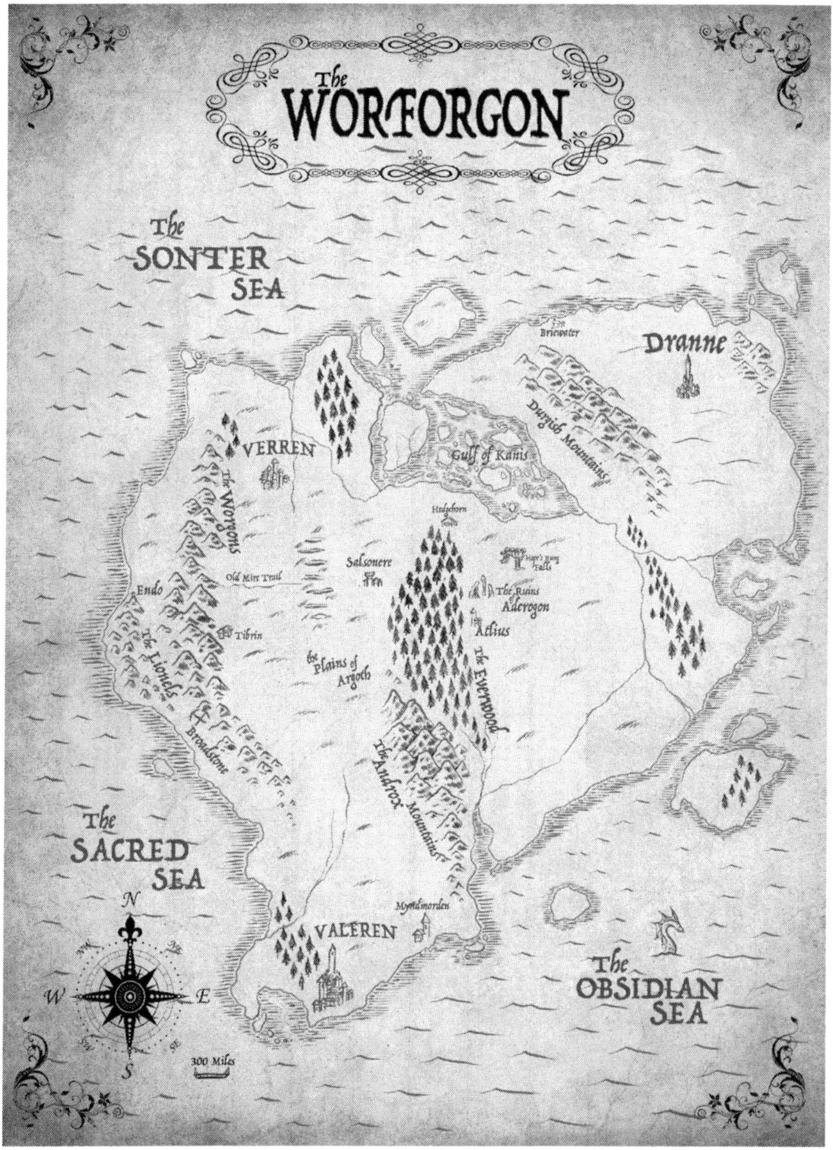

The WORFORGON
The SONTER SEA
Briewater
Dranne
VERREN
Gulf of Kanis
Durgish Mountains
The Worgons
Hedgehorn
Salsonere
Old Mitt Trail
Endo
Tibrin
The Lionels
Broadstone
the Plains of Argoth
The Ruins of Adcrogon
Atlius
The Everwood
The Androx Mountains
Myndmorden
VALEREN
The SACRED SEA
The OBSIDIAN SEA
N
W
E
S
300 Miles

PART I
BORN OF DIRT

Chapter One

There's a saying in this part of the world and no one knows if it even contains the original meaning: *Though in life struggles create the man, in death; those struggles, define the man.* But for some, death is not the end. And in this part of the world, where there is life, there is always struggle.

A rumbling noise like muffled thunder filled the dark, stagnant air. It came again seconds later, this time louder, causing the air itself to surge with vibrations. It was black, as black as black can get. Like the sun had burned out ages ago and the secret of fire had been wiped out by the gods themselves.

But in this darkness, there was a man. His limbs were sore, his mouth dry, with bits of musty, black dirt on his lips, and he was stirring as he lay on his back. His eyes were open, but he wasn't sure in this pitch-black darkness.

Am I blind? Where am I? How did I get here?

The sound above roared again, this time shaking the man's bones. He could feel the raw power from the sound, like a volcano exploding with hot, molten lava pouring down. In fact, the man could feel a warmth beginning on his chest and torso.

He lay on his back, he was certain of that by the scratchy wood on his elbows. His limbs felt as if they've been asleep far too long, as his fingers filled with pins and needles as he moved them, stretching them out, and feeling the wood beneath them. He groaned, then pressing his elbows firmly down into the wood, he attempted to lift himself up. His forehead hit that same, splintered wood mere inches above. It hit with a dull *thump*, and he fell back to his original resting place.

Any pain he felt from hitting his head was quickly replaced with a new, intense worry. In the complete, lonely darkness, his hands and legs moved around, scanning for what his eyes couldn't see. Then the realization set in, this was indeed a lonely place.

Oh no, I'm in a box. Not a box, this is a fucking coffin… I've got to get out. I've got to get out! The man gritted his teeth, as tears of worry formed at the corners of his eyes. He shook the tingling sensation out of his hands and feet, getting his blood to move. His chest heaved as he took deep breaths.

There's got to be a way, I've got to get out of here. I can't die in here…

He pounded his fists on the wooden ceiling as hard as he could, but the lid was on tight, and hardly moved from the hits. He turned to his side, forcing his shoulder into the top, trying to spread his chest and arms out as wide as they could go. He held his breath as he pushed with all his might, letting out a loud groan as beads of sweat rolled down his forehead, but the lid didn't budge. He pressed on though, heaving with every ounce of strength in his body.

The roars overhead filled the black air as he sobbed.

"Help me." He struggled to get his hands to his face to wipe the tears away. His elbows hit the sides of the rough wood, he bent his wrists upward, and he pulled his shoulders into his chest to get them up. "Somebody, please help me… I don't want to die in here. I don't want to die alone."

Minutes passed, as his mind struggled to find another way out. There had to be a way out, after all, no person deserved to die like this. So, he yelled out in the darkness. His voice reverberated in the coffin, filling the void. As he yelled out, begging and pleading for help, his voice grew raspy, and his eardrums buzzed.

"Help me, please! Anyone? Can you hear me? I'm stuck, I don't know how I got here but, someone, anyone, please…"

But nothing happened, and no one called back. He could be six feet underground, or in a morgue on a table, or in the deepest, darkest cave in all the lands. Out of pure frustration and determination not to die in this hell, he balled his fists and beat them again against the top of the casket. He kicked his legs and boots up and down as hard as he could. It was a wild tantrum of desperate blows. He couldn't tell if he was doing any damage even, he just wanted out. He *needed* to get out.

Then, he felt something strange on the top of his right hand; he could feel the wet blood trickling down his knuckles, but dirt seemed to be sticking to the blood. He reached up and felt the wood had cracked, and dirt was now sifting into his casket like sand in an hourglass. Not only that, but the dirt felt warm to the touch. That was unusual but perhaps it was a good sign there wasn't much dirt above, because maybe the sun was warming it. At least that was what he *hoped*.

The roar above came in this time with monstrous energy, shaking the wood around him. He looked around nervously in the darkness as his heart pounded heavily in his ears with a thick *thump thump, thump thump*. He had no idea what the sound above was; it almost sounded like a battle was happening. He imagined catapults launching fiery explosives onto a battlefield, *perhaps that could be what was causing the noise?*

Whatever was happening overhead didn't really matter to him though, he could deal with whatever that was, when—and if—he could get out of the prison he was in.

So, again, he yelled. He yelled as loud and for as long as he could. He took in deep, long breaths and let them back out in raspy, strained cries for help. He beat against the top of the casket with his boot and fists again. He screamed for so long, it felt like it had been a half hour, but perhaps it was more like five minutes. Then he fell back and wept once again. His body was fatigued, his head ached, his throat was sore, and his spirit was crushed. He sobbed with his head to the side, he felt as helpless as a newborn babe; he had no power to overcome his fate. He'd either die of thirst or lack of air soon, he thought. He really didn't even know how there was air in the coffin, but whatever was in there, was going to run out soon, he knew.

His mouth was dry, and his tongue was gritty as it moved to the top of his mouth. The taste of dirt still lingered around his mouth, and now he could taste the saltiness of his tears as they streamed down his face.

This is it… This is where I'm going to die…

The sound of that familiar, muffled roar shot out over him again, but he just continued to sob. The sound however, felt different this time… he couldn't tell why. It was more distant now, but there was a trailing sound after the roar faded, it was like a light thumping sound, muted and barely audible in his already-ringing ears, but it was there.

He felt as if his eyes were wide open as he focused on the sound, and his mouth was agape. His body was completely motionless as his head was slightly raised from the floor of the casket. Every ounce of his body was focused on that thumping sound. Hearing the roar again, this time more distant, he didn't flinch, as he continued to listen to the constant sound above that hit with a rhythmic beat.

"Hey! Anybody out there? I need help, I need—" He stopped short as the noise rang out clearer and clearer. It was not only getting louder; it was getting sharper. The roar rang out again, muffled, yet still powerfully terrifying. The rhythmic, cutting sound was getting closer, and the man inside the coffin beat upon it with a wild fury now, that was until…

As the sound had gotten louder and louder as it approached, all that halted as the familiar sound of metal hit the top of the coffin. It was as glorious a sound as he'd ever heard in all his life. The sound above had stopped, and the man's heart raced. Blood rushed to his chest and shoulders as he inadvertently held his breath, waiting to hear what would happen next.

In the darkness, there was a pale silence, a nervous silence that seemed to last far too long. Then, as quickly as it faded, the sound above picked up again, this time though, it was quicker. Mixed in now with the cutting sound of metal into dirt, the man heard the long scraping sound of that same metal dragging across the wood. Then he saw it… that one thing that was so gone and distant he thought he may be already dead… he saw light.

It crept into the interior of the coffin light a ray of light from the Golden Realm itself.

He felt a wide smile cross his face, and the tears formed again as he let his head fall back.

The sounds of the metal above had halted, and were replaced with a brushing sound on top of the coffin as the light streaked through, running down between the boards.

And in a voice, as sweet to him then as that of a God-sent angel, he heard a woman's voice say, "Is there someone in there?"

"Yes! Yes! I'm in here, please help me, I'm stuck."

The woman's voice paused, and he could tell she was taking in heavy breaths. "You…" she said. "You promise you're not dead?"

"I," he began, but wasn't quite sure how to respond. "I don't think so. I'm fairly certain I'm alive."

"OK," she said. "You promise? If I let you out of there

and you try to eat me, I'm gonna bash your head in with this shovel."

"Let me out, please," he said, leaning up. "I'll do anything you ask."

The tip of the shovel shot into the corner of the box, just about his waist to the right, and he heard the woman grunt. Light then poured into the box in a blinding, brilliant wash of white. He had to close his eyes as he was overcome by its intensity. As the top of the casket was lifted, with a sharp, creaking sound, he lifted both his sore, bloody hands over his face to shield himself from it.

He took nearly a minute with his eyes closed, and he groaned as he sat up, and he coughed deeply. He felt a hand pat his back as he did so, and as his eyes adjusted, he looked up at the sky, overcast and cloudy with thick, pillowy gray clouds. Then he turned and looked behind himself. His gaze was met with a pair of green eyes the color of fresh moss in a deep forest. Straight, golden hair framed both sides of those kind eyes. Her skin was pale and freckled but covered in a thin layer of dirt and dust. She held no smile on her thin lips, her look was much more confused by her furrowed brow.

"Well," she said. "You don't look like you're dead."

He smiled, letting out deep sigh of relief. "Those are the best words I could have hoped to hear from anyone." He moved to stand, but he found the side of the shovel resting on the side of his neck, its cold steel making him feel weak again.

"Don't move," she said, holding the other end of the shovel. "I don't know why you were buried like you were, but just because I got you out of there doesn't mean I'd trust you with even a hair on a mouse's ass."

His jaw dropped. "I'm not going to hurt you, you just saved me. I owe you my life."

"You owe me nothing," she said, but then raised an eyebrow, "unless… you have something to give?"

His hands scanned his tattered pants for pockets or a purse of any kind, but found nothing, slumping as she pulled the shovel back. He simply looked up at her and shook his head. He felt his long hair flowing on his back.

"Well, so long then," she said, climbing up the shallow grave, "what's your name?"

"I... My name... My name is..."

She turned back to look at him with those mossy eyes, her thin frame silhouetted by the gray clouds looming behind, as well as a round tree with most of its leaves gone and badly burned. "You don't have a name?" Her voice was high-pitched and surprised.

"My name... my name..." He raised his hands to his head to concentrate. "I don't know my name."

Chapter Two

"You don't know your name?" the blonde girl with the dirty face and deep green eyes asked. "Who doesn't know their own name?"

"I—I don't know." The man stared at his torn knuckles now dyed with deep, dark blood.

They were standing in the middle of a graveyard as the girl threw the shovel to the ground. At least, it looked as if it used to be a graveyard. Each grave marker had been badly burned, and recently from the looks of it. Gray stone had turned to black, even the names on each had been washed away by fire. The ground was black and ashen, any grass had been burned away, and the dirt was left to smolder.

What could have caused such an intense heat? There wasn't a battle going on up here... it was more like a volcano erupting...

But there was no volcano in sight, but the decrepit burned away ruins of a city. A once-mighty looking palace loomed overhead, broken and battered on its eastern side. A long staircase rolled down its front entrance, but it was severed in half, leaving only the top stairs looming over the city floor. The city itself looked like something out of an old tale told by a traveling minstrel; destroyed by invading forces, torn inside out by corruption, and burned to the ground. Endless rows of toppled, roofless stone buildings and houses lay in rubble. The palace was hundreds of yards off, and looking around further, he saw forests to the west, and fields of grass before the mountains to the south. A large hawk with white feathers at the tips of its wings cawed as it flew overhead with a snake in its talons.

"My name." He scratched the sides of his head with his dirty hands. "Why can't I remember my name?"

He stood there, taller than the girl, but under the speckled dirt his skin was pale, almost stark white. His face was lean, but muscular at his square jaws. Thick eyebrows of black hair ran over his gray eyes, and his hair was pulled back messily into a wicker band, and he had a deep widow's peak that cut down his forehead. The man was perhaps sixteen or seventeen, near the girl's age, and all he had in that moment were the clothes he was wearing: a white, thin linen shirt, a black sash around his waist, tan cloth pants and a pair of leather boots that ran up halfway to his knees.

The girl let out a snarky laugh. "Who doesn't know their own name? That's a first… well…" she scratched her chin. "Who gets buried alive?"

"I—I don't think I was buried alive," he said, looking back at the hole in the ground the girl had just dug to save him. "I don't know though…"

She looked over at him with a smirk and a wink. "You don't know much of anything, do you?"

He glanced up at her with hard eyes. "I know that you saved my life, and I'm in your debt."

"You go on and stop about that," she said, with her arms out at her sides. "It was pure luck I dug you up, you don't owe me anything… well… I mean, since you have nothing to give." She looked south and began to walk away.

"Wait," he said, following after her. "Where are you going?"

"I'm going where I was going before I met you, the nameless one buried in the ground," she said, not looking back.

He stumbled after her with his weak legs. "What's your name?"

She stopped walking, letting out a slight sigh, then turned around to meet his gaze, her green eyes flashing a wild deep, grassy color. "Ceres."

He ran up to her side, looking down south to the mountain range cast in a blue hue.

"Ceres, nice to meet you," he said with his hands on his hips, taking in a deep breath. "I—I have so many questions… I don't even know where to start."

"You can start by asking someone else," Ceres said as she continued her walk out of the graveyard and down a cobbled road, leaving the broken city behind.

"Listen," the man said, walking with her, "I'm not going to burden you, I just… just let me accompany you until we get to a city. I'll find a way to make it up to you… I swear it… and well, I have no idea where I am either… if that's OK with you?"

She stopped again, looking him up and down. "Well, aside from being a bit funny lookin', you seem harmless enough. I'm going down south to Atlius, you're going to have to find your own food. You any good at hunting?"

He gave her a blank expression with a raised eyebrow.

"Let me guess," Ceres said. "You don't know?"

He shrugged.

She let out a deep sigh. "You're going to be a bundle-full of conversation, aren't you?"

"I think things will come back to me," he said, almost to himself. "I hope so at least."

"Well, first off, I'm not going to call you the nameless one," she said, looking at him with a playful gaze. "So... what are we going to call you?"

He looked around and down at his feet, trying to remember his name, and seriously questioning if he ever even had one.

"Well?" she pressed.

"I don't even have the slightest idea of where to start with naming myself." He looked up at her for some guidance.

"Peter?" she asked. "No, you don't look like a Peter... Robert? No." She crossed her arms over her chest and looked back to the hole in the ground with the burned away marker over his corpse, with the name erased by fire. "How about... Gravestone? That's unique, and if anything, you are unique."

"Gravestone?" He mulled it over, scratching his stubbly cheek. "Seems a bit grim, don't you think?"

"Maybe, how about just Stone then?" she asked, her eyes wide, as if she were proud of herself for coming up with it.

"Stone?" he said to himself, deep in thought. "I don't hate it. That'll work for now, until I can remember who I really am."

To the right of the cobblestone road was a narrow stream less than a meter wide, and Stone ran over to it, and as it looked clear enough, he cupped his hands together, kneeling down and brought it up to his mouth, letting the cool, crisp water coat his dry mouth and run down his sore, parched throat. He couldn't remember the last time he'd drank water. Perhaps it was the first time, but no, he thought that was a foolish thought. It wasn't as if he'd just been born, he was well in his teens, he just couldn't remember... well, anything.

He let out a satisfied, relieved sigh, wiping the water off his chin, turning back toward Ceres, who stood behind on the road, seemingly amused and anxious at the same time to be on their way again. Her hand was on the grip of her dagger on her hip, and her foot tapped impatiently on the stone.

"Ceres," he said, letting out a deep breath after inhaling so much water. "How did you find me? How'd you know I was underground there? I'm sure you don't make it a habit of digging up graves?"

A curious expression went across her face then, as her lips pursed, and her eyes narrowed. "That, Stone, is something I've been thinking about ever since you came out of that coffin alive. Let's walk and I'll tell you. I am hungry, and the sooner we get to Atlius, the sooner I—we—can have a real meal. I'm sure you're famished. Who knows how long you've been down there… and who knows when that mad dragon is going to be back…?"

"Did you just say… dragon?"

Chapter Three

"You have been underground." Ceres shook the dirt from her hair, now growing blonder as the soot fell. "Yeah, I said dragon. Couldn't you hear that bloody thing?"

He nodded. "I did but didn't know what it was. I wasn't underground that long, actually. It's as if I'd just woken up."

"You know that gravestone looked pretty old," she said. "I don't know what that means, but… you don't remember anything?"

Stone shook his head. "Trust me, I wish I did. I have so many questions floating around in my head, and not a single answer for any of them. I feel like I've lost my mind." He clutched the sides of his head with his bloody hands.

Ceres walked over and touched his back. "I'm sure you'll get some answers… Do you think… its possible, that maybe… you were dead?"

He was horrified by the thought. *No one comes back from the dead. Everyone knows that. The Dark Realm and Golden Realm were it—the final adventure—there was no coming back once there.*

"I'm not saying it's possible." She drew her hand back and

looked up at the gloomy sky. "But you were buried there a long time. There was grass over you, before the dragon burned it all away."

They walked together southbound with a warm wind blowing across from the west. The smell of singed dirt wafted past, the sky hung powerfully behind the thick cloud cover, waiting for its moment to bare bright sunlight upon the vast lands. Stone walked next to Ceres, his mind brimming with a jumbled array of flashing questions. He found it soothing to watch his feet move step by step as they walked. After all, it wasn't that long ago he couldn't even see his feet. How good did it feel to be above ground again? A wide smile crept across his face.

He felt a strong presence from such a young girl. There was something special about her, something he couldn't put his finger on, but something deep inside of her made him feel safe. She'd saved him, and he'd do anything he could to protect her.

"Why are you looking at me that way?" Ceres furrowed her brow.

He was instantly caught off guard. "Uh, well, I just haven't seen… anyone… in a long, long time."

"You'd better hold it together," Ceres said. "I'm only taking you to Atlius. I don't do comradery." She looked him square in the eyes with wild, fiery green eyes. "Don't be getting attached."

He feigned a smile and looked back to his feet as he walked. "Ceres, you never told me how you ended up finding me."

She sighed. "I'm still trying to figure that one out. I don't make it a point to dig up graves often. Even for the treasure."

"Could you try?" he asked. "After all, I'm only above ground because of you."

"Well, I was in the Ruins of Aderogon visiting my mother

and father's graves," she said, a tinge of a quiver in her voice. "Then the dragon came…"

"I'm sorry you lost your parents," he said, looking over at her as her hair hung over the side of her face.

"Yeah, well… it happens, lots of people died back then, back when the dragons first came… after the Nefarian first appeared."

"The Nefarian?" He scratched his forearm.

"The riders of the Dark Dragons," she said, turning her head slightly, one green eye peering ominously at him. "You really don't know any of this? It must be a whole year now since they came. Keep this in mind when you're traveling around; dragon with no rider—can kill you but mostly good, dragon with rider—run for your life."

Stone didn't nod or respond; he still couldn't believe dragons were real. *Is this all a strange dream I'm in?* He pinched himself and thought of a series of numbers. *Nope, not a dream, this must be happening to me…*

"So," he said, after a long moment, "how'd you find me? You were visiting your parents, and then?"

"I was having a bit of a breakdown in front of the two markers," Ceres said. "That's when I heard its roar. It was a big one, dark red with black stripes down its back and tail. You haven't seen one yet, right?"

He shook his head.

"Its head is big enough to chomp you clean in half with its sharp teeth, its fire is hot enough to sear flesh from bone. They fly fast and are ferocious. A dragon's eyes are that of pure hunters; predators that seek only what will satiate their appetite. This one, was searching for one of the Nefarian I'm guessing… But anyways, back to what I was saying… I heard the roar of the dragon, so I searched out a place to take shelter. I was actually going to run for the burned-out castle, but then a strange thing happened."

Stone's eyes were fixed completely on her as the rays of sunlight lay a golden aura upon her.

"What at first I thought was a hummingbird with pale, blue wings darted past me, right in front of my eyes! I shooed the thing away at first, but then it came back to me, this time hovering right in front of my face. But I could clearly see it was no bird, it was…" she gulped. "Well, Stone, I think it was a fairy."

"A… fairy?" Stone paused in place on the cobblestone path.

Ceres stopped, turned to face him squarely, and nodded. "Tiny person body, completely naked with butterfly wings. You know… A fairy?"

He laughed, a deep hearty laugh. "Well, I didn't believe in dragons until a couple of minutes ago, I guess I can believe in fairies now too."

"Trust me," she said with a slight smile, "I didn't believe in them either until I saw this one."

"So, you saw a fairy," he said, "then what?"

"You won't believe this." Ceres shook her head. "But the thing pointed me to your grave… it pointed to you…"

"You can't be telling me the truth," he said, folding his arms over his chest. "How'd you really find me?"

"Believe me or not, but I'm telling you the truth."

He sighed. "Well, I'm grateful to whatever it was. Go on."

"I saw it, and couldn't believe it, so even with a red dragon flying the skies, I followed it, after all, they're supposed to be good luck. At least that's what my mother used to tell me when I was young."

"You followed it to me?" Stone asked with his hands out.

She nodded. "But that's when the dragon came. It had been burning the city, but its wings had shifted, and it was coming toward me. I ran as fast as my legs could carry me to the backside of the broken wall at the west side of the graveyard. And I only made it just in time, as the dragon burned the whole place with just one breath."

"I thought you said the dragons without riders were good?" Stone asked.

"Not good," she said, looking back at the decayed state of the once brilliant capital city of Aderogon. "Just not as bad as the riders. A dragon is a dragon. There's no sense trying to figure out why a dragon does what he does. They can do whatever they want. You'll see when you see your first one. You'll never feel so powerless."

"I don't know," Stone said in a grim tone. "I felt pretty powerless stuck in that coffin."

"When the dragon was far enough away, the fairy came back to me, urging me to follow it back to your gravestone," she said. "I did once I thought it was safe enough. The trees and bushes of the graveyard were burning, and the ground was still hot. But the fairy had an urgency in her pupil-less, black eyes. Standing by your marker, I didn't know what to do. I didn't know why the fairy had led me there, and as it spoke, it only came out as high-pitched chirping sounds. Not at all like a bird though, it was like a beautiful voice singing a soft melody. I looked around, not finding anything out of the ordinary. That was when I began to doubt the fairy, and doubt myself. I even started to walk away, but the fairy flew in front of me again, and as I watched it fly past it flew closer to the ground and sang with its chirping. This time, it was pointing to the ground."

"You followed it?" Stone asked, and she nodded.

"The dirt was still hot, and the smell of burnt grass was strong on it, but I went over, and lowered my ear to it. Nothing at first," Ceres said, "but after a couple of moments, listening to the ground and watching the fairy as it watched me anxiously, I did hear something… I heard you…"

Stone breathed out a heavy sigh of relief. He looked up to

the sky. "Thank you," he said clasping his hands. "Thanks to the gods for letting her hear my calls."

"I couldn't make out what you were saying," she said, "but there was something down there making noise. Not a single part of me wanted to dig up a corpse. But the look in those damned black eyes of the fairy, and its urgently pointing down to it, made me think of my mother and of how highly she'd spoken of their good luck in her old tales."

Stone smiled a wide smile.

"I'd seen a shovel resting against the back of that wall I'd hidden behind, so I went and grabbed it. I may have said some curse words, but I sent that shovel into the dirt, and I dug. And... that's it. That's the story. Seems strange saying it out loud. As if I'm confirming this strange story in my head. But that's how it happened. I ended finding some pale-skinned, weird-looking boy alive in a coffin four feet underground."

"Weird looking?" he asked, running his fingers along the sides of his face.

Ceres pulled her pack down from her back and rummaging around the side pocket of the leather bag, she produced a small, four-inch piece of what first looked like glass that reflected strong sunlight off it. She handed it to him, her expression was blank as she looked up at him.

"Go ahead," she said. "You don't know your name. I wonder if you know your face."

He took it from her, and as he held it up before his face, he knew then that she was right. Stone didn't recognize the face in the mirror. He was mesmerized. It was like growing up to be a young adult, and never once having seen your own face. His gray eyes looked back at him with a foggy look, a sort of uncertainty. Beyond the dirty, pale white skin, the hairline that dipped down to a sharp point, and the longing eyes—he looked... somber."

"What do you think?" Ceres asked with a pleasant tone. "Weird looking, huh?"

"If you say so," Stone said. "It is most certainly weird seeing a face I don't recognize as my own."

"You'll get used to it," she said. "We all do. In fact, I'm already getting used to yours, it's got… character."

"Is that a kind way of saying different?" he asked.

She looked at him, sunlight gleaming off her blonde hair as she put the mirror back in her bag with a wink.

That was when they both heard the dragon's roar return.

Chapter Four

The hairs on the back of his neck straightened, his body stuck in a moment of paralysis. Heavenly streaks of sunlight receded behind the thick, gray cloud cover. He and Ceres scanned the sky together, neither speaking a word. Although he saw nothing, that roar high above came from nowhere… There was something up there… looming, monstrous, and its roar rang far clearer than it did before when he was deep in the ground.

Then something out of place came through the clouds, dipping just below them—it was a long shadowy body with wings spread out wide. At that height it was difficult to tell how big the creature was, but he could see the unmistakable long neck and tail of the beast as it flew high overhead. He'd never seen a dragon, but he felt he'd heard enough stories of them from somewhere to know what they looked like.

His body was still in a state of panic—stuck where it was. But then his head turned to Ceres, and her eyes met his. There was a wild tension in her eyes, as they glazed over, and her face turned pale. Then they both jolted to life again as the dragon roared monstrously from the sky, leaving a long echo looming through the air.

"Ceres?" Stone said.

She reached out and grabbed him by the wrist, startling him. Her face shot close to his, so close that their faces were only inches apart, and in a voice as serious as he'd heard from her, she said, "Run!"

Ceres jerked his arm as she ran south, breathing fresh energy to him, and his legs moved quickly over the cobblestone road. She let go of his arm and they both sprinted as quickly as they could. His eyes were scanning for somewhere to hide, but all he found was a toppled over stone building a few hundred yards off.

"You see it?" Stone asked through heavy breaths.

"Yep," she said, running slightly ahead of him.

The dragon screeched loudly overhead again, sending Stone's legs to motion. The stone building laying solemnly in the grassy field grew closer, but it didn't seem to be getting close enough.

"Don't look back," Ceres said, "we'll make it. Just keep going."

But Stone couldn't help himself, even with her warning. He looked over his shoulder to see the dragon sweeping down at an astonishing speed... and it was diving toward them. "Good God. It's coming right for us."

They were both panting now, running as fast as they could. She said, "I told you not to look."

The dragon was frightfully stealthy as it glided down toward them. Stone couldn't hear a thing from it as it swooped down between its mighty roars. The collapsed building was only strides off then as they ran off the road into the tall, green grass.

The building was a scattering of dark gray stones, but the four walls were still somewhat intact, but leaned at a steep angle, and the wooden roof still rested on top. They scurried in through a window at the building's base. Once inside, they found the shadowy interior not much of a shelter at all.

"You think we're safe in here?" Stone asked, wiping the sweat from his forehead.

Ceres shook her head.

Looking around at the leaning walls, Stone said, "Feels like a strong fart would knock this place clean over. I think this was a mistake."

That's when they heard the heavy landing of strong feet hit the grass next to the building. Both of them gasped, sending a heavy silence in the dim interior of the musty room. They could hear the slow, long breaths of the dragon draw in deeply, and exhale in a manner like a horse's breath, but with a deep rumble. Its wings flapped, causing Stone's knees to wobble.

Ceres dipped down slowly and carefully, kneeling, and Stone did the same. They were both peering under the window they'd crawled under. Stone could see its strong, thick muscled legs covered in black scales that held a blue shimmer in the sparse sunlight. Its claws were a pearly-white as they pawed into the ground, easily ripping through it. The dragon walked slowly, growling low. Its tail followed behind, snaking its way through the green blades.

"That the same one?" Stone whispered to her.

She shook her head. "No. This one is a different color… and smaller."

"What do we do?" he asked. "Just sit here?"

She sighed, turning her gaze away from him and looked back out to see the thick wings of the dragon rustle by. "Pray."

The dragon, almost out of view, as it appeared to be about to circle the structure, turned around, heading for the window they were looking through. He gasped, holding his breath, to not make a sound. He reached out and grabbed Ceres' hand, which she quickly embraced. They looked deeply into each other's eyes as the dragon's claws dug into the ground, now directly facing them. Then, it let out an ear-piercing roar that shook the foundation of the stone building, causing both of them to reach up and cover their ears.

I escaped a box in the ground, out of pure fortune to wind up here? To be burned or eaten by a dragon? What a cruel fate. I never even got to know my own name...

The roar faded, and the dragon outside growled again low as it had paused just outside the window. It couldn't fit through with its size, but it easily could knock that wall over, he knew.

"Thank you for saving me," Stone said, not able to look away from the dragon's claws pawing at the ground just feet away. "I only wish I could've returned the favor before this."

"Stone... I..."

Then the dragon fully paused, stuck in a long moment of tension. Stone noticed he was fully holding his breath, unintentionally, and a thick nervousness ran through him. There was something else out there, something faint, but... familiar.

The dragon's black legs shifted then, turning to the side, facing away from them.

What is that sound out there? Is that...? Is that a dog?

He looked at Ceres, who held a confused expression on her face with a furrowed brow. She seemed as confused as him. But then, as the dragon walked slowly away from the window's slit, he could see it. It was a dog. A black dog with a white chest and one white spot over its right eye. It was on the cobblestone road to the north, and it was barking wildly at the dragon.

"Brave bugger," Ceres said, "c'mon, we've got to get out of here."

The dragon was striding fluidly toward the dog as its tail slithered behind it. Stone could see the back of the dragon's head now— scaly with dozens of white spikes down the length of its neck.

"Where do we go?" he asked. "And what about the dog?"

"We'll head for the trees on the other side of the road." She crawled under the window's opening quietly.

"What about the dog?" he asked again, himself scooting under the stone wall.

"The dog's on its own," she said, "now, be quiet, but swift."

The dragon spread its wings out wide, sending out a deafening, rippling roar at the dog, who only continued to bark ferociously back.

Fearless dog. Run, run away!

Together, they crept back over the cobblestone road as the dragon neared the dog with its teeth exposed, letting out a loud growl, and the dog continued to bark with a vibrant energy. Ceres made her way into the thick brush, ducking low, but just as Stone's boots left the stone and entered into the grassy knoll before the trees, he paused.

"Hey!" he yelled, and the dragon snapped its head toward him. "Hey, leave that dog alone!" Stone walked back toward the stone building. *What in the Dark Realm am I doing?*

The dog took steps toward the dragon, continuing its frantic barking. The dragon's eyes shot back to the dog, and then to Stone. Its eyes were a vibrant yellow, with streaks of oranges and reds like fire emanating from the long, black, thin pupil.

Stone continued walking backward toward the building, not knowing what to do even if he made it back inside, but he knew he didn't want to see that dragon eat that dog.

"Hey," he yelled. "Why don't you come after something bigger than that little runt over there?"

The black dragon with the blue sheen and white horns lumbered toward him then with strong strides and its wings clutched in tightly. It opened its mouth wide, showing its long, slithering tongue and sharp teeth. It readied itself to let out a roar before it ran at him, and Stone's footing slipped as he stumbled backward over a large rock on the side of the road, and he fell to his back. Behind the dragon, the dog continued its bark.

But before the dragon let out its roar, another roar echoed out from above, startling all on the ground. Stone's worry over his own position turned to watching the dragon before him scan the sky. The dog had quit barking, looking up itself, and before Stone could get to his feet, the dragon spread its wings out wide and flapped them mightily, sending strong winds down on him. He had to shield his face with his arm and close his eyes from the dirt flying up from the road.

He managed to open his eyes after a couple of seconds to see the dragon flying up toward another shadowy figure gliding high up in the clouds. That's when he felt the sting of a boot tip crash into his shoulder. The dull pain shook him back into the moment.

"Ow! What the?"

He looked up to see Ceres standing over him with a heavy scowl on her face. "You are the dumbest person I've ever met!"

The dog was in the same spot it had been as it looked upward at the flying dragon.

"What happened?" Stone asked. "Why'd it leave?"

She glared up at the dragon flying up to the other. "That's one of them," she said with a dark tone. "That one up there, that's one of the Neferian. The dragon wants to kill it." Her green eyes shot down at him with heavy worry. "We need to leave, right now!"

Chapter Five

They hurried southbound. Even as Stone looked back over his shoulder at the dragon chasing after the other silhouetted creature his pace didn't slow. The look in Ceres' eyes had been enough to startle him into an immediate sprint. The dragon growled high up in the heavens, snarling and letting out a crackling roar. Ceres was faster than him, and he struggled to keep up with her pace. Even with his longer legs he found his lungs gasping for breath.

"Wait, wait," he gasped, his chest heaving in and out heavily as he placed a hand on his knee and waved at her with his other hand. "Just a second, just a quick second…"

She slowed and shook her head, her dirty blond hair brushing from side to side. "I should just leave you—your head must be full of wool with what you did back there." Her gaze rose over him, and past. "And what are you following us for now? Shoo! Go away!"

Stone looked behind him and saw the dog the same distance he was from them before—thirty or forty meters. The mutt stood there, looking still and vigilant. He took two small steps forward.

"Go away!" Ceres yelled again. Meanwhile, the dragon began a great sweeping arc to follow the Neferian, who was now descended with its wings outspread wide.

The beast let out its own cry—a roar that began like an explosion of fire, and finished with a long, crackling sound like a shattering of thick glass into thousands of shards. Stone's eyes were fixated on the Neferian as it shot down with frightening speed, ripping through the air as the dragon was falling behind quickly then.

"Hey," Ceres said, with her arms out wide.

He shot up. "I'm ready." His boots made quick work on the cobblestone path.

Ceres sprinted up ahead, he heard the broken roar of the dark beast behind, followed by a screeching howl. The two were intertwined in the air—scratching, biting and clawing at each other. That's when Stone saw his first Dark Rider. To him from that distance, it was just a speck on the great beast's back. And he now saw that the Neferian was larger than the dragon that had almost killed him; much larger actually. Possibly three or four times larger as the dragon howled and roared amid the brutal attack that was being laid on it.

The Neferian's head was so much larger that as it snapped its jaws, it looked as if it could fit the whole dragon's head easily in its maw. An anxious feeling grew in his stomach then for the dragon, even if it had almost just roasted him alive for supper. And if he had to pick, he'd most certainly pick for the dragon to win just from the small input Ceres had given him about the two.

As the Neferian turned from a shadowy, silhouetted monstrous beast that towered over the already large dragon, its features came into view. Its head had thick muscles on its brow and jaws, it had a crimson red head with beady, serpent-like yellow eyes that pierced. The red head gradually turned to a smooth black body, with its scales glistening like glass in the sunlight. Its wide, enormous wings that draped behind its long arms were streamed with a gold like yellow, and the flaps of the wings were colored with a matte black.

"What is wrong with you?" Ceres called back to him, now far off, as she'd apparently just now discovered that he'd stopped again. Actually, he hadn't known he had stopped either—he was so stuck in a trance at the brutal battle hovering back over the burned city.

"Well," he said, shrugging, "I did just come back from the dead. My legs aren't what they used to be…"

"You're on your own," she yelled, and started back running south again.

"Wait! I'm coming," he said as he ran again. *Don't stop. Don't stop again. She's going to leave you behind…*

A flurry of vicious roars and ear-piercing screeches continued from the two behind, but Stone had now decided—that whatever happened, he was going to follow Ceres. He had to stay with the one who'd saved him, and the one who knew these lands far, far better than he. The battle behind was just that—behind him.

Eventually, she saw that he was running again, and slowed herself a bit so that he could catch up, but she also noticed that the dog was running after them, keeping itself at the same distance as before.

"Another mouth to feed," she said, between her labored breathing.

Stone almost asked what she meant by that, but then looked back to see the dog. He let a sly grin rise on the right side of his face so that she couldn't see it.

"You know it's only following us because its thinks we have food to give it," she said.

"Well," he said. "It did sort of save us from the dragon."

"No, it didn't," she responded. "That dragon would have flown off eventually."

A great roar echoed behind them in the air.

"That dog stalled it just long enough." Stone wiped the sweat from his brow. "You know just as well as I do that the dragon could have knocked that rackety shack onto our heads with a gentle blow."

Her gaze went forward again, and she scowled.

After a long minute of running then, he asked, "How far? To Atlius, I mean."

"From Aderogon, a day and a half roughly," she said. "We're going to have to camp the night, after we get the hell away from those two."

That was when they heard the loud roar of the Neferian behind, it was a roar that broke the air itself into shattered pieces, and as much as Stone tried not to look back, once he saw that Ceres had turned her head to watch, he gave in. It was a display that shook his nerves so much he tripped, falling onto his palms, and quickly moved to his backside, shuffling backward.

The Neferian had clutched the dragon in its claws and was spewing what looked like what he thought looked like 'fiery smoke.' It was a blasting black fire, bursting with an excruciating heat as it shot out of the beast's mouth onto the head of the dragon, which writhed and flailed trying to break free. Ceres stood there with her hand over her mouth.

"Not another one," she said behind her hand in a muffled voice.

Then the black fire extinguished, and from the distance, they watched as the Neferian's sharp teeth cut into the dragon's throat, and with a strong jerk, ripped its head clean off. Its jaws released and the head went tumbling down onto the ruins of the city. The dark beast then released its grip of the dragon's body, and that plummeted just after.

Stone was stuck in that kind of horror where your limbs just seem to shut down. But the newest call of the Neferian's victorious cry sent his feet quickly back under him, and he followed Ceres, who'd already been running to the tree line. They both dove in eagerly, with Stone landing much more awkwardly than her.

"Get in deep and stay still," she whispered as they pushed their way through thick brush and sharp pines.

They'd gotten in roughly one-hundred yards, when she finally motioned for them to stop and sit quietly on a downed tree.

"That was terrifying," he said, staring at the ground between his boots. Shaking his head, with his hands clasped around it, he couldn't believe what had just happened wasn't from some story but was real. "I just have no idea what is going on. Part of me thinks this is all a dream I need to wake up from, but I'm very certain it's not."

"Trust me—" Ceres said, looking out into the shady woods. "With the way the lands of the Worforgon have gone the last few years—I wish this was all a bad dream too."

Chapter Six

✦

A squiggling earthworm lapped in a muddy pool at Stone's feet. Heavy raindrops pattered on it and his head as he sat by the fire, as it struggled to stay alive. His entire body was soaking wet, that kind of wet that was impossible to remove unless you're indoors with a clean set of clothing. It was the kind of wet where he may as well have been laying himself in a pond.

Hours had gone by, and in the dimly lit clearing surrounded by tall oak trees, cool winds whistled through their makeshift camp. Ceres sat at the other side of the fire, staring coldly into it with her normally vibrant green eyes now a darker shade like that of thick, shady grass. The dog was there too, laying back in the tree line, surely just as wet as they.

Stone was miserable to say the least. He was happy, and felt lucky to be alive, but it was still only the early part of the evening then. They had all night still to sit in their wet clothing; waiting for the light of the warm sun to give them any semblance of relief, because lord knows that measly fire wasn't doing anything.

They'd returned to the cobblestone road and continued

after they felt the Neferian had flown back off east from its calls. Once the sun had begun its descent and cupped the horizon, they wandered back into the brush, finding this small clearing, still covered by the many layers of leaves overhead. But once the storm rolled in, the soft, dry grass was now a soupy mess of scattered puddles.

Ceres offered him a handful of stale bread once the fire had been started, but now they were stark out of food. He felt honored to have been offered anything at all. She still seemed annoyed by his actions throughout the day—their first day together… Maybe not annoyed, he thought… more like confused or bewildered. There hadn't been enough food for the dog, but Stone hoped that he'd been able to find something for himself along the way, and hopefully hadn't succumbed to eating any of those bulbous white mushrooms that were scattered throughout the forest floor.

His eyes crept up from the wriggling earthworms at his feet to the blond-haired girl on the other side of the fire with a thin hood held up over her head. He saw that she was shaking from the wet cold. He thought of her then as the one that saved him, and he wanted to help, so he stood and walked over to her; his boots squishing in the mud with the deluge above running through the thick leaves and falling in heavy droplets all around.

"Here. If we sit next to—"

"Don't you dare even say it," she interrupted.

"I didn't mean anything by it." Stone took a step back. "I only saw you were cold, and myself too."

"If you even dare touch me with those wet hands, yer gonna lose 'em."

"All right, all right," he said with his hands up. "No ill intention meant; I was just trying to help."

She finally looked up at him with a glare that made him question his own intent. "Any time a boy your age wants to offer help by touching, what other intent is there?" She groaned, looking back down to the fire and casting wet kindling onto it. "Always thinkin' with that stick in yer trousers."

"What?" he gasped. "That's not true at all!"

She gave a bored sigh, and then he slunk back over to his spot as the heavy rains continued, they even seemed to pick up then.

There was a long pause as he listened to the droplets hit the fire, each making a soft *hiss* as they landed.

Then, the stark reminder of the danger out there revealed itself from the distant echo of a terrifying screech of the Neferian out there. Stone was astonished that such a dragon could have been killed so violently by that monster. And as the Neferian let out that roar from wherever it was, the lasting trail of its brittle-glass sounding call left even the raindrops afraid to make noise when they landed. Everything was still and silent as the monster roared. Then the noise faded off like a distant nightmare after waking up to a soft pillow and blanket.

"I didn't think he was still around." Ceres scratched the sopping wet fabric on her shoulder. "Thought they'd be long gone by now."

"How many of those things are out there?" Stone asked.

"Who knows." She sighed. "Ten? A hundred? A thousand?" She leveled her eyes to his. "One thing I know fer sure... they never die."

Stone sat up straight—startled—not knowing what to say. So, she answered his unasked question...

"Yes, Stone, you dimwit, they don't die. The dragons... they keep going after 'em, and they keep dying themselves. No one knows why. No one knows where either the Dark Riders or the dragons came from, we're just stuck in the middle of this new war."

He still longed to ask a question, or make a statement of any kind to her, but his mouth refused to move.

"You're quite the poet you know that?" she asked, laughing. "But I'll say it, right out flat, I prefer a boy who'll learn to keep his lips shut o'er one that can't keep 'em closed ever."

"Thanks," he managed to say finally.

That night was a long, miserable one. The rains let up eventually in the wee hours of the night, but the cold had already sunk its claws into both of them. Sleep was fleeting, even with the heavy fatigue each of them carried. Stone's eyelids felt like thick wet cloth lay over them, forcing them down slowly, making it more and more difficult to keep them open. He didn't want to though—he wanted to sleep, but sitting up upon that fallen tree, up off the muddy ground, there was nowhere to lay his head comfortably. Especially nowhere dry.

Finally, when the sun had finally decided to creep back out of her slumber, that was when the rains decided to slip away—leaving a rather thick air hanging around them in the brush. To his side though, as he sat up with his back to the log, he felt a heavy, soft thing on his right thigh. He looked down with his foggy eyes, and at first thought it was a heaping mound of mud that had formed there, a round, textured formation of what was quicker and quicker, to Stone, revealing itself to be something that was breathing…

Looking down, he saw the animal's chest moving, and as Stone sat up slightly, he saw its dark eye open, looking up at him, a hint of white fur surrounded it.

"You're completely covered," Stone whispered to the dog, with a smile coming to his face. Stone could hardly speak though, as he himself was caked in mud, as it was the only way he'd managed to find sleep that night—by sitting in the soaked ground. He reached over and gently—and warily—pet the dog's back. "You got a name little guy?" Ceres was slumbering peacefully on the other side of the smoldering fire. "Guess not." The dog's head popped up as Stone stroked the dog's fur, but then its head lay back down after he continued to pet it. "I don't have a name either… At least I don't know what it was if I ever had one… I'm Stone now… named after the gravestone I was buried under. I feel like I should give you the same form of name now… something appropriate… Maybe Dragon, because you saved me from one? Or Mud… for obvious reasons? I don't know… I'll think about it… I'll just call you Mud for now until I come up with something better. That OK with you?"

The dog didn't respond, as it just laid there curled up in a ball, nestling in closer to him, trying to take in more warmth from him.

"Ceres is not going to like this," Stone said, looking down at Mud as he stroked the black fur hidden beneath the wet filth layer above. Ceres stirred, yawning lightly as she moved from one side to the other. "Best be off back to the trees boy, she's about to wake up."

Somehow—whether the dog understood what he was saying or not—it rose, stretched out its hind legs, and trotted back off out into the trees. Stone sat there with a smirk on his face that was unable to be washed off by the interrogative look in Ceres' scowl.

"What's that sly look for?" she sneered.

"Don't know what you're going on about," he said with his hands firmly planted in the mud on both sides of him. "Not much to be happy about here in this mess."

She cocked her head, looking for what was on the other side of the smile he was trying to hide.

Hours later, after he'd not revealed the secret to his joy and she'd seemed to have forgotten it, they were growing nearer to Atlius. The dirt road had turned to smooth stone, and more and more people had found their way upon the road. People of all sorts too. Those with small children on their backs, others with wagons pulled by tall horses whose inhabitants looked out with wary eyes. There were those dark-skinned, pale-skinned, those with earrings in strange places, those with eyes wild from travels and long-lived lives, and those with a wildness brimming throughout them, eager with youth and adventure. Mostly though, soldiers in heavy armor and with hardened horses became more in number as the high peaks of the towers of Atlius finally came into view.

PART II
BLACK EYES

Chapter Seven

The city of Atlius, under the warm afternoon sun, didn't reflect the sunlight like he would've expected. The dull, matte gray stone of its walls gave off an ancient aura of somewhere that had stood so long that it had far too many tales to tell. The city was framed by two mountain ranges farther to the south that both broke where the city stood. Looking up at the pair of towers at its center, Stone wondered how many times they'd been taken in a siege. But he couldn't deny that past the thick layer of horse excrement that wafted in the humid air, the smell of freshly baked bread lingered on the other side of those high walls.

"Hold you hither," called one of the guards who stood at the front gate. "What's yer business here?"

Ceres answered, "We're here for trade and rest. A fine cup o' tea or six."

The gruff-looking guard looked her up and down, noticing the filth the two were caked in. He ruffled his mustache that ran past his upper lip, and looked to the guard next to him, who only shrugged.

"She's not too bad on the eyes," the other guard said. "If she cleaned the ragged, gutter look off 'er."

"Go on," the first guard said, seemingly annoyed, yet looking to the family behind them, looking to enter upon their cart drawn by a pair of strong donkeys.

Stone went through the front gate after her, where the horse's smell dampened, and smells of the city caused his stomach to tighten and his mouth to salivate.

Entering into the city, running perpendicularly to the entrance, a vast market full of bustling people walked slowly down the long road, eying the wares and goods of the dozens of vendors resting in shade under the canopies of their stands or yelling out into the crowd. Stone had little to no memory, and this place gave him nothing to aid that—he had the feeling he'd never been to this place. He didn't even know if he'd had a life before that coffin, or if that was the dirt's womb for him.

That same mustached guard behind him yelled out, causing Stone and Ceres to spin around, "Catch it! Don't let it through." Stone watched as Mud burst between the two guards, running directly between him and Ceres as the guards bickered between themselves. "Ya should've gotten it! They said no more mangy dogs! You let it through ya slug!"

Ceres looked at Stone, "Ya better not be feeding that dog. Just leave it be. Let it live in the alleys here. It'll be fine, livin' off trash."

Stone shrugged, not really answering her. "What's first? Now that we're here."

"What do you mean?" she said, shuffling her feet away. "This is where we split. That's what I told you, remember?"

He folded his arms over his chest. "That's not what I agreed to. You saved my life. I'm here to help you however I can. I owe you a great debt."

"You can help me by bothering someone else," she said, turning to walk away.

"Hey," he called out past all the commotion of the busy marketplace. "I'm not kidding. I'm not going with you to trouble you or bother you—I'm here to help you. I insist."

She sighed. "Fine, while we're here let's go get something warm to eat."

He trailed behind her as they entered into the crowd. There were so many bodies mashed together, he was surprised that she glided so easily between them. She was like a shark fin cutting through choppy water. There was something about her though, something Stone couldn't quite put his hand on. Ceres wasn't like the other customers of the market. She faded in like a sand snake buried in sand, only its green eyes showing.

Through the crowded road, people barged through, knocking into women carrying children and old men that walked with canes. A few of these rustling into Ceres at the lead, and to Stone's surprise, even at her slim state, she stood firm. She slid off them like butter on a warm knife. Stone couldn't quite understand what was going on in the moment, he thought she was seasoned in traveling through cities like this. He thought she excelled at blending in.

Eventually, a couple of roads down, as the crowd had thinned a bit, she led him to a purveyor on the right side of the market. The vendor had a lavishly colored banner over his table, which was filled with exotic-looking candies, chocolates, and taffies. The table's items glowed under the soft sunlight like a scattered rainbow. Stone's mouth watered, and he had to swallow several times.

"Why here?" he asked Ceres, as the vendor smiled, showing his gleaming white teeth.

"I like to start out a city with sweets," said Ceres. "It's always just sorta been a thing… ever since I was a kid. Go ahead, pick something out."

"I've got cocoa from Tibrín, sugar from Alocade, honey from the bees of Nardoth…" the vendor said, nearly singing the words. "Try the taffy, made with salt from the Great Sea itself!"

"Two of those." Ceres pointed to two striped sticks of hard candy. "One of those, oh and one o' those too!"

Stone raised an eyebrow. *She wasn't kidding, she's going all-in on those.*

"Well, pick some out because you're not gettin' mine," she said.

Eying the table, he picked out a pouch of vanilla taffies.

"Fine choices, lass," the man with the white teeth said. "One quort and two denins that'll be."

From her left pocket, Ceres pulled a pouch of weighted metal. The bag was a tan canvas and Stone could see the inside lining resembled a soft violet velvet. She put her hand in, clanking around the coins inside and produced one silver quort and two copper denins. The man took them with a smile, and as she put the bag back in her pocket, Stone saw the letters RL branded on the side. *Are those initials?*

Ceres and Stone took their sweets from the front of the table, and she quickly popped one of the chocolates in her mouth, letting it melt slowly in her mouth as she closed her eyes and let out a deep, welcoming sigh. No, more like a guttural groan of joy.

Stone ate one of the taffies, it coated his dry throat as he chewed it quickly, letting it slide down his throat. The next one, he let sit in his mouth a little longer.

"All right," Ceres said in a relieved voice, "now we can go an' look for real food and bedding."

Stone nodded, looking for Mud, which he didn't find. He hurried after Ceres, farther down the long marketplace before eventually turning left onto a narrow road with buildings of old glass and taverns with musty smelling fellows, some worse for the wear.

"Let's stop in here," she said, looking up at a hanging sign that had a hand-painted mermaid and crescent moon behind letters that read, *Serenity's Pub and Tavern*. "Stayed here once, years ago. Good lamb if I remember right."

They walked through the swinging doors into the smoke-filled tavern in the warm afternoon. Most of the windows were covered with drapes, leaving Stone with a calming, cool feeling. There were only a handful of patrons at the polished, dark wood bar. A man with heavy wrinkles on his face smoked an earthy-smelling tobacco out of a curved pipe at the end of the bar. A man and woman sat side by side, not speaking to one another, but her hand was on his thigh as they drank red wine from a shared bottle. A boy about their age sat with his head down, swaying slightly as his hand cupped a glass with an amber liquor of some sort. There was an aged, weathered woman behind the bar, glaring at Stone and Ceres as they sat onto two stools that creaked between the couple and the young man with the greasy brown hair that hung over his eyes.

"What'll it be?" the woman asked, the gray whiskers of her sparse mustache catching Stone's eye until the light poke of Ceres' elbow caught him in the ribs.

"Ale," said Ceres, nodding up at the barrel behind the bar.

"Uh, dry wine," he said, "and some bread will do—to start. Oh, lots of butter too, if you have it."

The woman turned around and poured their drinks.

"Don't tell me that's her," he said to Ceres. "The woman from the sign."

"You betcha it is." Ceres grinned. They both took their drinks and took a sip as they both giggled, looking at each other. The bartender didn't say a word or smile as she laid down the drinks. *She's about as far away from serene as I can picture.*

"Wine?" Ceres asked after a few moments in the tavern that had streaks of sharp sunlight creeping through cracks in the thick drapes.

"Yeah." He shrugged. "What's wrong with that? Don't know if I've ever had a taste for ale…"

Ceres erupted in bright laughter, causing the gloomy boy with the brown hair to stir awake. "How do you know that? You've only been alive for what? Two days? Haven't seen you drink anything but water and mud since then."

Stone feigned a smile. "I guess that is funny. I don't know, I sort of just feel it. Like, ever since I was a child, I never liked the taste of it."

Her laughter waned, and she slid her frothy mug to him. He grimaced a bit, but took the glass up to his lips and took a sip. He took it back down quickly with his lips pursed and his brow furrowed.

"It's so bitter, ugh," he said. "I don't know how you drink that."

Ceres took another drink, smacking her lips after she put the mug back on the bar top with a *click*. "I just have good taste, I suppose."

They sat there another couple of minutes, drinking and enjoying the calmness after the commotion and noise of the market. Serenity came and laid down a half-loaf of a decently-looking fresh white bread with a knife and a mound of deep-yellow butter two fingers high. She glared at Stone with a look that asked, 'that enough butter you glutton?'

He nodded, and she went back off to glaring off into space, leaning up against the back of the bar.

As Stone cut into the bread, Ceres leaned over to him and whispered into his ear, "That boy o'er there, he's been staring at us."

Stone looked over and indeed saw the boy with the brown hair was glaring at them. His gaze was foggy, and he lifted his amber booze up to his mouth and took another gulp. He stood up from his stool, it was more like staggered up from his stool and moved two down to lean on the bar next to Stone.

He gave a somewhat charming grin, as he struggled to stand up, even with the bar to lean on. "What are you two doing in this dank hole of horse shit?" he asked. "Plenty of other, nicer places than this in the city. You new here?"

Serenity gave him an icy, cold glare, which he didn't seem to notice.

"Just passing through." Ceres took a piece of bread and slathered butter on it before putting it in her mouth. "Place don't seem so bad."

"Ha." The boy laughed. "I've had better food in the bin behind a brothel." Serenity growled, threw her towel on the bar next to the boy and stormed off.

"That was rude." Stone glared at him. The boy had brown hair that hung past his brow, his skin was lightly tan, and his eyes were a light blue color. He wore nice clothing, with a leather vest with fine leather straps and a still-fairly white sleeved shirt that was cuffed at his wrists.

"Oh, pay no mind to her," he scoffed with a wave of his hand. "I'm just giving her a hard time because she's always trying to charge me for more than what I've had." He put a finger up at the side of his head. "But she don't know that I never forget how much I've had."

"How much have you had?" Ceres asked with a mouthful of bread.

The boy counted on his fingers, looking up at the rafters. He seemed to make it to seven. "I'd rather not say, it may make me look like more of a lush than I am." He laughed.

"Well, we're still on our first," Ceres said, taking another gulp of her ale.

"What are you all in the city for?" the boy asked, looking down at their mud-stained clothing and dirty hair.

Ceres and Stone looked at each other, as the boy took up his drink and polished off the last finger.

"He just rose from the grave," she said, "and we almost got

killed by a dragon and a Neferian up north, nearly drowned in a storm o'er night, and just looking for a place to wash up and rest. Then you came along…" She polished off her drink then.

The boy gave them a cold, inquisitive stare, and then chuckled. "Nice to meet you both, whatever your story may be, you definitely could use a warm bath, the each of you." He put out his hand, "Name's Adler, Adler Cauldcron."

"Ceres Rand, and this here's Stone."

"Stone," he laughed, "what kind of name is Stone?"

"What kind of name is Adler?" Stone spat back.

"I'm a killer," Adler hissed. "A full, cold-blooded assassin. At least… at least I'm supposed to be."

"What does that mean?" Ceres asked with a raised eyebrow.

"Hey, Serenity!" he called out. "I'm getting dry again, and I'm still counting!"

What a prick…

"Ask me again another time about that," Adler said, taking a seat at the stool and waiting for his next drink. Ceres scooted the bread toward him.

"Eat," she said.

He reluctantly took a small bite of bread.

"Stone is what we named him because he don't remember his real name," she said.

Adler looked up at him with his eyebrows lowered. "You really don't remember your real name? Don't tell me you really rose from the ground, right?"

Stone nodded.

"You two are real interesting," he said. "I can already tell."

Serenity came back to the three of them. She glared heavily at Adler, but asked what Ceres and Stone wanted. They got another round, and Adler said that one was on him… but he was still keeping count.

Chapter Eight

"That boy was weird," said Stone.

"He was just drunk," Ceres said. "I sort of liked 'em. Seemed real enough I suppose."

Both of their boots walked heavily up the stairs of Serenity's Pub and Tavern. The greasy floorboards creaked loudly as they made their way up. Ceres had paid for a single nights' stay in one of the four rooms of the inn, and it appeared that the only other room that was rented was Adler's who'd been there for the better part of a week.

They arrived at the door, and Ceres drove the key into the keyhole, turning to look at Stone one more time over her shoulder. Her green eyes glared heavily into his.

"You're not sleeping on the bed, you can buy your own if you want one," she said with narrow eyes. "No way you're going to sleep next to me. I sleep alone."

He nodded quickly.

"I could sleep on a cactus right now," he said. "I am just grateful for anything. I'd give anything for a change of clothes and a bath is all."

She opened the door inward and the warm sunlight kissed

their faces. It was a pleasant change from the dreary bar down below. Inside the four-walled room of dark wood, a single bed lay with clean, cotton sheets underneath the window at the left corner of the room. A rickety-looking desk was by the door, and Stone saw his resting place for that night—a rocking chair by the window on the right side of the room. A well-crafted cabinet rested between them with finely carved edging.

They both took their boots off, leaving them by the door, she put her hand on his shoulder for balance.

"I'm off to bathe first," Ceres said, letting her heavy boot fall to the wooden floorboards with a *thud*.

She exited back out of the room, going across the hall to the single bath in the tavern.

Stone went and sat in the chair, rocking as he looked out the foggy window. He saw the marketplace down below as it had slowed down as merchants were closing down their shops. Beyond, he saw the walls of the city and beyond. He saw the cobblestone road that they'd taken to get here from his hole in the ground, still with a great pile of dirt lying next to the dragonfire-burnt gravestone. He then wondered where Mud was at that very moment. He hoped he was digging into some tasty leftovers of meat.

He rocked back and forth, letting his head fall to the side, and the few wines he'd had aided him to fall into a deep slumber.

STONE WAS LOST IN A DREAM—a dream of being pulled away from someone, kicking and screaming. He tried to fight and run, but his legs felt as heavy as tree trunks and his arms were held back by iron vices. He yelled until his throat cracked. But then he awoke, his eyes opened wide, finding Ceres standing by the door with it partially open, the doorknob in her hand as she prepared to exit.

"Stone?" she asked in a soft voice.

Her clothes were clean from a wash, her pale, freckled skin and heavenly golden curls glistened in the warm sunlight that wafted in the air. He breathed heavily as he felt the sweat beading down his forehead, but he was so awestruck by the transformation a bath and rest had done for the girl that had saved him—he was left speechless.

"Everything all right?" She closed the door slightly.

"Um… yes," he said, leaning back in the chair and gathering his wits again. *It was just a dream, but it was so powerful. It felt real.* "What time is it?"

"It's the morning," said Ceres, with an uplifting tone in her voice. "You slept all night, you even snored for a bit. You'd better get cleaned up, then we'll figure out what's next."

Stone looked down to see he was wearing the same, dirt-covered outfit, and his hands and arms wore that same dirt. He grunted as he rose from his 'bed' as Ceres turned and left the room. He stretched his arms out wide with a yawn and made his way to the bath.

An hour later, he had a cloth wrapped around his waist while his clothes hung outside the windowsill of their room, drying in the sunlight. He caught his reflection in the glass then as he leaned in to see his face again. His skin had been kissed with a slight tan from their walk, and his silky black hair hung down both sides of his face, radiating down from the widow's peak that ran halfway down his brow. His gray eyes glowed brighter now, with the blue sky showing beyond the foggy glass. He leaned back and saw his body, lean with long muscles in his arms and his ribs shown slightly.

How long had I been in that coffin? Why can't I remember anything?

He sat in his chair, waiting for his clothes to dry. He thought about the dream further, about where he'd been before the coffin, and about what would be next for him. What could be his purpose. He decided that until he remembered who he was—Ceres and Mud would be his purpose. They'd be his closest friends—his only family—if she'd let him, that is.

Stone went back down the stairs a little later, his stomach growling, but soft cloths caressed his clean skin. He felt like a new man—reborn, if you will. He was surprised to see that at the bottom of the stairs, nestled at the bar top sat Ceres, but that wasn't the surprising thing—she was sitting next to Adler, who gave him a wide smile as Stone approached.

"Back from the dead again, I see?" Adler announced as he stood up and opened his wide arms at him. This was the first time that Stone noticed that for being a killer, Adler had a stout build and a round belly.

Ceres nudged Stone with her hand for him to come sit with them. He went and sat on Ceres' left side, as Adler sat back down on the other.

"Go ahead and order," she said to him, "I've got it."

He leaned over and whispered into her ear, "I've been meaning to ask, where'd the purse come from? Who is RL?"

She then whispered into his ear, "None of your concern."

He ordered pan-fried eggs, bread, and a soft, nutty cheese. Adler had an ale, but seemed much more sober than the day before. Ceres sat with her hands in her lap, without a drink.

"What are your two's plans while here?" Adler asked later in their conversation.

"Just passing through," Ceres said. Stone looked at her, as he was eager for an answer too.

"Where's the destination?" Adler asked.

"Don't have one," she replied.

"Drifters, then?" he asked, leaning back and folding his arms. "I like that."

"So, Adler," Stone asked. "You from here? You got family?"

Adler's eyes looked to the cracks of sunlight wafting through the curtains. "No, and no." His tone was stoic, devoid of emotion.

There was a long, heavy pause for many minutes after that, as Adler drank his ale, and Ceres looked around.

"Let's go for a walk," she said finally. "Get some fresh air."

Stone had already inhaled his food, and Adler had finished his drink, so they were all off quickly back into the streets of Atlius. And as soon as they were out into the crowds that walked in the roads, Stone saw something familiar—out of the corner of his eye, he saw a black dog with a white spot over his right eye staring at him from an alleyway behind a small cart. Stone smiled as they walked.

They made their way south toward the three towers at the epicenter of the city. Two roads down they found a round fountain at the intersection of six roads, and they stood there, marveling at its features. There seemed to be somewhat of a maritime theme in the city, as landlocked as it was.

At the center of the fountain, a marble figure was carved emerging from a great wave of water, he had a long, wavy beard and a trident in his hand. He was muscular, with veins running down his arms, and in his other hand he grasped a large squid with its beak open, ready to bite into the man. The squid was so large it could be the true definition of a sea-monster.

"What about you?" Adler asked. "You got families?"

Stone had no idea, and he assumed Adler knew that because they both looked to Ceres for her answer.

She only shook her head.

"No family at all?" Stone asked.

"Not anymore," she said, looking coldly at the fountain.

"Welp," Adler said. "Looks like we got a pack of three orphans, destination-less and drifting. The orphan drifter's trio, rather."

Ceres seemed unsettled by that. She looked back to the entrance of the city, back by the marketplace. "I'm gonna go back to the market to get something real quick."

"Let me go with you," Stone said.

"No. I'll meet you back at the inn later. I want to be alone." She then hurried off, alone.

Stone's fingers fidgeted over his knuckles.

"Did I say something wrong?" Adler asked.

Stone didn't reply but watched her as she walked back north in the bustling crowds, until she disappeared back into the city—alone.

Chapter Nine

Sitting on the edge of the fountain with the epic scene of the seaman battling the giant squid, Stone couldn't shake the uneasiness he felt with Ceres being gone. Even with Alder's words being directed at him, he kept wondering—*did she leave for good?*

"…And that was when I insisted…" Adler said, Stone catching the words through the myriad of stories he'd been telling. "…You either get out of my seat or I'm going to send this butter knife straight into that hand!"

"Sorry," said Stone, itching his forehead. "What was that first part again?"

"You sure are the foggy type, aren't ya?" Adler shifted his hands under his thighs. "Sheesh, don't worry about it. You missed all the important parts. Hey, where are you two off to after this? Or are you planning on staying awhile in the city? I could show you around more, can't say I've got much to do. Trying to bide my time 'til I figure out my next adventure."

"Before…" said Stone shyly, rubbing his hands together, "…the other night, you said you were an… assassin? You didn't mean that, did you? Another one of your jokes, and you appeared a little worse for wear."

Stone looked at the boy sitting next to him as he let out a deep sigh. For all his talking, Adler didn't look as though he was interested in talking about that part of his life.

"I'm trained," he finally said. "At least... well enough..."

"Trained? Where did you train to be a... you know... assassin?"

Adler cleared his throat and stood up. "Don't really feel like having this conversation."

Stone rose as well. "Why all the interest in what we are doing here, and where we are going? You've asked a few times now."

"Seems like most people are coming and going in the inns here," Adler said. "Most are boring old men with exaggerated tales, or the battle-worn looking to drown their memories away. You two however, I don't know... I guess it's just because we are the same age. Don't seem many our age out on our own—not living on the streets."

Stone thought about that. *Battle-worn?*

"Is there a battle going on?" Stone asked, looking around at the scores of people around, many of them looking haggard and tired.

"You have been in a hole in the ground!" Adler laughed, but then looked into Stone's eyes. He chuckled until he finally noticed Stone wasn't laughing. "The civil war that's been going on for decades?" His eyes were looking for any flicker of recognition from Stone. "King Tritus? Queen Velecitor? The Battle of Brigon? Any of that ringing a bell? The armies of Dranne?" He paused. "Well, anyway, it's all pretty much been on hold since the Neferian showed up. Everybody's reeling trying to figure out how to kill the awful things."

Stone shook his head, trying to remember something...

anything... but his head was full of what looked like a shattered mirror. Bits and pieces of scattered, blurry images cascading throughout. Not a single thing Adler had just mentioned to him felt familiar.

"I'm sure you'll get some memories back at some point," Adler said with a clap on the back. "You probably just need a good whack on the noggin'. Maybe that's how you lost everything in the first place... Care to try?" He balled up a fist playfully.

Stone just stood there, glaring back toward the market. "I wonder if we should go after her?"

There was a long pause.

"You know—" Adler scratched his chin. "I only just met you both, but I'm a pretty good judge of character. She doesn't really seem like the 'I like to be followed type.'"

"You may be right about that," Stone said. "But she saved my life, and I feel I owe her a great debt."

Adler brushed away all concern with a wave of his hand. "She can take care of herself. I see it in her. Scrapper, that one."

"Come," Adler said, draping his arm around Stone's neck. "I'm thirsty. Let's go see what the old witch has got for us."

Stone didn't really feel like going with him so Adler could start his night early; not to mention his thoughts were still with Ceres, but Adler nudged him with his elbow, so Stone followed.

They were soon back at the tavern, where Adler was quickly on a second drink, and Stone was slowly sipping on water. Standing outside while Adler continued to tell him stories about his time in Atlius, Stone scanned the crowds for her—and although he knew it was nothing—*and* that he'd only just met her, he knew that she was his only real friend. The only person that he even sort of knew, and he felt a pit in his stomach that she was away.

Adler was mid-sentence when Stone said, "I'm going to go and check in on her."

He was already a few paces away, when Adler tried to stop him, but Stone assumed he knew he was tired of being reassured that she was fine, and Adler set his drink down and followed Stone. Continuing back down the long road and winding up back in the marketplace, he found himself standing in the middle of the crowds. Adler was at his side, and they were both looking for her.

"Gonna be tough to find her in the middle of all this," Adler said, loud enough for his voice to be heard over the crowd. "Look for blond hair I suppose. Why are you so worried? She'll be back later."

Stone kept looking both ways down the long market. Now that he was cleaned up, merchants were yelling for him to come over and check out their stock. Elegant rugs, shoes with leather laces, extravagant flowers with colors he'd never seen, and one woman was even selling bones—he had little idea what use bones had of value.

They'd walked down a few hundred feet when Stone felt something at his side, something with rough, scratchy fur. He saw that it was that same dog with the dirty black fur and white spot over its eye

"Mud!" he said, kneeling and petting his neck. *I was wrong, I do have another friend here.*

Mud looked up at him, panting, with his wide eyes looking into his.

"You know this mangy thing?" Adler snickered.

"Yes, he's really something actually," Stone said.

Then Stone noticed that Mud's eyes went to the vendor with the bones sitting on the table. The merchant was calling out to other people perusing wares, while Mud whimpered quietly.

"Oh, are you hungry?" Stone asked, still kneeling by the

dog. "I don't have any money, but I can find you something back where we're staying if you come. But I think you're a little scared of Ceres. I don't blame you." He laughed. "I'd never want to be on her bad side."

He stood and walked over to the merchant, and Mud crept behind him, out of sight.

"Hello," he said, "odd request, but you don't have any of these that you'd be willing to part with for a favor, would you? I can do some chore for you if you're in need."

The woman's wide grin fell to a look of sheer unpleasantness with a scowl.

"Young man, you wouldn't be knowing what exactly you're looking at I'm supposing? These are not mere bones. These are shards of dragon bones. Their uses are many, and no, I don't have one I'm willing the *part* with. Now if you've no money to…"

Just then, Stone caught a glimpse of a white spot of fur moving up to the table on his right side. Mud opened his jaws and bit down onto a six-inch bit of bone and bolted off into the crowd.

"Stop him!" she yelled. "Stop that bastard! He stole from me." His glower went to Stone. "You know that dog? Is it yours? You wanted that bone for him. Get the soldiers!"

"Miss," Adler said, moving up to the table at Stone's left. "We don't know that nasty thing. My friend here was asking for a bone for teeth-picking is all. And I'll point out he was offering a barter. We've no need for handouts."

She eyed them both heavily. "You have money?"

Stone shook his head. Adler nodded, jingling a pouch at his side.

"Well, that one bone cost six tabers." Her chin rose as she said that.

"I'm not paying you for what a homeless dog took from you," Alder said, letting the purse fall back at his side. "Come on, let's go. Maybe you shouldn't leave dog scraps on the end of the table."

Stone stood there, confused, and impressed by Adler.

Adler grabbed his arm and pulled him away, the opposite direction that Mud had taken.

"You fool," Adler said. "Don't be asking for handouts here. Beggars get thrown into the alley. Literally thrown. You could even end up in the dungeons for asking for money to feed your children. They want this to be a safe place for those more fortunate."

They walked back by the entrance to the city and saw a line of dozens trying to get in, and they saw the same guards who let him and Ceres in.

"You know," Adler said, "she's probably back at the tavern now wondering where we are. We should go back. I'm working up a hunger anyways. Whatd'ya say?"

Stone took one last look around and couldn't find his friend. He gave in, and they made their way back.

Once there, Adler fished out a gnat from his drink and finished it in two big gulps. He took an uncomfortable shiver. "Ale sure does lose its allure when it sits in the sun."

"I'm going up to go see if she's here," Stone said.

As he was going back toward the tavern, Adler said, "You know, girls don't like being chased too much, makes you look desperate."

Stone turned with a scowl. "It's not like that. Don't think that it is."

He really knows how to irk me sometimes.

He went up the stairs and into their room, and opening the door slowly, he found that there was no one there, but her things were still.

Well, I suppose she hasn't left. Maybe I should just enjoy my time.

He caught something strange out of the corner of his eye though—something out the window. He saw what he thought was a figure on the rooftop next to the tavern. It was so brief and so faint; he couldn't be sure. But he couldn't shake the feeling that a pair of black eyes were fixed straight upon him through the glass before they disappeared.

Stone felt a complete, overwhelming feeling that something wasn't right. No. Something was very wrong

Chapter Ten

❧

He rushed down the stairs, back into the main entryway to the tavern, and Adler's eyebrows raised high. Stone made no motion to Adler, instead he ran straight for the doorway, back out into the city.

"Hey!" Adler called after him.

Stone sprinted down the long road back toward the marketplace.

I don't know what it is, but those eyes... Those black eyes... They held a certain look of old wisdom... and pain.

Behind him, he heard the quick footsteps of someone trailing shortly after. Adler called out through his deep, heaving breaths, and eventually Stone slowed so that he could catch up.

"What in the heavens is the matter, man?" Adler asked.

"I don't think we looked hard enough," Stone said, running again at a fast pace. "She's out there. I can feel it, and she needs my help."

They continued to run without a response for a long moment, but then Adler simply said, "Let's find her then."

They were soon back on the busy marketplace road, slightly less populated now, but still brimming with people.

"Ceres!" Stone called out, pushing his way through the crowd, scanning for her golden hair.

"Ceres?" Adler peered out into the vast crowd of thousands.

They made their way the same way they'd gone before, but Stone had the feeling that perhaps he hadn't gone quite far enough. He deeply wished he'd just missed her, and that she was now back at the tavern—wondering where they were now.

Passing past the wicked eyes of the bone vendor who sent a menacing scowl at them as they rushed by, and the other same merchants they'd seen only a little bit ago, Stone shoved his way unapologetically through the crowds. His mind was racing with worry, and all the while those black eyes still burned into him. Had he really seen them? Or were they just a figment of his imagination? Perhaps it was just a tapestry or some linens drying on the rooftop before being blown behind something? Either way—his gut was telling him to head out deeper into the market, telling his legs to move faster, and his eyes to keep vigilant.

"Hey," one man said with the whites of his eyes large as Stone pushed him out of the way to get through, but he didn't apologize. Adler moved quickly behind him.

"Where we goin?" Adler asked. "I know you know this, but we've already been down this way."

"I don't know," Stone replied instinctively, "just follow me…"

Adler gave no response but followed behind as Stone moved closer back to the city entrance. Once they arrived there, they found half of the gate was closed, and fewer guards were there with torches in their hands, waiting for the sunlight to fade. They stopped once at the gate, their feet stopped on the stone road. Each of them looked around as they gasped for breath. Above were high turrets with archers who glared down at them. The soldiers at the entrance seemed not to notice them—they were too busy turning away travelers eager to enter the city, which they seemed to slow the stream of later in the day. There was shouting from the other side of the walls by those frustrated by their denial of welcome into Atlius.

A strong breeze hit Stone's back then. It seemed to propel him forward, if not physically... spiritually. His eyes locked in that direction, and he was off at once.

"Hey, wait up. Damn fool is quick, I'll give him that," Adler said, heading off after him briskly after only seeing him shoot off after a few moments while looking in the other direction.

"Ceres!" Stone shouted out into the loud crowds. "Ceres!"

He soon found himself in the middle of a giant square with another wide road intersecting with the market one, and he was unsure of which direction to go. In the square, there were inns with lines out the doors with customers waiting on a hot meal, brothels with ladies and lads peering out the tall windows seeking new customers, and lurking eyes of those who wished to prey upon the weak—mostly by collecting the coins in the pockets.

Stone spun in the confusing crowd as dozens passed by in the middle of the road, and he suddenly found himself with the question: did I make a mistake? Yet, that deep pain in his gut remained.

"What now?" Adler asked, and Stone looked at him unsure. Sweat pooled over his eyebrows and again, Stone found himself lost.

"I don't know, just give me a moment..."

They both looked around again, and self-doubt began to creep in. *What am I doing here? This is silly... There's nothing wrong... she's probably...*

A faint noise caught his ear from somewhere he couldn't tell. It was so faint and so distant beyond the noise of the crowd; he could hardly recognize if it was of any importance at all.

"You hear that?" he asked.

"Hear what?" Adler responded, looking around, and watching which direction Stone was moving to.

"I... I think..." he said. "Maybe this way..."

Stone continued down the road of the market, directly down the middle of the crowd. The sound he'd been hearing was constant, yet faint, but perhaps getting louder. He thought he heard it clearer then, and a flash of recognition shot into him. He was quickly back into a wave of desperation and moved as fast as he could forward. Adler was just behind.

Indeed, he could feel the sound getting louder, and his heart began to pound powerfully in his chest. Then, the sound muffled, and he stopped, wiping the sweat from his brow, looking around. He saw a couple of alleyways that he'd just passed and ran to them quickly. One was behind a bakery, but he knew once he heard the sound again that it was down the opposite alley.

Adler had been hearing the sound too, and as it was becoming clearer, and as they ran down the alley with wet linens hanging from windows above, he asked, "That's not the same dog from earlier barking is it?"

Stone didn't answer, but he knew deep down that it was.

They both took a sharp right, and just a few hundred feet down they saw Mud barking ferociously into a crevasse behind another building. They couldn't see what he was barking at, but they ran to him immediately. As they were only halfway there, they watched as Mud shot forward, trying to bite something out of view when a heavy leather boot kicked the dog in the ribs, knocking him away, but only causing him to bark wilder.

Stone and Adler were in a complete state of shock and worry when they went to the dog's sides.

Before them, in a deep recess in the buildings that were dark with age and trash were four soldiers in full uniform, but most terrifying of all was a glimmer of the color they'd been searching for, for hours—that golden sheen of Ceres' hair at their center—on the ground.

There was the one soldier who was standing tall and strong in front of them—the one who'd kicked Stone's friend, and then there were three behind, all of them crouched over her.

Ceres kicked, screamed, and fought to break free of their strong grips. She hadn't seen Stone and Adler yet, but the pain in her voice cut through Stone's heart like a hot knife through butter.

"Let her go! Get the hell off her right now!" Stone yelled as Mud continued his tirade of vicious barking. The tall soldier standing before them in light chainmail and a silver chest plate gave both of them a deep grimace.

"Get tha' fuck outta here," he grumbled. "This be royal business."

Stone then belted out a loud yell from down in the depths of his stomach. "I said leave her alone or I'll kill the lot of you!"

"Stone!" Ceres called out from the middle of the soldiers, who now had their sights on Stone.

The soldier before them balled his fists, while his sword was still nestled powerfully in its sheath at his hip.

"You heard him," Adler said, with a shakier voice than Stone now. "You get off her, ya hear?"

Behind the soldier they could see the other three get fully back on their feet—except one—who still had his hands clasped onto Ceres, who was fighting frantically to break free. Stone saw that her shirt was torn, her eyes were wild with rage and fear, but her clothes were mostly still unremoved.

One of the soldiers behind—Stone now recognized—was the exact same guard who'd let them into Atlius, the one with the mustache. "Ya heard him. Get on your way at once, or it'll be the dungeon or the casket for ya!"

Stone, thinking only of her and that she'd saved him from his own prison, surged forward with an explosiveness that sent the first soldier reeling to unsheathe his sword. The guard had it halfway removed when Stone bouldered into him, sending him onto his back as Stone's shoulder careened into his chest. Stone was on top of him then, and slightly surprised by his success, and not knowing what to do next, he got back to his feet and ran toward her.

The two guards left standing quickly drew their swords, and Stone found himself in a very serious predicament. He didn't care though. He ran at them ready to strike both of them down with his fists.

Ceres yelled out for him. "Stone!" It was as much a cry for help as it was for worry. There was a tone in her voice that was almost saying to him, 'No, you'll die, what are you doing?'

He ran at them, his fists in balls, his teeth tightly clenched, and his mind in a murderous rage. *I'll kill all three of you with my bare hands. You touch her again, and I'll burn this whole city to the dirt!*

Behind him, he heard Adler's footsteps following him.

"I've got the one on the right," said Adler as he leaped over the downed guard, kicking him in the cheek as he struggled to get up.

The two boys were almost upon the two soldiers as their two sharp sword blades were drawn back to hack into Stone and Adler. The soldier who was pinning down Ceres looked up at them with a certain curiosity, as if watching two mice go in to scare off two fat cats. A wide grin crossed his aged face, waiting for those two mice to become a nice meal.

As the boys were only feet from them, Stone and Adler jumped at the two with wild abandon. The two soldiers swung their swords, and even with Stone's speed, he knew that he'd be able to knock the soldier over, but that sword was going to find its mark. *You won't be able to save her if you're dead... But you can't save her by standing back there in the alley either. This is your shot. This is your chance to save her… Make it count!*

Time slowed, and Stone and Adler were about to barrel into the two guards on their feet, when an explosion of light tore into the alley. It was if the sun had exploded into a bright burst just above. The thing was—it wasn't a white light, or a golden color like you might expect—no, it was a brilliant, red the color of heavenly dusk.

Stone was blinded but felt the metal of the soldier's armor as his shoulder knocked into it. They both fell to the ground in the alley filled with a thick, crimson red. The soldier landed with a deep grunt, as if the air had been crushed from his lungs. Immediately, Stone grabbed the soldier's wrist that held the sword and began to pummel him in the face with his right fist. The blinding red had faded from an overwhelming light, to now a sort of funneling twister in the alley. He beat the soldier's face harder and harder as the red faded, and he saw the worry in that bastard's eyes.

"Stop at once!" The last remaining soldier had gotten to his feet, pulling Ceres up with him. She was standing before him with her back to him, and he had his sword to her throat. It was if everyone had forgotten the influx of red light that had just occurred, as it rose back to the sky like a fading dust devil.

Adler was on top of the other soldier next to him with his fist raised over his face, now looking up at Ceres in her new predicament.

"Let her go!" Stone yelled at him. "Release her, and we release them."

"We can all walk away from this like it never happened," Adler snapped.

"There's no walking away from this," the final guard said, clasping onto Ceres' upper arm tighter, shaking her. "You attacked soldiers of the king. You're gonna hang fer' this."

"No," Stone said. "You're going to rot in this alley for this, if you don't let her go, right now."

By then, the guard behind them was back to his feet with his sword drawn. They were surrounded, and even though they had the two beneath them pinned down, the soldiers were stronger, older, and much more armed.

I could run to her. I could go for it, but his blade is up to her throat. But, if I do... she'll die... or I'll die... but if I don't, then they'll take me... beat me and hang me... and they'll have their way with her... Better to die fighting for the one who saved me I guess...

Stone shot to his feet and ran with every bit of strength he had, and at his side he saw that same dirty fur with that white dot over his eye.

If we die, I guess we die together, eh buddy?

The soldier's face was stricken with a sense of surprise as his eyes widened and his eyebrows raised, but then his brow furrowed as the muscles in his arms tensed.

He's going to kill her! There's no way I'm going to let that happen!

"No!" he yelled out, ready to kill that god-damned soldier. "No!"

The soldier's sword twisted in his hand, ready to slice Ceres' soft skin, that same flourishing red light filled the recess of the alley, washing them all in its powerful light. This light was different than the first time though, it held a heavy aura of power. It clung to Stone like vines wrapping around his arms and legs, and he found himself unable move—or at least that's what he felt, as his eyes were shut tight.

The others around him yelled in confusion, and Mud barked madly. All this was silenced by a thunderous sound. At first, Stone thought it was another soldier moving in, but it seemed to come from above.

"You will cease your barbarous actions now," the voice boomed. Stone felt the voice deep in his stomach as it echoed in the crevasse of the alleyway. "You will let the three of them go, and you will do it now!"

The red light faded to that same swirling twister all around them, and Stone could see then that indeed vines had wrapped around his arms and legs, but not only his, but all of them! The soldiers fought and squirmed to break free with their swords, but their swords were covered in them too.

Ceres was looking up to the sky in a way that showed him there was something more important up there than breaking free of her own vines. He looked up and couldn't believe his eyes.

Perched upon the ledge of the building to their right was a figure cloaked in a dark shawl and hood. She had a dark complexion, had thick ivory bones pierced in her ears, and she had deep, dark black eyes. *It's the same person from before, that one on the rooftop by the tavern!*

"What've ya done, ya bitch!" the soldier over Ceres yelled up. "Get this thing offa' us. We're soldiers of the court. We'll send you to the gallows fer…" His voice then turned to a groan of pain as the vines on his arms and legs tightened, squeezing his blood vessels tightly.

"You'll do no such thing," the woman said as her cloak tails rustled in the wind. "I'll let you heathens live, although, don't make me regret it. Even if you do all deserve to rot where you are…"

Stone, Ceres, and Adler were all in a state of shock as the vines unwound from their bodies.

"Now," the woman said, "You three come along. We have much to discuss."

Chapter Eleven

❧

Stone leaped up from his position over the soldier and ran to Ceres. He grabbed her arm eagerly, hoisting her up from under the soldier who was still struggling to break free. Ceres leaped up and sent the tip of her boot into the soldier's groin, sending a deep, heaving grunt from the depths of his gut. She spit in his face once for good measure. Every part of Stone wanted to take the soldier's sword and run him through. But he'd have to pry it from the wrinkled hands of the soldier and tear the vines off.

Adler had run next to them, standing with his eyebrows raised—staring up at the woman with the black eyes. The red mist had faded, and the soldiers yelled out for aid. Stone turned and—in a great arc of his right fist—sent it into the soldier's face. He hit him so hard in fact, that the soldier's body went lip, being held up from the vines then.

"You ever try that with another," Stone said, "and there'll be no one to save your miserable hides."

One of the standing soldiers looked into Stone's eyes after he said that, with a deep, hateful stare.

"We see you again," he said, "and we're gonna kill ya. Yer as good as dead. Ya just wait, boy."

"You won't be seeing them again," the woman on the rooftop said, sending a look of fear into the men still held in the thick vines. "And I will say, if you intend to pray on those like you just did with this young woman here, those vines aren't going to stop their squeezing. They'll crawl into your mouth, ears, eyes, every hole they can find until the pain will be so great you won't be able to breathe." The soldiers gasped and their tanned skin turned pale.

As the three of them turned and left, Ceres spat in the faces of the other soldiers. They turned the corner and waited for the woman to come down from the roof, and they watched as she leaped down from the ten-foot roof, landing next to them with a gentle kiss as her boots touched the dirt next to the cobblestone.

Up close, the woman held deep wrinkles at the corners of her eyes, and her black eyes didn't look so black then. They were dark brown like tobacco leaves.

"Let's be on our way," she said, her voice then was calm and soothing—very different from the commanding voice that thundered down from the rooftop. "We don't want to risk a spat of their comrades finding them, and then us."

They walked with quick footsteps behind her. Ceres looked at Stone with a look of disbelief in her eyes. He shrugged. The woman's dark cloak tails whipped behind her in the breeze. She was nearly silent as she walked, leaving no sound to her footsteps. Stone thought that he'd like to learn how to do that.

They'd been walking behind the swift woman through alleyways for the better part of ten minutes before Ceres finally asked her, "Miss, what's your name? Who are you?"

"We're almost there," the woman replied.

The alleyways of the city were a myriad of short stretches like a forking river. Stone had no idea where they were after walking down them in a seemingly random pattern of rights and left. Men playing card games stared at them, woman hanging wet linens from above glared at them, and even eyes from the dark crevasses seemed to loom upon them.

Then, the woman darted to the right, ducking into a narrow space between two buildings, and she had to clear cobwebs out before them. She knelt once they were halfway down the stretch of twenty feet or so, placing her fingers underneath a hardly noticeable ledge that stuck out from the side of one of the dwellings. She rose just part of the wall popped open an inch, a door had just opened from the seemingly smooth wall on the right building, and as Stone was still trying to figure out what was happening since he'd found Ceres fighting off the soldiers back there, the woman disappeared into the side of the dwelling. Ceres followed behind her, and then Adler followed.

Stone stood there, contemplating what he should do, and whether he should trust the woman or not. After all, following strangers into dark rooms wasn't a great idea, but honestly… he thought, *almost everyone is a stranger to me. I've got to trust somebody, and Ceres is in there.* He knew he trusted her.

The inside of the building was dark, as thick tapestries hung over the front windows to the tiny dwelling. It was furnished with five wooden chairs around a round, wooden table at the corner of the room by the windows. As the door shut itself behind them, Stone wondered how a door could shut itself like that. But there was a lot of new things happening to him since he'd risen from the ground.

"Take a seat," the woman said, going to the other side of the room, where a small bed with a dull red blanket lay in one corner, and a kitchen was in the other—which comprised of a wood-burning stove set between two white-painted cabinets presumably full of spices, flours, and sugar. She went to the kitchen and grabbed a clay pitcher and four cups down from a shelf. The woman pulled her hood down and ushered them to sit at the table with a wave of her hand. They sat, and then she sat in the wooden chair with a creak. From behind the tapestry, Stone could see Mud's eyes looking into the room, as his front paws were on the outer windowsill. She took her arms from the sleeves of her cloak and let it fall back onto the chair. She poured a glass of water for each of them and took a deep gulp, giving a sigh of relief. She stared stoically into Stone's eyes. "I'm glad to have finally found you."

None of them said a word, although they all knew she was staring at Stone.

She looked around at each of them with her brown eyes like shaded, old oak. Her flowing silver hair was then rustling at both sides of her thin, weathered face. Her skin had seen much sun, although she was already dark in her complexion. The smile that wanted to grow across her mouth, but didn't, showed a restraint at some energy that was brimming beneath the surface. She was excited, excited for something.

"What do you call yourself, young man?" she asked, scratching her throat. "What's your name?"

"Stone."

"Stone, eh? What about your friends here?"

"This is Ceres, and he's Adler. New friends of mine." Ceres and Adler both looked confused by their stillness. "What's your name? I believe we owe you a good deal of thanks."

"Marilyn," she said, finally letting out a kind smile.

"Back there." Ceres leaned forward with her elbows on the table. "Back there with the soldiers. How did you do what ya did? What was that?"

"A simplish enough spell," Marilyn said. "Casting *Juniper's Red Haze* isn't complicated as one may think, if any were trained on how to cast such a spell. The *Vines that Hold* takes years to master though."

"Spells?" said Adler, moving back from the table, leaning

back on the two legs of the wooden chair. "I saw what happened back there, and still don't believe it. But spells? There isn't any magic anymore. We all know it's been forgotten. You're talking about things back from when the Old Mothers ruled."

"Oh, hush you," the old woman spat. "I always detested that term… Old Mothers—as simple a description as I've ever heard for some of the strongest who ever lived."

"Well, what would you have me call them?" Adler asked, his tone mildly sarcastic.

"You won't understand my language, but in the common tongue it means, The Majestic Wilds."

"The Majestic Wilds?" Adler mouthed, with his eyes wider. "Hmm…" He stared up at the ceiling in contemplation.

Ceres then spoke, "I don't know if ya know much, if anything about Stone here, Marilyn, but he doesn't know much about nothin'. So, this may as well be in your foreign tongue to him too."

"I know just enough about him to have been searching for him wide and far," Marilyn said, with her eyebrows raised, and lips pursed. "That's what's brought us all here together, to be sitting in this city, in this room, at this table, sharing water, and having this conversation while your dog perches on my windowsill. Stone, there's something special about you, whether you know it yet or not."

"Yeah," Adler scoffed. "I'd say! He's only like a week old but looks like almost a man. Give him another week, and he'll be bent at the back, strapped to a cane!"

"Oh, shut up Adler," Ceres said as she whacked him on the arm with the back of her hand.

"Hey," he gasped.

Marilyn leaned forward to Stone; she was so close then that he could smell the peppermint on her breath. "You may be the one I've been looking for… There's a group of us, high up in the mountains, we hold old knowledge and although we lean more toward the private, spiritual side of the life that's given to us, we also feel the need to intervene when we deem it necessary to keep that life continuing." She looked at the three of them, one by one, and that's when they heard *his* name for the first time. "He's come to do nothing but kill. We think what he's doing, he thinks he's doing to save his people, but he'll do nothing but destroy until there's nothing left. That's what we see. He brought them here, the Nefarian, they belong to him. And I can see in your eyes that you've seen him, whether you knew it or not. Yes… he killed a dragon right before your eyes, didn't he? He's a ruthless and sly bastard, even if he's only got one eye. You see, Stone, you're part of the song that tells about *his* coming, and *his* possible ending. King of the Riders of Dark Dragons: King Arken Shadowborn."

"Was it him we saw kill that dragon back in Ruins of Aderogon?"

When Ceres said that word, Aderogon, something flickered in Stone's mind—something faint, hardly noticeable. It felt like a shiver from the cold, or a pinprick on your finger. It was a quick surge of energy that rushed through him, but then vanished as if nothing was ever there. *Was that a memory wanting to come back? It felt like it, but I saw nothing…*

"That was Arken," Marilyn said, "You saw the king himself."

"So, why are you after Stone then?" Adler asked, his obnoxious self had seemed to quiet down, and he gave a serious look at Marilyn, eagerly awaiting an answer.

"We never *knew* if the King of Dark Dragons would come, but now he's here." Her wrinkled hand clasped the mug of water like a statue's. "But we knew if he ever came, we needed to search out the answer to something of a riddle we'd been pondering for generations. It was something we knew we'd never be able to find an answer to until that time came, and here we are now—the four of us."

"Well—what was it?" Ceres asked quickly. "What was the riddle."

"Again, it's in our language, as old as time just about, but it means something like—When the King of Dark Dragons comes, the dead will aid in his end."

"The dead?" Stone asked, sitting back in his seat with his hands hanging limply at his sides. "What have I got to do with the dead?"

Ceres smacked him on the arm with the back of her hand. "You know anyone else who's come back from the dead? You daft?"

Chapter Twelve

"Was... Was I dead?" Stone asked in a soft voice, as if asking himself the question.

"You were certainly... something... down in that coffin," Ceres said, running her fingers through her long hair. "That grave was burnt by the dragonfire, but that dirt was hard. It had been there for a long time. Years even."

"Years?" Stone gasped.

"Marilyn," Adler asked. "What did you mean, that the dead will aid in the death of King Arken?"

"Now," said Marilyn, "I didn't say the King of Dark Dragons would die. We know so little about him. We only know he is old... very old."

"Everything dies," Ceres said, wide-eyed. "Right?"

"There are trees that are thousands of years old," Marilyn said in a whimsical voice. "The great mountains of the Nordconds are as old as the oceans themselves nearly. Turtles that cross the seas can live well beyond our years."

"Mountains aren't alive," Adler whispered under his breath.

"Are they not?" Marilyn shot back. "There's much you

don't know about this world young man. Did you know the mountains move and shift in their age? They crack and break when angry, spew fire when their infamous rages erupt, and most of the time they lay peaceful, asleep. The Dark King has slumbered long enough too, and now he's here. He's here with the wrath of the erupting volcanoes. The dragons have come to fight him off, but they're all going to die trying unless we can figure out the answer to this riddle. You, Stone, are the answer, at least we believe you may be."

He lowered his head into his hands and swayed from side to side. "I don't even know who I am," he said, with his head still a jumbled mess. "Marilyn, do you know who I am?"

Marilyn sat back in her chair and looked up at the ceiling with a deep sigh. "No. No, I do not."

"How'd you find us?" Ceres asked. "How'd you know about me and Stone?"

"Why… I felt it. We felt it."

Ceres' eyebrow perked up.

"Life flows through a spider's web of energy, and each birth and death are a pluck upon those silk strings. It's really a beautiful melody if you ever get to hear it. But when Stone awoke from his slumber or whatever it was, it was like a big, hairy moth bursting through that web, shaking it to its very foundation. I was simply taking a walk when I felt it. It nearly sent me reeling over onto the ground. Then I came after the source, until I found you. At first, I thought it was you Ceres. That's when I found you back there, but then I felt Stone's presence. I've got to get you all back to my home. You must meet with the elders, and quickly."

"Your home?" Stone asked, looking out of the foggy windows to catch Mud's eye as he peered in. "Where is that?"

"To the west," Marilyn answered. "High upon the slopes of the coast in a city that few know exist. You will be safe there. We can have time to prepare for what will be to come." She eyed the three of them as their next question was on the tips of their tongues. "And no! I'm not going to tell you what's to come. That's for us to decide once we are all in Endo."

"Endo?" Adler asked with a slight tinge in his voice. "Never heard of it. You sure it's there? And we're going to have to go all the way to the coast?"

Ceres gave him a wicked glare that sent a tingling sensation down Stone's back.

"Did you not see what she did fer us back there? Are ya not hearin' what she's doing fer us now? She's trying to help us you slog. Listen to her, or don't. I don't care fer what you want to believe. But I believe her, and I think Stone does too. I'd bet anything that muddy dog's gonna be after us as well." Her eyes rolled back, and she gave a deep sigh. "We're never gonna be rid of that mutt, are we?"

Stone smiled. "I hope not. I like him."

"So, you'll come?" Marilyn asked, leaning back into the table and staring at Stone, as she quickly began to tap her fingernails on the table back and forth, from index finger to pinkie, and back.

"I don't know if I believe that I'm the one that you've been searching for," he said, sitting up straight in his chair with his shoulders back. "But if there's anything I can do to help, I'm in." He glanced over at Ceres, who seemed to be looking at him with a brimming anticipation. As her eyes were held wide open, and her mouth hung agape. But once he said this, her eyes beamed, and she smiled a wide smile. She nodded. "Are you going to come?" Stone was now looking at Adler, whose mouth was twisted at one side, as he returned Stone's gaze with one that held deep thoughts behind those light blue eyes.

"If you need me, I'll be there with you," Adler said with a nod.

"You surprise me," Stone said, "we've only just met, and you'll come with us, all the way there?"

"If I'm not mistaken, all three of us, actually four—" Adler said, "I guess, make that five of us, with the dog, have only just met. I never gave much of a second thought to fate…" He shrugged. "But life's short, maybe this is something like destiny, if Marilyn really believes this mystery prophecy of hers?"

"It's real. I'm absolutely certain of it," Marilyn said. "Because if it's not, and there's no way to stop King Arken, then we're all going to see what the afterlife holds, and I'm afraid to say… before too long."

"So, what's next?" Stone asked, scratching his chin. "Do we leave now? The streets are sure to have eyes out for us."

"No," Marilyn said, standing up suddenly, grabbing her cloak from her chair and whirling it around her back to her shoulders. "I will leave you now. You will find food and drink enough for the day, and when I return when the moon is at its brightest, then we will be off. But know this…" She leaned down to peer into each of their eyes. "It's not an easy road. We'll be sought after by not only the guards of this city, but the flying Nefarian, and others that lurk in the shadows. Be prepared for what may, and will come…"

Marilyn strode away from the table, walked over to the door, opening it only an inch so she could peek through the opening, pouring a slit of sunlight into the room that fell upon Adler. She opened the door wider, to step through, but then closed it quickly back again to a sliver.

"One more thing," she said in a low-pitched voice.

"Yes?" Ceres asked.

"Don't let that filthy dog into this house. I don't want my brethren dealing with fleas." She then slipped through the door, closing it with the latch of an iron lock, and the three of them found themselves sitting alone at the table in the shade of the dark room.

Adler clicked the bottom of his mug on the table, somewhat obnoxiously. "It's a long way to the coast, and she mentioned nothing about us getting weapons if we're going to be hunted down like she said."

"I'm sure we'll find something," Stone said, "or maybe she's going to use some of her magic to help us stay out of sight."

"Magic..." Adler said. "I still can't believe it. If I wouldn't have seen it with my own eyes..."

"But you did." Stone sat back tapping his fingernails on the table. "So, we know it's real, and in Endo there's sure to be plenty of people who know how to use it. Maybe they'll even teach us a little."

"Not me," Adler said, "I don't want to be a part of any of that witchcraft."

"Witchcraft?" Ceres said with an insulted gasp. "That *witchcraft* saved us, you twat."

"Twat?" he said, seemingly insulted with his eyebrows raised.

"If I didn't know any better," Ceres said. "I'd say you were highborn, where you grew up in a house with thick, warm stone walls, hot food every night, and a plush blanket to rest yer spoiled head on!"

Adler pursed his lips and folded his arms. "You don't know me."

"I feel like we are finally getting to know each other," Stone said. "I don't care if you're highborn. What does it matter anyways? You lost your parents. We don't have any either. In fact, what does it matter where any of us came from? Nothing really matters now except where we are going. We're going to speak with the elders of Endo. The more we can learn about their prophecy and what we can do to help the better."

"Maybe somewhere along the way too," Ceres said, "you can find out who you are."

Stone sighed, while the others sat in silence.

Then, upon the terracotta roof above, the sound of dull,

thick raindrops pattered down. Stone stood and walked over to the door. He unlatched the door and began to open it inward.

"What in Crysinthian's sake are you doing?" Ceres asked loudly.

Stone opened the door wide enough to look down both ways of the narrow alley.

"Stone!" Adler shot up from his seat.

Stone opened the door wide then, letting the graying sky fill the room with its thick aura, as the sound of the falling raindrops sounded like a soothing melody of an old song. He knelt and held his hand out on the other side of the wall.

"He's not—" Adler sat back down with a thud.

Stone stood back up and stepped back into the room, behind him entered the black dog with the white spot over its right eye.

"Stone." Ceres snickered with her arms over her chest then. Her brow was furrowed, and Stone could tell she was perturbed.

"Don't worry," Stone said. "I'm going to bathe him before she gets back. He deserves that before we all head out on the road. After all, he nearly scared a dragon off on his own. Which one of us can say that? We'll need his protection. We'd better treat him with some dignity, right?"

Ceres sighed, and turned her head away.

"You sound like a child," Adler said. "But criminy, who knows, maybe that mutt may look like a dog underneath all that filth. Here, let me give you a hand." He rose, walked over to the kitchen area and began to fill a bucket with water from the barrel on the floor. "Ceres, you want to collect some soap?"

"Collect some soap?" Ceres said. "I'll tell you where you can shove some soap, I'm not touching that thing." She pointed a shaking finger at Stone. "If that thing gives me fleas, I'm gonna show you a hundred ways you're going to regret it."

"So, that's a no?" Adler walked over to Mud, who was panting, but seemed to be smiling.

"Yeah," Stone said, with a smile of his own. "I believe that's a strong no."

Adler laughed, throwing his head back, and Stone joined in on the laughter.

Ceres frowned and turned away from them again. "Children, just a couple of children I arranged myself with. Good looking out for yourself, Ceres," she whispered. "What've I gotten myself into?"

"Don't worry," Stone said. "We may not be the most grown up yet, but we will look out for each other. That's what friends do, right?"

PART III
THE BLOODY SWORD

Chapter Thirteen

The winds whistled through the cracks of the dim interior of the shack that belonged to Marilyn and her people. Stone rustled uncomfortably on the creaky, wooden floor. Scratchy splinters poked their way through the thin blanket beneath him, poking into his spine and the soft spots on his side. He turned to his side, staring at the tapestry that covered the one window of the room.

Outside the strong winds howled, gusting from west to east, blowing in with them pouring rains that fell on the building like basketfuls of thimbles falling on a thin sheet of silver. Somewhere out there, Mud was left alone in the cool winds, but Stone figured that he'd at least had the skills to find a dry corner of this city that had suddenly, and swiftly, fallen against them. He turned over, looking at the single bed in the room that was occupied by Ceres, whose hair rose from the top of the cotton blanket like a bundle of soft, golden silk, and her tan boots stuck out of the bottom of the blanket—he assumed she left them on so that she could leave at a second's notice.

And then there was Adler... whose snoring filled the room with a constant thunder that seemed to compliment the pouring rain. It wasn't a loud snore, but just enough to keep Stone awake. That wasn't the only reason he was awake at that hour, he worried he'd never find out who he was... or even *why* he was. Marilyn seemed to think he held some importance in the world... and he certainly hoped so. He wanted to cause some greater good in the world... but as of then, he only had two friends and a dog that seemed to care about him. He had no family though, or purpose except for what Marilyn had given him.

He missed the soft bed of the tavern too.

Wondering when the moon would shine at its brightest, he lay awake, trying to trick himself into sleep, but sleep wouldn't find him that night, as the latch of the door unlocked and twisted. He stirred to his feet at once; Ceres too... Adler's snoring stifled but continued again after only a moment. Stone grabbed a chair leg in his hand that had been resting in a corner of the room, and Ceres drew a knife. Neither of them spoke as the door handle moved, and the door itself opened.

Stone twisted the chair leg in his hand, feeling the oily stain lubricate his palms, and the sweat was building from them as well. He shifted his weight back and forth, ready for anything, although he knew his makeshift weapon held no chance against an armored soldier with a sword.

His shoulders relaxed once he saw the dark eyes and silver hair of Marilyn as she drew her hood back, letting the soaking wet cloak fall to the floor. "Son of Crysinthian," she said in a voice that echoed through the room. "That's a lot of rain! I nearly thought I was going to wash away in that storm."

"What happened?" Ceres asked with her hands out. "Where were you?" Adler was stirring awake finally.

"I went out to see what our situation was," Marilyn said, taking her boots off and placing them next to the door. She paused, eying the floorboards by the door. She shot a glare right at Stone then. "You didn't let that dog in here, did you?" Her tone was as serious as he'd ever heard her.

"No, ma'am! I would never."

"Yeah, he did," Ceres said. "I told him not to."

Marilyn sighed, shaking her head. "Well, when someone comes to me complaining about a flea infestation, I'm sending them your way to cast whatever spell they wish upon you."

"Fair enough," Stone said. "I just wanted to wash him up before we go off."

"I'd leave you here," she said. "If it wasn't that I needed you. Are you all ready? We should leave now. In the morning, Lord Borendür will send out his scouts in the early morning with hounds to search for us. He's not all too pleased about our attack upon his soldiers."

"What about their attack upon us?" Adler said, wiping the sleep from his eyes with his hands balled up.

"You think he cares about that?" Ceres asked. "I guarantee he didn't hear no peep about that from them."

"So, we leave now?" Stone asked.

Marilyn nodded.

"I need to get my things first," Ceres said. "There are some things I need at Serenity's Pub I have to get b'fore we're off."

"I'm afraid we can't do that," Marilyn said. "If they figured out who you were, they most likely found out where you were staying."

"Then leave without me," Ceres said as matter-of-factly as Stone had ever heard her speak.

"Fine," Marilyn said, returning that same tone.

"No, no, no." Stone shook his head. "We go together. Ceres, what's so important there that we have to risk our lives for?"

"Doesn't it sound to you like we're gonna be riskin' our lives from here on out?" asked Ceres. "I need to go back to the tavern. I'll go alone. It'd be better that way, anyways. I move best alone."

"We can give you fifteen minutes," Marilyn said. "I will take you all as close as we can get, and then you are on your own. If you're not back in that time… we're leaving, because in that case, you'll most likely be caught. And I'm not going to be breaking you out of no prison cell."

"Fine." Ceres nodded.

"Now, before we head off, I've got some things for you," Marilyn said. "You all ever swung a sword?"

Stone couldn't believe that with everything happening in the dark he didn't notice the four swords in scabbards she'd laid on the floor on top of her wet cloak in the dark. She picked them up and took them out one by one, handing them to them, keeping one for herself. The first thing that Stone noticed was the wet leather in his hand of the scabbard. Wrapping his fingers then around the wet, black leather-laced grip of the sword, a wide smile crossed his face.

He pulled the sword six inches out of the scabbard and stared at the metal as it reflected the faint moonlight that trickled through the window.

"Stone?" Ceres asked. "Are you all right? You seem…"

"Dazzled," Adler said. "You look awestruck. Have you ever held a sword before?"

Stone thought about that with a pause. "I have no idea."

"Ready?" Marilyn asked, breaking the conversation. "We need to leave, now."

***

THEY QUICKLY FOUND themselves with those heavy droplets falling upon their hoods and cloaks. As they followed behind Marilyn with their boots trudging through deep puddles, Stone had wrapped the sword belt around his waist, and his right hand held it tightly. His eyes scanned the dimly lit alleyways and Marilyn glided through them like a horned owl swooping down upon a field mouse; silently and powerfully.

They'd been scuttling down the short stretches of gaps between small homes for the better part of ten minutes before Marilyn finally made a real pause. She ducked down, putting her back to the clay wall while her silver hair crept out of her hood, reflecting the brief moonlight that threaded its way through the dark clouds. Each of them knelt behind her. She slowly peered around the corner, hiding most of her face with her wet hood.

Stone's heart pounded as he stared at her. They were only halfway to the tavern, and she appeared to have already stumbled upon something concerning. He couldn't wait to get out of this city, after their run-in with those bastard soldiers. Marilyn looked back at them, with Ceres kneeling next to her.

"Three of them," Marilyn whispered. "They're looking for us." She looked back around the corner, watching the three guards as they roamed the city streets at night. For Stone, it felt as if they were waiting forever, as he twisted the grip of his new sword in his hand. But then, suddenly, Marilyn turned back to them. "OK, let's move."

She rose to her feet and darted down the alleyway, making as little splashing sound as she could, as they all tried not to run. The sound of the storm though proved to be a sort of blessing, as the thunder boomed, drowning out all other sounds, and the constant deluge masked their footsteps well. Not to mention, how many soldiers would be walking around in this?

They made their way to the tavern, with Mud trailing not far behind. Marilyn stopped them fifty yards off, tucked away in a nook between two single-story homes with no lights coming from their interiors.

"All right." Marilyn glared at the inn. "You don't have much time, make every minute count."

Ceres ran back out into the rain, but Stone grabbed her arm.

"I'm going with you," he said.

Ceres returned this with a cold glare.

"You're staying put," Marilyn said. "This is her decision, and her risk. I can't risk losing you."

"Let go of my arm," Ceres said, pulling free from his lose grip. "I'm gonna be right back. I move better by myself anyways. But I need to go. I need to do this." With that, she was off into the shadows of the city. Stone was always impressed with the way she moved when she was on her own. She moved like a ghost, he thought.

She made quick, light footsteps as she wove her way around the building that led to the inn. As she disappeared behind the tavern, Stone caught a glimpse of something… something in one of the windows on the second floor. It was in their window! It was the distinct reflection of metal coming off a gauntlet as someone separated the curtains to gaze down onto the street below.

"You see that?" Adler said to both of them.

"It's a trap," Marilyn whispered She looked around them nervously. "We need to go. She's on her own now. I can't risk…" But as soon as she looked back at them, Stone and Adler were already running toward the inn, following the path Ceres had taken.

"Damned fools!" Marilyn spat, as she went off after them.

Ceres scaled the backside of the tavern's rear wall, gripping onto the framing of its back windows. She had less than an inch to grip onto, but that proved to be of little concern to her as she approached the window to her and Stone's room. With the sheer strength in her fingers she pulled her way up to look into the room. It was dark, with both curtains covering every bit of the interior. Putting her ear up to the window, she listened, but the rain was still strong and made it difficult to tell if there was anyone in the room or not.

But then she heard something loud and clear—below—Adler whistled like the call of a robin. It was loud enough for her to hear, but hopefully not loud enough to alert anyone else. Ceres turned her head and looked down at them, and Stone was waving his hands over his head, calling for her to come back down. She shook her head, raising an eyebrow as if to show she didn't understand him, but then, she quickly realized what he was saying when two strong hands clasped onto her wrists from out of the window, and pulled her in.

"No!" Stone yelled into the storm. He drew his sword from the sheath and ran around to the front side of the inn. At this time of night there were no patrons or things being served to them. The bar only had a single candle glowing from a corner of the room. Stone was quickly at the front door and clicked the latch to find that it was unlocked.

"Slow down," Adler said, "just a moment. Are we going to just rush up there?"

"Yes." Stone opened the door and slid into Serenity's Pub and Tavern. He heard the scuffle happening upstairs.

"Let me go!" Ceres screamed.

Stone and Adler flew up the stairs. He flung the door open and found six soldiers in full armor, all with their swords drawn. One at the back, that same mustached guard who'd attacked her before, was holding onto her with his arms wrapped around her, pinning her own arms to her chest. He was smiling a wicked smile.

A rush of rage shot through Stone then, and he wanted to yell out for them to let her go, but instead he burst forward with unexpected speed, catching the nearest soldier off guard. The guard nearly didn't get his sword up in time to block the swipe of Stone's. The metal of the swords clanged in the dimly lit room, as Stone laid blow after quick blow on him.

The other soldiers moved to surround him, and two of them stalked Adler, who was striding slowly down the wall.

"Stone," Ceres cried. "Behind you!"

He turned just in time to parry away a strong thrust by a soldier at his back, and Stone quickly found himself surrounded by three guards. They each attacked with swipes of their sharp swords, but his own seemed to move on its own. He twisted, turned, and his feet lightly shifted on the floor as he let his sword fly. He knocked away their thrusts, pushed back their arching swipes and dodged their strongest blows, but out of the corner of his eye he could see that Adler was struggling to stave off the other two's attack.

"We don't need you alive," the mustached guard said in a spiteful tone. "I'd rather prefer you dead anyway. It don't matter to our lord, and besides, I don't like it when my pretties get away from me." His slimy tongue then slid out of his mouth and he licked a long line up Ceres' neck.

"You son of a bitch," she cried. "Get off of me!"

Stone continued to fight off the blows of the guards, but then Adler said, "Stone, I could use some help here."

It was then that the bright red glow that had appeared in the alley before to save them filled the room.

Stone couldn't see the soldiers that were only feet away, but he quickly slipped away from their circle, making his way to where he thought Adler was.

"It's that witch again," one of the soldiers called out. "Find her and cut her throat!"

"Let them go," Marilyn said in the red mist. "Or this time I won't be letting you walk away."

Stone heard her that she seemed to be talking from just outside the doorway, and he heard the distinct clacking of the soldier's armor as they shuffled over there. In the red mist, he ran as well as the vines started to crawl up his legs, and certainly up the soldiers'.

"Quick, kill the bitch!" one of them yelled.

Stone pushed through the vines that clung to him, and was nearly at the door, when the red mist faded. The five guards were at the door as well, where each of them had paused, staring at Marilyn at the door. Stone's jaw dropped when he saw her brown eyes darken as she looked at him, then her gaze faded down and she gripped the bloody sword tip that had plunged into her back and was sticking out of her chest.

"Marilyn!" Ceres cried, stomping onto the mustached soldier's foot and flinging her head back to blast into his nose. That's when he loosened his grip, sighing in pain, and she ran from him toward Marilyn.

Stone and Adler were stuck in horror at the scene as the sword was drawn out of her as she winced and fell to the floor.

The soldier's held their swords out at the three of them, many of them with wry smiles on their faces.

"We got you now," one of them said.

"Now that your nasty witch is dead," another said.

Another soldier took a big step over Marilyn, who laid motionless on the ground.

Another one? How did I miss him? You're so stupid, Stone, this is all your fault. You should have checked first!

The last soldier joined the others, with his sword tip still covered in her blood. The soldier with the mustache grimaced as the blood ran down his nose. "Kill the boys and fuck it. Kill the girl too…"

Stone, think! What do I do? I can't fight them all off before they get to Adler and Ceres. Think!

Then, he noticed Marilyn shift on the floor, and she raised her hand out at the soldiers as she looked into the eyes of the soldier with the mustache.

"Excindier," she said in a weak voice.

Stone gasped and jumped back as smoldering smoke began to creep through the breaks in the soldiers' armor—all of them.

"Kill her!" one screamed in pain.

Stone watched as the smoke turned to a black ashen tone that covered their bare skin, moving up their necks to their faces, and then a hot fire burst from each of them. All of them fell to the ground crying out in pain. Marilyn had cast a spell on them, and then they were all burning alive. The flames rose from them as they yelled out for help. It was a grueling thing to watch, and Stone had to look away as the skin burned up from their bones, their hair was engulfed in flames from underneath their helmet.

The smell… the smell of burning flesh caused Stone to cover his nose and stride backward. Ceres ran around to Marilyn.

"Come on," Ceres said, "help me get her up."

Stone and Adler went over and helped. The soldiers had all stopped moving, each of them still burning with hot flames, but then the flames had moved away from them, and had then caught the drapes and furniture on fire. The whole place was going to go up!

They helped her up to her feet, but Ceres let her go. "Get her out of her," she said. "I've got to get something first."

"Ceres, no, we're getting out of here, the floor is going to collapse," Adler said.

"Go!" she said.

Stone and Adler each put one of Marilyn's arms around their necks as they carried her back downstairs. She was unconscious, but still faintly breathing.

"Don't die on me, Marilyn," Stone said. "We're almost outside. We'll get you fixed up, just stay alive!"

Chapter Fourteen

❧

As they carried Marilyn down the creaking stairs, the heat of the fires upstairs filled the dark corridor. Stone's head was flooded with worry for her, as her head bobbed as it rested on its right side in his hand. Below, in the tavern, he saw Ursula with a hand over her mouth and her eyes wide, holding a brass chamberstick with a single candle in her other. At the closed front door to the tavern behind her, there was a loud, frantic barking and clawing at the wood on the other side.

"Open the door," Adler said to her, but she only stood there in shock.

"What's happened?" she asked. "Where'd that fire come from? We've got to put it out!"

"Open the door!" Adler shouted. "We've got to get her away from here."

The stunned Ursula turned and opened the door, letting Mud fly into Stone's side.

"There's no putting out the fire," Ceres said as she rushed down the stairs. "The whole rooms ablaze." She gave her a paused look, touching her on the shoulder. "I'm sorry. The floor and ceiling are going to come down soon. I'm very sorry. Grab what you can, while you can."

While the old woman rushed behind the bar, out of sight, Stone and Adler carried Marilyn outside and into the alley two houses down. They laid her down gently on the dirt. There were dark bags under her eyes and her skin was pale; ghost-like. Adler bent his ear down to her mouth.

"She's breathin', but only slightly," he said and his voice cracked slightly.

"Marilyn?" Stone jostled her shoulders. "Marilyn, wake up."

Adler took his shirt off and placed it on the wound on her chest. He pressed down on it firmly.

Ceres had heavy streams of tears rolling down her face, with both her hands clenched inward over her mouth.

"Marilyn," Stone continued. "You have to wake up, you can't die on us, not now."

Mud then ran out of the tavern, darting over to them, and he started licking Marilyn's cheek.

"Mud, go away," Adler said, nudging him away with a shove, but Stone looked down in surprise to see Marilyn stirring awake, and blinking slowly.

Each of them hovered over her, and Ceres dropped to her knees, grabbing onto one of Marilyn's hands.

"Wh—Where am I? What happened?" she asked, staring off into the sky, as the rains had slowed to a soft trickle.

"You… You're injured," Stone said, "but we're going to get you better, you've just got to hold on until we can find someone to…"

Marilyn's eyes closed, her face strained, and she winced in pain. After the long strain of the rush of pain, she looked down and saw Adler holding the bloody shirt with both hands on her.

"I'm so sorry," Ceres cried, squeezing her hand and

holding it up to her mouth, kissing it. "It's my fault, it was all my fault."

A strained, but warm smile came to Marilyn's face then. "Did... did you get what you sought?"

Ceres closed her eyes tightly, letting thick drops of tears roll down, nodding. Her mouth was pursed, her wet hair stuck to the sides of her face, and she was sobbing.

"May I ask, my dear?" Marilyn struggled to say. "What was it you needed?"

Ceres' head dropped down onto Marilyn's hand, letting out deep sobs.

"It was..." said Ceres, "...letters from my mother and father... before they died..."

Marilyn smiled again. "Good," she said as her eyes closed. "Good... I'm glad you got them back..."

"Stay with us, Marilyn," Stone said. "You can't go to sleep. You've got to stay awake."

"I got 'em, didn't I?" Marilyn said. "Haven't used that spell in an age... Not a pleasant one..."

"Marilyn!" Stone shook her shoulders.

That's when her eyes popped open wide, and she gave an unsettling stare into his eyes. "You've got to reach Endo. Corvaire, you must see him. He can help you fulfill what it is you must. The elders at Endo, they can show you your path."

"You can take us there," Stone said. "We'll get you better, we will..."

"West to the shores of the Sacred Sea," she said. "Where the mountains kiss the sea waters and a sharp rock like a shark fin breaks the warm waters, pointing to the heavens. A white streak is painted down its front side. Climb the mountain there, and search for an olive tree where there shouldn't be, follow the path there up, and you will find Endo. Learn the ways of the sword on your travel, not only the Nefarian and King Arken are out there thirsting for blood. You must find Corvaire… find him… find him before…"

Then, Marilyn's fiery eyes closed, her head rolled lifelessly to the side, and they'd never hear another word from her again.

As Ceres sobbed, and the tears rolled down Stone's cheeks, Mud howled. It was a hollow, somber howl that broke the rain, silenced the wind, and filled the sky with a broken sadness. They'd lost their friend, giving her life to save theirs. And now —she was gone.

They sat around her body, as the watered-down blood pooled beneath her. Of all the things they'd gone through together since Ceres saved Stone from his underground prison, a certain kind of gravity fell over him like a thick veil casting a dark shadow over him. He then realized what was truly at stake now. He'd almost been killed by a dragon and the king of the Nefarian himself, but now Stone realized that people were going to die in this war. This wasn't a nameless person out in the fray, this was a person who cared about him, and a person he cared for.

Staring at her pale skin, and the silver hair matted to her face, he brushed it back behind her ear.

"Farewell," he said. "Thank you for everything. Even if you were wrong about me, you gave me purpose, and I promise I'm going to do everything I can to get to Endo and find what is there for me."

The growing heat of the top level of the tavern was now a blazing inferno. Everyone in the city could see the bright glow, Stone thought. The scattered rain did nothing to alleviate the high-reaching flames. As he watched Ursula spinning in circles frantically before her torched tavern, he told himself he'd help her rebuild someday, and he worried for her safety, but figured the soldiers had no reason to harm her once they arrived.

Mud's howling faded, and his head snapped to the north,

he lowered his head and the fur on the back of his neck straightened. Stone laid Marilyn's head to the ground and rose, looking north.

Ceres' lip quivered as she said to herself, "It's my fault, I'm so sorry. It's all my fault."

"It wasn't your fault," Adler said. "I should've seen that soldier that got her. I should've known to check."

Mud growled.

It didn't take long for Stone to realize that Mud's instincts hadn't proved wrong yet.

"Guys," he said, taking a step backward. "I think someone's coming. We should be off now."

Ceres continued to sob on Marilyn, but Adler's senses perked as he gazed north.

"Yeah, I reckon we should probably be off," Adler said, waving for the others to follow.

Stone went over to Ceres and placed his hands on her arms.

"C'mon, Ceres," he said in a soft, yet urgent voice. "There's nothing we can do here for her now. Worse off, she wouldn't want us getting killed hanging around."

Ceres leaned down and pressed her lips to Marilyn's head. "I'll get him to Endo. I promise."

Stone began to hear the clanking of metal and the shuffling of thick-soled leather boots coming from the road to the north.

"Come on," he said as he helped Ceres to her feet. "We need to get out of the damned city."

She wiped the tears from her cheeks and they both started off after Adler. Mud followed.

They turned left into an alleyway quickly, running through the shadows of the city at night. Rats raced along the bottoms of wet walls, and the smell of soaking wet linens and human excrement filled their nostrils as they went along. As the sound of the crackling fire dimmed, the sounds of the soldiers yelling back at the inn did as well.

"How are we supposed to find a way out of this place?" Stone asked Adler as they crept around another corner, their boots sliding on the wet stone of the alleyways of Atlius. "They're not going to let us just walk out of the front gate, especially now with all that smoke rising from the tavern."

It was then that he heard the horns blow from the city center.

"Damn," Adler said, looking both ways down a new alleyway. "The front gate ain't gonna be open now, not with the horns going off. We're going to have to use another way."

"Another way?" Stone asked. "You know of another way out?"

"I think so," said Adler, looking deep in thought as he scratched the side of his face. "My master told me about it, but it was years ago, I'm trying to remember."

"Well, you'd better remember quickly," Stone said. Mud was behind them, peering down the alleyways behind. Ceres had a blank look in her eyes that conveyed that she was only a shell of her normal self—at least for the time being.

"I know—" Adler said, seemingly talking to himself, "—it is to the west. I think it's by a cobbler's house, or was it a tailor?"

The muffled sounds of soldiers came from the north alley, and the dull glow of torchlight crept around the corner.

"West it is," Stone said, urging Adler forward, and grabbing Ceres by the wrist, pulled her after him. They ran down the slender alley, with Mud behind.

They soon turned another corner that veered to the right, still heading west-ish, and as they ducked underneath a line of wet clothing someone forgot to bring in before the storm, Adler reached up and nicked a white shirt from the line. Stone wanted to say something, but he felt bad for his friend running in the cool drizzle with no shirt.

"I can't believe she's dead," Ceres said softly as they ran. "I can't believe she's gone. I wish I could've done it differently. I shoulda' known they'd be up there."

"Just keep running," Stone said. "We'll have time to grieve later, once we're out of this place."

"Or was it a baker's house?" Stone heard Adler say at the lead.

"You're joking, right?" Stone asked.

"I'm pretty sure it's a cobbler's house. I think I remember it has a red-painted sign above the door. That much I'm sure about, I think. I'll know it when I see it."

The horns continued to blow. Their call was brassy and bellowing as it rang out within the walls of the city. It was then that Stone wished the rains would pick up once again so that they may find fewer watching eyes out in the streets. But they ran, ducking under open windows, sliding through slender pockets between homes that no armored guard would be able to squeeze through. It seemed to Stone that they'd run through the city forever. His mind was on Marilyn, who lay in a pool of her own blood, but also for his friends' safety. They couldn't stay in the city any longer. He knew they needed to leave before the light of the sun rose over the city walls and the sky was already beginning to lighten.

Chapter Fifteen

※※※

Another twenty minutes or so rolled by, and Stone could tell that not only was the sun's light emerging from its deep sleep, but the city itself was stirring to life. The horns had died down from the center of the city, but the glow of candlelight was growing within the homes they were running past, and the rain had all but died.

"How much farther?" Stone asked, his breathing was more labored and heavier.

"Don't think it's much farther," Adler replied, his eyes darting down long stretches of road, and down short, jutting alleys. "I think it's just down this way. Can't be that far off now."

Ceres followed behind Stone, she'd been silent the whole time they'd been running, not uttering a single word. Stone worried for her, but there'd be plenty of time to worry once they were safely out of the city. Mud, good old Mud, followed behind her.

The alley they were running down was about to end, Stone could tell. It opened into a wide road that a horse and wagon jotted down, walking past the mouth of the alley ahead. But something caught his eye, even past a hobbling drunkard that staggered down the road, a muted flash of red above a door swayed in the breeze. It was only a small sign, hidden underneath a shaded overhang, but he got a warm feeling that ran from his stomach up to his shoulders.

"That it?" Stone asked.

Adler didn't reply immediately, but after they'd taken another dozen steps he looked back and nodded to Stone. "I think that's it. We gotta cross the road and get around to the backside of the house. There's something back there that should let us out."

"Should?" Ceres finally spoke.

"Yup, should," Adler said. "Remember, this was years ago that he told me this."

"What do we do if it doesn't work?" Ceres said.

"Pray for wings," Adler said.

"I don't know why I ask you anything." Ceres sighed.

As they approached the end of the alley, Stone put his back to the right wall, his hands gliding along the rough, moss-coated mortar, it smelled of pungent, wet grass. The sunlight had grown to a point where it had cast a shadow, letting its light seep into the alley.

We've got to get out of this city, and fast! He then heard a barking sound that made his heart beat wildly: dogs. A pack of hounds was behind them in one of the other alleys. Stone looked at Mud behind them, and the dog whimpered.

"Let's go," said Stone to the others, and each of them nodded.

"Just walk casually across the road," Adler said. "We're just normal people crossing. But don't draw any unwanted attention."

He poked his head around the corner, scanning for soldiers, but after not seeing any, left the safety of the alley back out into the eye of the public. Stone went after, and then Ceres. Each of them hung their heads low as they walked straight across the street, meanwhile, the sounds of the barking and howling hounds on their trail was growing louder. Stone's heart continued to beat strongly, pumping warm blood in his shoulders and neck. He felt like he might burst aflame.

They were nearly across the alley, and Stone looked up at a group of young men walking down the road. Each of them, four in all, were looking in the direction of the pack of hounds approaching. One of the men looked at Stone then, into his eyes. The man's gaze was hazy, as if sleep hadn't found him that night. If he'd been up all night, he surely heard the horns blow, and knew something had happened, especially with the blaze, Stone thought. He put his head down and continued following Adler out of the road and around to the backside of the house.

Once out of view of the road, they ran around the house and Adler quickly scanned the wall, which was the outer wall of the city. It was a rough stone patch of wall that showed no sign of any door or secret passage through.

"What are we looking fer?" Ceres asked.

"There's supposed to be some sort of latch or something..." said Adler, running his hands all over the still-moist stone from the rains.

Stone felt a sense of tension in the air, as Adler frantically searched for the latch he vaguely remembered was there. The air was thick and muggy with the warmth of the sun filling the nooks and crannies of the city. Stone then felt the urge to peak around the backside of the house, checking to see if anyone was following them, and indeed, once he looked, a feeling of dread welled up in his stomach.

The pack of four men had stopped in the road, and were holding a conversation, while the one who'd seen Stone was pointing to the back of the house, to where they were, and the barking of the hounds was louder still.

"Hurry, Adler," Stone said, turning back to see Ceres now checking the wall. "We're gonna have company soon."

"I'm looking, I'm looking," Adler said. "Give me a minute."

Stone looked back to the road and saw the four young men were walking toward them, walking to the backside of the house.

"We don't have a minute," Stone said.

Adler gave a strained sigh, frantically looking for anything that would get them out of this mess.

Mud leaped to action, jumping into the alleyway on the side of the house and barked at the four men with wicked aggression. The four were startled, as Mud came off like a rabid dog with how angrily he was barking. The four of them paused, confused as to what they should do next, and as Stone was getting the feeling that they wouldn't want to deal with a mad dog, his hope faded as one of the men picked up a rock from the road and hurled it toward Mud. Mud moved to the side, letting the jagged rock hurtle past, and he snarled; again, barking his vicious bark. But then another stone flew, and Stone felt a sense of rage wash over him, as all nervousness about their situation was extinguished.

"Hey!" he yelled, leaving the safety of the backside of the house. "That's my dog, leave him alone you drunks!" He picked up one of the stones the boys had thrown, and he held it over his shoulder, ready to let it fly.

The four paused again, unsure of what to do, at least for a moment.

"Adler..." Stone heard Ceres say in a soft voice. "Find anything?"

In the narrow alleyway, Mud continued to snarl and bard as the standoff between the four and Stone loomed.

Then one of the boys spoke, "You have anything to do with a fire last night?"

"I saw the fire, sure, anyone who was awake did," Stone said. "I didn't have a thing to do with it though."

"Why are you hiding back there then?" the boy asked, turning the rock around that was in his hand at his side.

"Looking for something," Stone said, not sure what else to say about why they were back there.

"Looks like you got hounds after ya," another boy said. "Sure to be a reward for ya if ya ain't telling the truth."

Stone wasn't sure what to do next, as he wasn't the best liar, and the boys didn't seem to be buying what he was selling anyway. That's when Ceres emerged into the glow of sunlight in the alley, walked over to Stone's side, wrapping her arm around his. Stone caught her wink at the boys, and without a word pulled Stone out of the alleyway and back again to the backside of the house. He saw at least one of the boy's smirk.

They were now out of view, and Mud continued to bark.

"That may have given us a couple minutes," she said to Adler. "But if there's nothing here, we're going to have to run."

"Run where?" asked Stone.

"I don't know," she quickly responded. "But we're sure to be caught if we stay here much longer."

Stone then went to the wall, running his hands up and down it, looking for a latch, but he sensed that Adler, whose forehead was covered in nervous sweat, had checked the wall well already. So, he took his hands down and started to look at the grassy ground at their feet. Looking around, he didn't see anything that looked out of the ordinary. Ceres peaked around the side of the house.

"They're still there," she said. "Only now they aren't looking this way, they're looking the other way in the direction of the dogs. They're... they're waiting for them."

Stone noticed something then. He wasn't sure if it was anything, and it wasn't on the wall, or in the grass, but on the backside of the house itself. The back of the house was constructed with small stones held together with a gray mortar, but one stone, about knee-high, had a gap around it. The stone was only the size of an apple, but more oblong. He didn't ask Adler for his input, instead he put his thumb on the rough stone and pushed. Nothing seemed to happen, but as the sound of the hounds was almost drowning out Mud's barking, he dropped to a knee, pressed his knuckles against the stone, and pushed hard.

The stone gave way, moving back only a half of an inch or so, but he heard a click.

Next to his feet, he heard another click, and a small gap had formed in a patch of rocky ground free of grass. By this point Adler noticed too, and he ran over and dove his fingers into the gap, lifting up.

There it is… a passageway underground! Thank the heavens, and not a moment too soon! Those hounds are in the road.

"Ceres," Stone said over to her, still looking around the side of the house; her fingers were nervously tapping its stone wall. She turned and saw the hidden door as Adler had lifted it up, the back side of which was hinged. She ran over and went in first, climbing down a narrow set of stairs into the shadows below. Mud noticed too and ran in after her.

"Go," Adler said to Stone, who didn't hesitate, and Adler climbed in behind, letting the hinged door seal behind him, and with it, a solid blackness surrounded them.

Chapter Sixteen

❧

With the snap of the hidden door closing behind them a veil of near-total darkness enveloped them. Stone laid his hand on Mud's coarse fur, stroking it gently. Above, the muffled patting of heavy footsteps caused an echo in the shadows. The hounds barked wildly too, letting their confusion show in their high-pitched yelps and low moans.

Stone felt slender fingers slip in between his and begin to pull. Ceres led him through passageway underneath the wall to the city as he'd taken his hand off Mud's back and let it slide along the wall to his right. They were careful to step lightly, even with all the noise above, Stone figured if they found the door in the ground it wouldn't take much to pry it up with a couple of strong swords. They continued along that straight path for a few minutes before the wall to their side veered right.

They walked another ten minutes or so as the sounds of the moaning dogs drowned out behind them. Eventually, after walking in the cool, yet moist, passageway—they stopped. He heard Adler whisper from in front of Ceres. "It stops here."

"Can you feel anything?" Ceres asked. Stone heard her

hands searching the walls for a clue as to how to get out of the tunnel.

"Not yet," Adler said.

Stone turned and searched for anything that may lead them out of the darkness, and out of the wretched city. He was surprised to find his hands wrapped around a rickety, wooden ladder.

"Found something here," he said, as he climbed up. The ceiling wasn't high. Ceres and Adler were both below him, waiting.

Stone pushed on the ceiling, it was paved with smooth stones, and cold to the touch. It didn't seem to move, as hard as he pushed. "Ceres, get up next to me and help."

She climbed the ladder, and as they were pressed together on the thin ladder, they both pushed together. As they groaned, Stone thought he felt the ceiling budge, if at least only by a little.

"You feel that?" she asked.

"Yup," he said. "I think it's the exit."

They both pushed together, this time harder.

"That's it," Adler said from below. "You've got it."

The door moved a little more this time from Stone's side, and this time, a crack of light ripped into the darkness, cutting it like a sharp sword.

Once the door was slivered open, he found the door open easily, and once it was open only wide enough for him to peak through, he climbed another rung of the ladder. He could barely open his eyes at all to the blinding light. Stone found they were in the middle of a grassy field, with a road one-hundred or so yards off, and tree line just beyond.

"What do you see?" Adler asked.

Stone didn't see the city, so he assumed it was behind the door.

"There's a forest out there," he said. "We could make it there pretty quick if we run."

"Anyone around?" Ceres asked.

"Don't see anybody." Stone scanned the road. "But it's bright and sunny out there. Someone from the city walls would be sure to see us. If I had to guess, we're less than a mile from Atlius."

"Should we wait until nightfall?" Ceres asked. "None of us have had a wink o' sleep in a good span."

"I sure don't want to sleep down here," Adler said. "Not if the guards are gonna find that door eventually."

"So, we run?" Ceres asked. "If they spot us, they'll be sure to send the hounds out again."

"What about Mud?" Stone asked.

"What about him?" Ceres asked with a slight groan in her voice.

"We could let him out first," he said. "We could see if he notices anything…"

"The dog doesn't speak our tongue," she said sharply. "What's he gonna do? Wave his paws in the air if a dragon comes? Or is he going to bark five times if there's soldiers, four if it's a mother breastfeeding a toddler?"

Stone sighed as Adler chuckled. "Just hand him up here."

Adler reached down and lifted the dog to Stone as Mud moaned from being picked up so awkwardly. Stone lifted him and pushed him out of the opening. Mud quickly looked around, and after a few seconds, shook as if to shake off the darkness from below. He then sat on his side and scratched his ear with his hind leg.

"Looks pretty good to me." Stone took another step up and rung and opened the door more.

"Damn dog better not have lice." Ceres scratched her hair nervously.

Stone put his boot up on the grass patch above, and slowly

rose out of the passageway—the scabbard of his sword knocked onto the stone underside of the door as he did. He knelt low and quickly looked back at the city's walls. He was impressed with the distance they'd made. They were in fact easily a mile or more away. They must have been down in the corridor longer than he'd thought.

"Come on up," he said, reaching our for Ceres' hand.

"I've got it," she said, helping herself out into the field, and Adler followed.

"The forest?" Adler asked quickly, his eyes were narrow from the sun, but there was a great sigh of relief in his voice.

"I can't believe we got out of the city," Stone said. "Praise to the Golden Realm you remembered that way out."

"Aye," Adler said. "Glad my memory's not all rubbish."

Stone looked over and saw Ceres was already making her way toward the forest, and they all quickly followed. They ran through the tall grass as it whipped behind them. There was little breeze in the warm afternoon as three ravens circled them overhead. Stone's boots were soon running over the road and they were quickly in the safety of the trees just beyond.

Once they were a few hundred feet from the empty road each of them found a spot to sit upon a fallen tree two feet in diameter. Stone breathed heavily, catching his breath, and Mud gulped water out a stream just behind them.

"Well," Adler said, wiping the sweat from his tan brow with the back of his forearm. His crisp blue eyes glistened in the sunlight that spotted the forest floor through the thick tree cover overhead. "We are on the west side of the city. That's a good thing. We won't have to go all the way around to make our way toward the sea."

"Where are we?" Stone asked, looking around the increasingly thick woods.

"Everwood forest," Adler said. "Said to be haunted…" His eyes grew wide as he said this.

"Stop it," Ceres said. "Not everything is a joke."

"Fine." Adler waved his hand. "Stone's too gullible as it is. I can't help myself."

They each took a moment to enjoy the fresh breeze that blew past then, and Stone then felt the exhaustion roll over him. His muscles ached, his feet burned, and his eyelids felt heavy.

"I'm hungry," Adler said. "We got anything to eat?"

Stone shook his head, and Ceres too.

Adler looked around at the trees. "I'm not hungry enough to eat grass yet…" He looked at Mud as he lay by the stream, snoring. "Meat does sound pretty tasty, though."

"Don't even think about it," Stone said.

"Stone. You really need to work on not being so easy to tease, it's not becoming." Ceres sighed and looked back at the tips of the highest points of Atlius that were only just visible through the trees and from that distance. "Poor Marilyn," she said with a crack in her voice. "I hate to think what they're doing with her body now. You think they'll bury it eventually?"

"Not sure," Adler said. "She did attack the soldiers with her magic. There's a strong chance they're gonna label her a witch."

"Was she…?" Stone asked. "A witch?"

"Suppose so." Adler scratched his head. "But a good one, no doubt about that."

"I'll remember her forever," Ceres said, rubbing her arms up to her shoulders. "She helped me when I needed it most. I never felt so vulnerable as I did then." She looked into Stone's eyes. "Thank you, you two for coming to help me too. That was brave of you. You could'a died."

"That's what friends are for," Stone said with a smile. "You would have done the same for me I bet."

Ceres nodded, and Adler smiled. "Aye, we would'a," she said.

Tears rolled down Ceres' cheeks. "We gotta reach Endo, if for no other reason than to honor Marilyn's last wish…"

"How far is it?" Stone asked, pulling his black hair to the back of his head.

"Far," Adler said. "We've got to make it to the Sacred Sea. It could be weeks to get there, depending on what path we take. The road is quickest, especially if we had the coin for horses."

"Once we get far enough from the city," Ceres said. "They won't be looking for us. We'll have other things to worry about out in the open."

"I really don't want to run into anymore Neferian out there," Stone said. "That's for certain. I could die a happy man never seeing one of those dark monsters ever again."

"I'll second that," Adler said.

"You think it's safe to rest here?" Stone asked them, as Mud snored behind. "I feel like I could sleep for a week, but I sure don't want to wake up to a battalion of soldiers making their way through the trees."

"You two go ahead and rest," Adler said. "I'll watch out for a few hours. Gotta look for something to eat anyway. I'm more hungry than tired at the moment."

"Sounds good to me," Ceres said as she sat with her back to the fallen tree, put her hands behind her head, closed her eyes and slunk down.

"Is that comfortable?" Stone asked.

"Not really," Ceres said. "But right now, I could sleep in the middle of a battle if I had to."

Stone moved to sit on the grass, with his back to the tree. His eyes almost closed themselves, and he fell into a deep, soothing sleep. He woke moments later to an itching sensation on the side of his head.

Chapter Seventeen

A crack of thunder and a gentle patter of rain on Stone's forehead caused him to stir awake. He slowly opened his eyes, and after rubbing them, and letting out a grizzly yawn, he scratched the back of his head. The itchy sensation felt as if it could never be satiated. He looked to his side, and in the dim light of the sun cast behind thick clouds, Ceres lay on her side, itching her head under her golden locks.

Luckily enough for them, Adler had returned and was sitting on the fallen tree eating a red and green apple, morsels of which were flying from it as he took big bites. Next to him was a mound of them, placed upon a wide, green leaf on the ground. Adler noticed Stone was looking at him and tossed him one. Stone took a bite, and its sweet juices caused him to close his eyes and smile.

Ceres pushed herself up from the ground, and then she got to her feet. She was itching her head with one hand, and then with a low groan she itched with both hands, showing her irritation.

"What did I tell ya?" Ceres asked in Stone's direction—her teeth were nearly clinched.

He sat there silently, eating his apple, hoping to avoid the blame. More raindrops fell around them through the dense tree cover above.

"Stone." Ceres waved her arms to get his attention. "You know we got this from that mangy mutt over there. I told you!"

Her just talking about it only made his head itchier. He tried to resist but thinking about it made the skin on his head feel like thousands of tiny pinpricks were causing a small fire—so he itched with one hand, while shrugging with the other.

"Could've gotten them from somewhere else," he said.

She gave a heavy sigh with her mouth pursed. "You really are thick. Aren't ya?" Looking over at Adler, with his mouth full of apple, he had a slightly amused look on his face. "Don't tell me you don't have this too?"

His mouth turned forcefully from a smile to a straight mouth, and he shook his head.

"Mother of mercy, of all the men... *boys*, I mean, in this world, I get stuck with you two." She scratched her head again.

༻❀༺

HOURS LATER, they were walking through the forest, just deep enough into the trees that they could still see the road that snaked along the side of the Everwood. As the sun was about to set behind the countless trees to the west, the forest stirred to life. Stone didn't know what to think of it. From deep within, exotic bird calls echoed like they were in a wild menagerie. Beasts howled, bats swooped overhead, and the overwhelming sound of insects buzzing made the forest seem like the last place he'd want to rest for the night—especially with no blankets or pillows. Ceres and Adler didn't seem to share his concern though; Mud neither.

"Should we camp out here?" Ceres asked suddenly.

Stone was about to reply, but instead, he caught Mud's sudden attention shoot to the eastern sky. He was looking past the trees to the clouds that were still thick and glowing a warm orange hue. The scant raindrops were still fluttering in the trees above, and the forest seemed to crawl back into slumber. Stone felt a heavy stillness behind him. The sounds seem to have all but faded to a thick silence. Mud let out a low growl.

It took Stone a moment to see what was out there, but Ceres walked next to him and extended her arm out so that his eyes could trail from her shoulder to her extended finger out into the sky, and that was when he saw it—one of them… one of the Neferian.

It was only a silhouette from that distance, that much he was happy for. But he could see the many horns jutting out from its head, he saw the spikes on its tail as it whipped through the air, he saw its long arms with vast, spiny wings flowing behind them—one of the main differences from them and the dragons, as the dragons had short, strong arms that were separate from their wings—and of course, he could see the rider that was perched upon its back.

The monster in the distance let out that roar Stone hoped he'd never hear again. It burst out like an explosion, with the tinge of broken glass rippling out as it echoed throughout the miles that surrounded it. Stone could almost feel the resonance from it even at that distance. The forest itself felt as though it was holding its breath, trying to hide from the beast.

Each of them ducked down low, but it was desperately hard to look away. It was terrifying. Stone's hands sweat, he noticed he'd been holding his breath far too long, and his eyes went wide as his legs felt weak. But then and there, it was like watching a shipwreck—as horrible as it was, no one would look away, even if all they wanted to do was help.

The Neferian soared up and down through the thick,

orange clouds as it screeched and roared. It was heading north and didn't seem to notice them. Stone wasn't sure why such a monstrosity would waste its time on three people, when there were real dragons out there chasing after them, but it felt as though the Neferian would be continuing on its way without sensing them.

It let out one last call, it was faint, yet powerful as it was almost completely hidden by the clouds as it soared. Stone took a deep breath and sighed a sense of relief. He looked next to him and saw Ceres with glassy eyes and her hands covering her mouth. Adler's mouth was completely agape with raised eyebrows, and Mud sat licking his paws. *That dog isn't afraid of anything! He's either dumb as a toad, or as brave as a badger.* Stone knew which was truer though.

With the deadly Neferian gone, they set to make a small fire. Small enough to raise their spirits, and give them something to warm the cold, damp forest from their clothes. They hadn't been expecting to leave the city like they did after all. All their warmer items were left back at the burning inn.

Stone collected kindling and firewood while Adler relaxed, and Ceres went off looking for food. While he was bending over, picking up sticks and bundling them in his other arm, many questions flowed through his splotchy mind—questions he hadn't had time to think about since… well… since everything. His life had only just begun, and there hadn't been many dull moments yet. So many questions… and almost no answers. *I pray to Crysinthian, the one true god, that someone in Endo can tell me who I really am. I don't want to live like this forever. I just want some answers. I want to know my real name…*

⁂

LATER THAT NIGHT, huddled around the fire which burned with warm oranges and slivers of blue flame, the three of them stared into the flames as it popped and hissed. Adler held his palms out to warm them, Stone had his arms draped over his knees as he sat on a log, and Ceres looked as though her mind was elsewhere as her eyes glazed over and her eyelids drooped.

Stone itched his head, and Ceres nervously did the same. Over by Adler, Mud scratched at the side of his muzzle, then he stopped and panted looking up at Adler.

"There's something I've been meaning to ask you," Adler said to Stone, breaking the silence.

"What's that?" Stone said as he prodded the fire, sending a stream of embers coursing up into the air.

"You—" Adler began, "—the way you handled yourself with that sword up there in the tavern. How'd you learn to do that? I've been training most of my life and… I ain't be able to do some of those things. Ah, cursed be the Dark Realm! You fought off three trained soldiers at once! How in the Halls of Gillry did you do that?"

Stone wasn't sure how to answer, but saw Ceres had a look in her eyes that showed she was curious for an answer as well. He shrugged. "Beginner's luck?"

Adler didn't feign a laugh like Stone expected. "I'm serious, what was that? How'd you learn to do that?"

"You want the truth?" asked Stone. "I have absolutely no idea."

"That doesn't make no sense," Adler said, scratching the stubble on the side of his face.

"But, I'll say this. I know it felt good holding that sword in my hand for the first time. I had no idea how to handle it, but my hands felt at home once I had it. I'll say this too, I'm sure glad my body and hands knew what to do when the time came, because I sure didn't. All I knew was that Ceres needed our help."

Adler nodded, and Ceres gave them both a look of gratitude with a warm smile as the light of the fire glistened off her rosy, freckled cheeks.

"There's another thing we haven't talked about yet either," Adler said.

"Marilyn's last spell…" said Ceres in an ominous tone.

"That was near… God-like," Adler said.

"That was terrifying," Stone said. "If we weren't on her side, I would've thought the whole world was ending the way those soldiers screamed and cried in agony."

"I—I want to learn it," Ceres said. "I mean… someday."

"Keep that rubbish away from me," Adler said, waving his hands out in front of him. "I don't want no magic even near me. You can have it all for yourself, Ceres."

"I think you'd make a good sorceress," Stone said to Ceres. "Maybe they'll teach us something once we get to Endo?"

"Don't get ahead of yourself, Stone," Adler said. "We've got a long way to go still before you start coming up with your, *Stone the… Whatever* name."

"How about Stone the Stonebreaker?" Stone asked with a wry smile. "Stone the Dragonslayer?"

"Stone the Stone-headed?" Ceres said, tapping him on the shoulder with her fist. "Stone the Too-Brave-he-almost-comes-off-as-foolish?"

"It does have a nice ring to it," Stone said with a wink.

Adler sighed. "I'm going to get some shuteye. One of you two take first lookout. I don't trust the dog yet. Wake me in a few hours. I just need to rest my eyes. We'll figure out our path tomorrow. I don't feel like we're going to have any more conversations worth remembering tonight." He laid on his side, facing the fire, and closed his eyes. "God, I wish I had a warm bed to lie on, and a barrel of ale right now… Where's a good forest tavern when you need one?"

Chapter Eighteen

The cool, crisp wind blew past the camp, sending dazzling embers floating up toward the rustling leaves overhead. Warm light cast on Stone's knees from the crackling fire. He smelled the smoke from the burning, thick logs before him as he picked up a piece of some possum meat Ceres had captured and cooked for them earlier.

She and Adler both slumbered soundly in the grass. Stone was happy they all weren't in cells beneath the keep of Atlius or strung up by their necks. Stone prodded the fire and saw Mud's eyes reflect orange as he glanced up at Stone, but then lay his head back down with a groan.

Stone could feel the exhaustion in his bones, but this night he had no trouble staying awake. There were too many questions to let his mind relax. He really, truly wished he could get some answers in the mountain town of Endo. But it was so far away, and he wanted answers right then.

He pulled the sword from its sheath at his hip, holding it out to inspect in the firelight. It glowed a majestic orange hue, flickering like sunlight through thick leaves. He ran his hand down the cool steel, feeling the new chinks in it from their fight back at the tavern. He remembered what it felt like to be in a sword fight like that. When it was happening, it felt like he was living someone else's life—like he was in somebody else's body... Then he angled the blade toward him, and as the glow of the fire faded, he caught his own reflection in the clean steel. His pale-skinned face held the warm hue of the fire. He saw his own gray eyes staring back at him, and he saw the unusual widow's peak that ran down most of his forehead. He hadn't seen anyone like himself yet...

An owl howled over to his right, high up in a birch tree. He looked over and saw Mud was still soundly asleep. Of everything he knew about his life at that point, Stone knew he could trust Mud's instincts, and he was grateful for that. He also knew without a doubt he could trust Ceres, even if she liked to put him down every once in a while. *It's probably something she's always done to protect herself. I've only been an orphan for a few days, I don't even know how long ago it was that her parents died... or how...* Adler was a trickier one to figure out, but Stone trusted him more than not, and he'd proven himself a good asset. He'd helped them escape the city after all and promised to help Stone reach Endo.

But there was one thing that bothered Stone more than anything, one thing that was so prominent in his mind that it resonated with him every waking hour... *Did I... Do I... have a family?* If he did, he'd find them. He'd *have* to find them. They could be looking for him right then, or they could think him dead. Either way, if he could do anything to get this answer, he swore to himself he'd find a way...

◈

IN THE EARLIEST hours of the morning, with the sun still not peaked over the horizon, a fresh morning dew clung to the grass at their feet. The fire had died down to a smoldering pile of ash with charred logs half-burnt away. There they stood, next to the dying fire, each with their swords at their side—no packs, no coin, no food—but they had a destination.

"Well?" Stone asked, pulling his long, black hair back and tying it with a strand of twine.

"We either go through the forest," Adler said, looking through the thick brush to the west. "Which will cover us almost completely but will take longer to walk through… or we take the road. He looked out to the dirt path that lay just outside of the woods to the east. We'd go north for a bit, curve around the forest, or if we're lucky, find a path through."

"What do you think?" Ceres asked Stone, with her arms folded over her chest.

Stone looked down at Mud that was next to his side; panting softly. "We're going to need to find food, and get some coins for the journey… right? We'll need something to keep us warm at night, and equipment for traversing the mountain. There's no coin in the Everwood, I'd reckon."

"There's a small town along the path to the north," Ceres said. "If we chose that way, I'll take care o' coin."

Stone eyed her inquisitively with a squint eye. "Is there something you're keeping from us? You know you can trust us."

She shook her head. "I've just got a nose for it. Don't bother yerself worrying about it. Just leave it to me. Hedgehorn is the town. Not near as big as Atlius, but they'll have prying eyes, nonetheless. We'll have to keep to ourselves. But… we could get a couple of nights in the tavern, not sleep in no wet grass."

"My vote's for bed and warm food," Stone said. "But it's not completely my decision to make."

"It is your quest," said Adler, his voice was low and strong. "This prophecy falls on you, not us. It should be you to make the decision."

Ceres and Adler both looked at him with waiting glances. Ceres brushed her dirt-covered golden hair back behind an ear with her fingers.

Stone didn't know what was best. Of all of them, he knew these lands the least. He looked down at Mud. "What'd you think boy?" Mud only leaned to one side and scratched the back of his ear. Stone instinctively scratched his own itchy head.

"You said it would take longer to get through the forest?" Stone asked.

"We'll cover less ground, yes," Adler said. "But who really knows, going around could take more time total, or less... It's been an age since I've been to that part of the country, and even longer since I've laid eyes on the Sacred Sea. But roads are always easier..."

Stone took a deep breath. "I hope I make the right choice here... Let's take the path of Hedgehorn, where at least we can bathe, and pray to god we don't see any more of the Dark Dragons."

PART IV
WARS OF KINGS

Chapter Nineteen

❧❧❧

Hours later, they were on the road that led north, and the warm sun raised their spirits. They walked next to one another, with Atlius far to the south. It was then that Stone thought of Marilyn and everything she'd done for them. His heart sank at the thought of the light in her eyes once he'd finally seen it. She cared for him, and she cared for these lands. He wished she was with them then.

Stone's stomach rumbled, and Ceres seemed to hear it with her head cocked, looking at it.

"I know," she said. "Me too." She scratched her head. "I don't know what I want more—food or fer this damned itching to stop! It may kill me before starvin' to death." She scowled at Mud. "You couldn't have picked a cleaner mutt to bring along with us?"

"To be fair," Stone said. "He found us, remember?"

She sighed, and Adler chuckled.

That was when they heard something approaching up ahead. Around a bend in the dirt road, they heard horse hooves pounding the ground. They shot over to the trees to their left, each hiding behind a tree, Ceres put her back to a fallen one. As the single horse came down the path, Stone saw there was a rider on its back. The rider was slumped over, as if taking a nap—and he wasn't moving.

The horse wore thick leather armor with silver rivets on its legs and chest, with thick straps. The man mounted on its back was in full armor, tarnished with splotches of blood, and his thinning, sweaty red hair was caked to the top of his tan head. Each of them watched curiously as the horse neighed as it marched slowly down the road. That was when the rider slunk down the side of the horse, falling onto his back with a grunt. The horse stopped and looked down at the man, who writhed on his back, letting out a long, low groan.

Stone then saw the horse's back and saddle was splattered with blood, and the man was clutching his stomach as he moaned. He then saw that Ceres stood from behind the safety of the downed tree and was walking up toward the man. Adler followed, and Stone too. They slowly approached the man, and Ceres kicked away the soldier's sword that lay next to him. She pulled her sword from its sheath and held it next to her.

"Who are ya?" she asked.

The soldier groaned with his eyes closed, not seeming to hear her at first.

"Huh?" she asked again, this time nudging him with the tip of her boot on his arm.

His eyes opened, they were reddened and glossy. Stone saw the man was injured in the stomach, as the blood pooled below him.

"H—Help me," he said in an agonizing voice. "Please…"

Adler, who had his sword at his side as well, sheathed it and knelt next to the man.

"Adler?" Ceres asked with wide eyes. "What're ya doin'? You don't know this man."

"Looking at the injury," he said, pulling the soldier's arms from his wound. He lifted the chainmail up over his stomach and tore a blood-stained white shirt apart to reveal a hole in the soldier's stomach made by a spear most likely. Blood pooled in his navel. Adler looked around and motioned for Stone to hand him the banner that was atop the back of the horse, it was a red banner with a red V and a yellow stripe across its center. Stone cut it from its mounts with his sword and handed it to Adler, who crumpled it and pressed it onto the wound. He looked up at Ceres and shook his head.

"He rides for the city of Verren," Ceres said, narrowing her eyes.

Adler sighed, pressing down the banner hard on his stomach as the soldier winced.

"Verren?" Stone asked. "What does that mean?"

"The castle in Verren is where King Roderix II rules," Adler said. "He's one of the ones leading this civil war you heard about. He's one of the warring kings."

"I thought the civil war was called to a truce," Ceres said with a furrowed brow… "at least for now…"

Adler leaned down to look into the man's eyes. They were a dark red at their corners.

"Where'd you come from?" Adler asked. "What happened to ya?"

The soldier groaned in pain, and Stone could tell he was in seething agony.

"War," the soldier said with a grimace. "War did this ta' me."

"War?" Stone gasped, as he looked north to where the soldier had ridden from, and from this new vantage point he saw two thin trails of smoke sifting up into the sky.

"What war?" Adler asked, still pressing onto his stomach.

"*The* war," the soldier said, closing his eyes and moving his head to the side. "We had 'em too. We had 'em!"

Ceres walked over to Stone's side and saw the lines of smoke rising into the sky.

"How—how bad is it?" the soldier asked Adler, moving his head up slowly to look down at his torso.

"It's deep," Adler said, with a faint tinge of remorse in his voice.

"I shoulda' seen that bastard," he groaned. "Coward came up from behind me…"

"Sir," Ceres said, turning back to look at him. "How far up ahead is the battle? How many?"

"Don't you be goin' that way lassie," he said, his voice clearer then. "It's the closest thing you'll see to the Dark Realm, I can tell ya' that. You… All of ya' will die if you head that way. If you're lucky, you'll only be captured, split up, and put in a life you'd never want… I can promise ya' that."

"We won't," Adler said. The soldier's body jerked then, shaky as he clenched his teeth, and blood rolled down both sides of his mouth.

"I thought the civil war was called to armistice due to the Neferian?" Ceres asked. "Have the warring kings decided to keep fighting each other even with such monsters in their own lands?"

"Ha," the soldier laughed. "You ever met the king? They're all the same. More arrogance and pride than all those in their kingdoms put together. Of course, they're fightin' again. Damned fools. We all knew it, but who would ever be foolish enough to test the will of King Roderix?"

"Don't they know we're gonna need everyone we got to fight the Neferian?" Adler asked, his voice grew angry when he said that.

The soldier's face grew deathly pale then, and his breaths grew shallow. He raised his head slowly, looking up to the sky. His eyes were wide, but unfocused. Stone knew he was dying. "Don't matter none if they can't be killed anyway… They're gonna kill everyone… They're gonna kill us all…"

The soldier's voice trailed off, his head slumped back, and

his eyes closed one last time. Adler let go of his stomach and rose, after wiping his bloody hands off on the soldier's pants.

"Damn," Ceres said. "There's a battle happening between us and Hedgehorn? When are we ever gonna catch a horse-sharten break?"

"Horse-sharten?" Stone asked. "Is that a real expression?"

She brushed him off with a wave of her hand.

"Speaking of horse," Stone said, looking at the horse still next to them on the road. It stood six or eight inches taller than Stone even when he was standing completely up straight.

The three of them all looked at each other, curious expressions ran over their faces.

"He's not gonna be needing it anymore," Ceres said, looking at the corpse on the ground.

"Stealing a soldier's horse isn't something we should be even amusing the idea of," Adler said.

"Like I said," she said. "It's not stealing if the man's soul is searching for a final place to rest. He's not gonna be needing it anymore, and we got a long way to go still."

"Could we take off all the armor and banner and get it to look like any other steed walking these roads?" Stone asked.

"If we re-saddled it," Adler said, but then something seemed to cross his mind as he raised an eyebrow and looked back at the horse. He walked over to it.

"What is it, Adler?" Stone asked, following him.

Adler lifted a flap from the right-rear of the saddle, and what he suspected of seemed to be there as Stone was looking at a large, circular brand with the same V and horizontal line as the banner of Verren.

"Yup, just what I thought," Adler said. "Not touching that horse within a stone's throw. That's a death wish taking that horse anywhere."

Ceres sighed. "Fine, well which way are we goin' now?"

Stone thought for a moment. He still very much enjoyed

the idea of a warm bath and a soft bed but didn't like the thought so much of dying on the road.

"What if we take the forest around the battle?" he asked. "Maybe it's far enough south of the city that we could still get in. I figure we might be able to round up the supplies we need still, before we head off to the sea?"

"We could," Ceres said, looking over to Adler for conformation. "It's risky, but if we stick to the deep woods, we should be fine. I'd say to do it in the daylight, to see if there's anyone else in the forest, ya' know… hiding out?"

"It should work if we stay deep enough in the Everwood," Adler said. "And I'm not sure what you two feel, but a bed would be a welcome treat."

"All right," Stone said. "Sounds like we're all in agreement then."

Ceres walked over to where they were, as Stone was unsure what she was doing, but he quickly realized what it was when she opened the pouches on the sides of the horse.

"What are you thinking?" Adler asked her. "You gonna take a dead soldier's things?"

She closed the flap on that one pouch, and then opened the one on the other side, promptly pulling out another canvas bag. She lifted out pieces of jerky and a large, round stale bread with the flour still baked on the top of it.

"The bugger had a sweet tooth too," she said. "There's chocolate in here."

Adler's eyes grew wide, and Stone's mouth watered.

"Search his body," she said. "There may be a flask for Adler."

"All right," Adler said, walking over to the fallen soldier. "We're only taking things that're gonna spoil. That's it."

Ceres looked at Stone, who was still in shock of the whole ordeal happening before his eyes. She threw a piece of jerky to him, and she winked his way. He popped it in his mouth and chewed. It was amazing: smoky, meaty and salty. It raised his hopes so his mind was set at ease for now.

He heard a whimper to his side, and saw Mud had a long string of drool falling from his mouth. Stone took half of the jerky, and just before tossing it to the dog, he instead held it out before him—to Stone's surprise, Mud sat patiently. He then gave the jerky to the dog, who took it eagerly.

Huh. I thought he was just another old street dog…

Chapter Twenty

※

With some food in their bellies, and fresh legs they crept back into the forest—deeper than before. It was still before the light of the high afternoon sun, and if the battle was still going on, it would have a whole day's worth of the light to keep going if it needed. Stone only hoped it was a small battle, and far done with and abandoned by the time they approached it.

There was something else that happened when they were by the body of the soldier; something that Stone had bittersweet emotions about… after they stripped the man's supplies of every morsel of food they could find, they also decided that a few coins wouldn't be missed. The soldier would have offered them with the help that Adler was giving him anyway! That's what Stone told himself at least. It was only five tabers, two quorts, and a dozen dinins… who would miss that? It's funny how the mind works though, because after they decided as a group that the coins wouldn't be missed, they continued to rummage, and now Stone had a dead man's socks wrapped around his feet. It left him with an icky feeling, but those socks sure were ten times softer than the damp ones he'd been running around in—after all, they did come from a casket with him in it.

Ceres had grabbed a pocketful of things from the soldier that Stone didn't notice. Adler only took a pouch of tobacco, a pipe, and two candles. Stone only took the socks. He left the boots. They left the body, as they figured there'd be a patrol after the fighting ended to collect the bodies and bury—or burn them.

They continued walking through the woods for the next couple of hours, northbound, and when they saw the first hints of the battle, they made their way deeper into the Everwood. It was not as Stone had hoped either—the battle was still going on—it was still raging. He wasn't sure how long it had been going on, but it appeared to him to be at its most brutal part… if there was such a thing. It was chaos without any discernible side to tell from the other. It was a sea of flashing metal, loud grunts and screams of dying pain out there beyond the trees. Stone wanted to crawl into his own skin from the sounds of the cries out there. He wished he knew some magic that would make him as small as a creepy, crawly insect so he could hide under the leaves on the forest floor, undetected.

"Wish we had an invisibility spell about now," Ceres said. Stone looked at her as each of them knelt side by side. It was as if she'd read his mind, or at least had seen enough death lately they both had thought about how useful a spell like that would be.

"I'll do fine just moving along," said Adler, heading north again with his hand on the grip of his sword. The other two followed. Stone began to pull his sword from its sheath.

"What're you doing?" Adler said, clasping Stone's hand and pushing the sword back in.

"Oh," Stone said. "The reflection…"

Adler let his hand go, and Stone fully sheathed it, but his hand didn't leave its grip.

"I can't believe they're daft enough to let this happen," Ceres said, shaking her head. "What a waste of life. We're going to need them in the battles to come. What do they hope to accomplish with this anyway? I swear… the egos of kings, eh? It's all about who's got the bigger pecker!"

"Aye." Adler snapped his fingers. "Nailed it there. That's what every war is about."

They continued through the woods, and even at that distance from the battle they were careful to not break the twigs beneath their feet. The three of them tried to stay as silent as fireflies in the night sky. There was an agonizing scream from the battle where at least a thousand soldiers battled wildly in the chaotic field. Stone was able to spot the soldier that had let out that horrendous scream and saw the javelin that protruded from his thigh. The soldier on the other end of it was twisting it in his leg, yelling himself in a mad rage. Stone picked up his pace, and looked behind, looking for Mud, who he didn't see.

"Hey, either of you two seen Mud?" he asked.

"Deep in the woods," Adler said. "If he's smart, and so far, he's proven himself certainly that. He's been in a hot spot less than each of us ever since we all met."

Ceres was silent, but scratched her hair, shaking fine dust from it.

"Once we're past all this," Stone said, scratching his own head. "We will get that bath!"

They walked for another twenty minutes underneath the shade of the great, tall trees above that swayed in the breeze. Rays of light speckled the forest floor like a shimmer on the sea, and Stone was able to appreciate the subtle beauty of the forest as the screams and roars waned. They weren't gone, more like drowned out by the slowly growing distance they were leaving behind them.

That feeling of security shriveled away quickly as another

sound appeared somewhere between them and the battle. They each heard the rustling of brush, followed by the low sound of a man's voice. The three of them quickly hid. Adler went stomach down to the ground behind a downed tree, Ceres knelt behind a short tree that looked like a bushy pine, and Stone ducked down behind a thick tree. He could feel his chest tighten, and he gripped his sword tightly in his hand.

Thus far, the man's voice was indiscernible, but this much had become clear to them—he wasn't alone. At least five men stumbled through the Everwood, and they were heading in Stone's direction. Stone looked at Adler and Ceres for what they were thinking to do; run, hide, or fight…

Adler had his sword's grip in his side, but was waving his hand at them, motioning for them to lay low. Ceres glared at the men through the pine, she was ready to fight if they needed, he thought. Stone hoped that if he needed it again, his sword would know what to do if push came to shove.

"I'd have not left the bloody battle," Stone heard one of the men say in a low tone and thick accent. "If it hadn't have been for such foolishness! What're a battalion of three hundred s'posed to do against five? If we woulda stayed we'd have ended up like the rest of 'em. We were right to leave!"

The other men grunted in affirmation. Stone now counted eleven of them. *Eleven* hardened soldiers. Wait… *twelve!*

"Aye," another said. "We would've fallen back there like our brothers. This way we live ta fight another day for our king. He'll see that. He surely will. He's just!"

"Here, here!" another said.

"Y'all are buffoons with cotton fer brains," another said. "We're all gonna have ropes 'round our necks before we even step foot in the palace."

"What're ya saying?" another said in a bitter tone.

They were getting closer now, walking toward Stone and the others in the shade of the forest.

"I'm *saying*... what do you think was gonna happen to us? We're deserters now! What? Do you think the king is gonna welcome us back with open arms just because he needs a few more swords? Come now, ya' know better than that... or do ya?"

"You're saying we never go back then?" the one with the growing anger asked. "What of our families? Verren in our home!"

The other said with a low rumble, "Ya shoulda thought o' that before you left yer comrades. I'm heading north... while I still have one attached to me shoulders."

They were close then; closer than Stone cared for, as he looked to Adler, who he could tell was getting uncomfortable as he was fidgeting with his sword and wiping the sweat from his brow. The soldiers were only twenty feet off then, and their course hadn't shifted. They'd be upon them soon, and it would take a miracle for them to not be seen.

Ceres then motioned for them, she told them with her fingers extended and lowered to stay where they all were, but to get ready to run. Even with Stone's newfound sword talent, they'd have little hope to best the twelve-or-so soldiers out in the open. Stone's heart pounded in his chest and his palms were slick with sweat. He could feel the sweat trickling down from his armpit under his shirt.

Run? Where are we going to run? We have youth on our side, and less armor, but that'll do little against arrows or spears at this distance. I'll stay and fight... give Ceres and Adler the chance to...

It was almost as if the gods heard Stone's thoughts then, as an arrow tore through the air, leaving a whistle behind it as it plunged into one of the soldier's arms. Then another arrow ripped through the air, narrowly missing one of the soldiers, flying past and landing in the other side of the tree that Stone was hiding behind with a *thunk*.

The men roared in confusion, fumbling to find shelter.

"Flank attack!" one yelled.

"Archers!" another said.

Stone, Ceres, and Adler didn't hesitate, as Ceres motioned for them to follow her and she quickly crept away, ducking low, and keeping to the shadows. They moved quickly north as the sound of arrows whizzing in turned to the clash of sword on sword. The battle had come to them, and it was far too close for Stone's liking. They kept their heads down and moved as fast as they could away from the fight.

Dry leaves crackled under his feet as his boots made their way through the brush. Ceres was at the lead, keeping her head low to not be seen by any of the soldiers they were hopefully leaving behind. One of them screamed in pain, cursing out vulgar words as a gurgling sound crept out from his throat. *Run. Just keep running!*

In front of Stone, Adler looked back at the fight as his eyes widened. He gulped then, turning back around, as they were all nearly in a full sprint, ducking under extended branches from tall trees, and leaping over fallen ones. The light that draped through the trees overhead flickered raindrops in moonlight as they ran. The battle was behind them by a good distance then, but Ceres continued her running. They ran like that for another twenty minutes, as Stone's breath was labored, and his chest was heaving. He stopped quickly to wipe his brow as the sounds of the battle behind had dimmed to a faint echo through the forest. Adler noticed Stone had stopped to catch his breath and called up to Ceres to slow.

She turned and Stone could see her breathing deeply as well.

"You think we lost 'em?" Adler asked. "That was a real blessing—those other soldiers coming... Even if it just about made my heart explode; as close as they were."

"We should keep moving," Ceres whispered. "I don't think

we could get far enough from the fighting. We've a ways to go 'til we reach Hedgehorn."

Stone took a great breath and exhaled deeply. "All right, I'm ready."

They were off again then, heading northbound; leaping and dodging as the nasty sounds of the battle faded to nothing. It was all just a close call, and they were making good progress through the wood as they were even able to slow enough that Stone found a pace where he could breathe easy. *I've got to get in better shape, these two could run for days. Of course, I was just buried underground for who knows how long…*

※

NIGHT FELL, and the forest came to life with the chirping of insects and the squawking of wild birds. The bats screeched overhead as the three of them sat in a tight, fire-less, circle. They were past the battle—but how far—they didn't know. The war could be raging still in the fields for all they knew.

A chill breeze blew in from the west, and Ceres had her arms tucked into the inside of her shirt as she shivered.

"You want me to…?" Stone began to ask.

"Ah-ah," she said with a wicked glare. "You stay where you are. I'm fine."

Adler giggled.

"What're you laughing at?" Ceres asked. "You know Stone, if you're cold you could always snuggle in with him."

"I'm fine," Stone said with a shrug. "I was just offering to warm you."

"Warm yourself!" Ceres said.

Adler giggled again.

"Anyone seen Mud?" Stone asked. The other two shook their heads. "I hope he got away from that fight. I haven't seen him since." Stone looked around in the darkness under the dark, wild canopy above.

"I sure wish Marilyn was with us still," Stone said, letting out a sigh. "I still feel terrible for how she met her end. I wish I could go back, and we could've done things differently. She could still be alive."

"Don't think like that," Adler said, with a serious tone in his voice. "There's nothing we can do now except fulfill her last wishes."

"These are hard times," Ceres said. "It could've been any of us that fell back there. Or *all* of us... but yeah, I wish she was still here with us. Who knows how many spells she knew? She could've even known a flyin' spell for all we know. She could'a flown us over the forest or made it so no one could see or hear us. We'd be like ghosts."

"Bad expression," Adler said.

"What?" Ceres asked with her brow furrowed.

His right eyebrow dropped as he glared at her. "You really want to throw around the word ghost right now?"

"It's just an expression," she said.

"Well," Adler said, dragging out the word longer than it needed to. "I'm just fine being alive."

Just then they heard a crack off in the forest. It was to the south.

"Mud?" Stone whispered.

Each of them sat silently, listening to the forest. Stone was nearly holding his breath as his fingers slid around the grip of his sword. Then there was another crack, and this one was definitely to the west. The first had been more to the south.

"I don't think that's Mud," Adler said softly.

Stone's gaze shot around them in the darkness, seeking out whatever had made those noises in the faint, scant moonlight. It was then he noticed the sounds of the birds and bats had faded away. "We need to go." He was slowly walking backward with his sword now unsheathed and glistening in the lunar lights.

"Yep," Adler said, walking backward also.

Each of them turned and ran north, away from the sounds they'd heard. It was then that an arrow struck the ground before them with a *thunk*. It landed just feet in front of Stone's stride. As Stone halted, Adler pummeled into his back, and they both fell to the ground. Ceres stood behind with her sword held before her, with both of her hands holding its sharp tip out.

"Who's out there?" she demanded. Then she whispered to the other two, "Get up to your feet."

They were both quickly back up in defensive positions, unaware of who or what was out there. They could see the black trees, and the rustling bushes, but still they saw no sign of who had shot at them.

"Drop yer weapons," a grizzly voice called out. It seemed to come from all directions.

"We'll do no such thing," Ceres said back.

"When you've got arrowheads aimed at your heads and hearts," the voice said, "ya drop your weapons, or we drop you."

"Who are you?" Adler asked. "We've not much coin on us. We're only heading through the forest for this night, we've got comrades meeting us here in the morning. You'd be best to leave us be."

"I said," the man called out as a large, burly figure emerged from the shade before them. "Drop 'em."

The brush around them rustled as a squadron of soldiers emerged stealthfully. Stone could tell they were soldiers from their reflective armor, but they didn't bare the colors of Verren, no, they wore the colors blue and gray on cloth that draped over each shoulder. It was a sigil that bore a blue crescent moon with a grayish-silver sword behind it, and pale white sky behind.

"They're from Dranne," Adler whispered. "They're King Tritus' men."

"I'm only gonna ask once more," the man said.

"What do we do?" Stone asked. "I may be able to fight some of 'em off."

"We can't dodge arrows," Adler said.

"I wish Marilyn was here." Ceres still held her sword out before her.

"Me too, Ceres," Stone said, "me too."

Chapter Twenty-One

❧

Stone could feel the bowstrings growing taught around him, and the tension hung thick in the air like a heavy tapestry falling slowly down on them. A heavy silence grew in the Everwood, broken only by the low chatter of the insects that lived within the forest. He could see the eyes of the soldier before them; brown as an old oak that had seen too many winters. The man was stern with his hands down at his sides, and one of them hefted his broadsword with dark blood still clinging to its cold steel.

He said he wasn't going to ask them to surrender again, and time was running short. At any moment then, an itchy finger could let loose an arrow that could strike any of them, and Stone wasn't about to let that happen—at least without a fight.

They looked anxiously at one another—Ceres and Adler uncertain about what action to take next, but none of them had dropped their swords. Stone had a flurry of thoughts and emotions happening all at once: *We can fight, I can take them, but what if they get to Ceres?, if only I take the leader out first..., can Adler hold his own while I take out the others?, and what if I can't fight like I was able to that last time?, what if that was only a fluke?*

Stone stared into the dark brown eyes of the man standing before them. He didn't know what to say though. If you're going to fight, do you say, I'm going to fight you! No… You simply attack. Stone dug his heals into the ground and readied himself for the fight of his life. After all, there were fourteen soldiers now that he was able to count. Fourteen! Fourteen against three, doesn't get much more dismal than that.

"We are travelers from Atlius," Adler suddenly said, catching Stone off guard. "We're just passing through, we hold no ill intentions against Dranne or your king. We only seek rest in Hedgehorn. Please let us pass, we hold no allegiance to your enemies."

"This ain't about enemies," another of the men said, spitting at the ground. "And anyways, how do we know ya ain't workin' for them." His wide eyes glanced around at the other men. "Make it suspicious that you'd say that you ain't with them. Makes me think you is!"

The other soldiers grunted and nodded in agreement. Stone looked around at them, nervously watching as one of the many bows could let loose a sharp arrow at any moment. It occurred to him then that that may be the opportune moment to attack, in the soldier's brief moment of distraction. His heels dug in farther and his sword's blade turned as he tightened his grip.

"My friend here says the truth," Ceres said. "We're just passin' through. We have little to no coin or offerings. We play no part in your war. If only you'll let us pass, we'll pay you tithing through praise for you and your king the rest of our days."

The brown-eyed soldier looked around at the others, looking for what their response was to her plea. He simply said, "Nah, it's not about praise. You're out here in the woods all by yerselves, outside o' one of the biggest battles in a decade. You aren't with us, which means you're against us, and until you can prove otherwise, you're gonna come with us. We need someone to wash our clothes and backs after all." He winked at them, causing a searing fury inside of Stone.

"We'll not do such as be your servants," Ceres said, causing the bowmen to pull their arrows back tighter.

"Then you'll soak the dirt with your blood," the brown-eyed soldier said. "And you'll be naught but food for the ravens and worms. If that's your wish."

"Better to die free than live as a slave," Stone said.

"Your wish…" the soldier said.

"Hold," Adler said, sheathing his sword and putting his hands out wide. "You want the truth?"

The soldier shrugged, as if he didn't care, but was willing to listen.

"We met a woman in Atlius, a woman who saved our lives. She saved us because of him…" He looked at Stone. "She'd been looking for him. She could *do* things—incredible things with her words. She'd come from the shores of the Sacred Sea just to find him. Do you understand? He's important. She died so that we could get out of Atlius so we could make it west, back to the rest of her kind. We're on a mission, we're on a quest…"

"Oh, a quest?" the man said in a markedly sarcastic tone. "And what's this quest? We did just come from a battle; we'd love to hear about the importance of this grand expedition."

Don't say it, Adler…

"We're going to stop the Neferian," he said. "At least we hope we are. That's what she told us. We're going to stop the dark dragons and their riders from killing at will like they are. That's why you need to let us go."

There was a brief pause, and then just like Stone expected, a burst of hearty laughter from the brown-eyed soldier, and then the others followed. Stone could tell Adler was wincing in humiliation as he took a step back.

"That's a good one boy," the soldier said. "Let us go so we can save the Worforgon." He stopped laughing just as Stone thought that'd be another good opportunity to lash out with a flurry of swipes from his sword, perhaps he could get a good thrust into his stomach before the arrows flew. The brown-eyed soldier now glowered at them.

"On your knees now!" he yelled. "I grow tired of this. Toss your swords aside and get on the ground. You're coming with us whether you like it or not. It'll be up to King Tritus to decide whether you're worth setting free or not. Now get on your knees!"

Stone looked at his friends, each of them shrugging their shoulders, unsure of what to do. He knew for sure that none of them wanted to be held captive. They needed to get to Endo, that was the real mission, whether these hollow-headed soldiers wanted to believe them or not.

"I'll only say this once," Stone said then with as firm a voice as he could muster. "My friend here speaks the truth. We must be on our way. Going with you, although you may think it wise, will impede our progress toward our goal. We made a promise to our friend to make it to the sea so that we may do whatever we can to stop this war from going on. All this war, all this death… Maybe there's a way it can end. If there's even a sliver of a chance, would you not take it and let us pass? What do you have to lose?"

The brown-eyed soldier's bushy eyebrows lowered and gave Stone a mean stare. He strode toward him with heavy footsteps. He then stopped only a mere foot from Stone's face. He had his broadsword in his hand. Stone was ready to defend himself at a moment's notice, and he wasn't finding any other way out of their situation other than fight or give in.

"You're either an actor in sheep's wool," the soldier said in a grumbly voice, "or yer' tellin' the truth." His head cocked to the side as he peered deep into Stone's eyes with those aged-oak eyes. "Either way though, you're gonna come with us."

"No!" Stone said as he let his sword fly at the soldier's throat, but the brown-eyed man's sword was up much quicker than Stone thought, holding Stone's sword in place just over the soldier's shoulder.

He's much faster than the soldiers I fought back in the tavern in Atlius...

"Men..." the soldier said. "Looks like the bloodshed ain't done for the day just yet..."

The large man pushed Stone's sword back, and Stone held a defensive stance only a sword's length distance from him.

"You and me," Stone said. "The winner gets to walk away."

The large brown-eyed man laughed. "Ain't no way in the Dark Realm that's happenin'. You can try but you're going leave this forest in pieces."

"If you're so sure about that, let's see what you've got."

"Stone, no," Ceres said softly.

"I've got this," Stone said, with his gaze fixated upon the soldier before him who stood a full head taller and was much wider at the soldiers. He easily had two decades of training over Stone, who honestly didn't know if he had *any* training...

It was then that Stone caught a flicker in the soldier's eye, and it was also then that he realized he'd been too entranced in the potential fight with him that he turned to see a horrified look in Ceres' eyes. Stone's anger flared as he saw the shiny, flashing metal of a dagger held to her throat.

How'd I not see that soldier? I was too distracted...

"Let her go," Stone growled.

"Drop your weapon," the brown-eyed soldier said, "or your pretty friend over there dies." He swung his broadsword at Stone, who had to jump back unexpectedly to evade it. "Or I just kill you right here and take her anyway. It's up to you, and I gotta say, I'm kind of enjoying this now."

Stone glared at the man with the full fury of his heart heavy in his chest, but then looked to Ceres, whose soft throat was being pricked with the sharp metal blade. He looked to Adler, whose head slunk, and he pulled his sword slowly from its sheath and dropped it to the ground.

"Adler?" he said.

"I'm sorry," said Adler. "We're outnumbered."

Marilyn, what do I do? Tell me, please. If only you were here with your magic to save us again, I...

Stone felt a strong pain on the side of his head, and everything went black.

Chapter Twenty-Two

A muffled voice crept into existence like a dream. It was soft and faint, holding a delicate echo as it repeated a single word in the darkness. The word drifted around his mind like a long-lasting spell, containing something important in that one word that rippled like rolling water.

It was then he heard the voice clearer; from a familiar friend. She repeated the word over and over, as he felt a thumping motion on his thigh.

"Stone," she said again, louder now.

Stone's eyelids peaked open, and a pounding headache drove them back to close again in pain.

"He's waking," he heard Adler say.

"Stone," said Ceres, again he felt the thumping on his thigh. It was her, he could tell, but it wasn't by her hand, no, it was hard bone like that of a knee.

"Yes, yes," Stone said, not remembering quite what had happened, or where they were. That was until he tried to take his hands up to hold both sides of his seething head but was unable to. His eyes opened wide and he tried to get his hands out from behind him, but he quickly looked over to Ceres to see what he feared was true: they were all bound with their hands tied behind them with strong, fibrous rope.

"Stone," said Ceres, her green eyes were open wide, with her straight blond hair framing the worry in them. "You're awake finally."

"Where are we?" he asked. "How long was I out?"

"A few hours." Adler sighed. "That little-dicked bastard snuck up behind ya while you were distracted with fighting the big fella. Cracked you on the side of the head he did. Coward."

"They hurt you, Ceres?" Stone asked.

"Nothin' too serious," she said. "Got tossed about, and my neck's still sore, but I'll live… hopefully."

"How are we going to get out of here?" Stone asked. To their backs was a canvas flap, as they were stuffed into a tent that stood less than six-feet tall. A single candle flickered within the tan tent, and they were sitting on wet grass. Stone's face was wet on his right side, and his hair burned with an itch he couldn't scratch. "Where is it?" His bound hands flew to his hip to find nothing there.

"They took our swords," Adler said with his head slunk.

"We can run," Stone said. "Surely we're faster than them. Our legs aren't bound."

"Possibly," Ceres said, shushing at him for him to lower his voice. "They're right outside." She whispered in his ear then. "They're listening." It was dark outside of the tent. Night had fallen and an owl hooted loudly overhead. "We could try to run. But they warned us if we tried, we'd be beaten and really tied up."

"We've got to try," Stone whispered. "We've got to get to the mountains, we promised her. We don't have time to be taken to Dranne." He paused and thought for a moment. "Where is Dranne?"

"To the east," Adler said softly, but his words resounded awfully in Stone's mind.

"Absolutely not," Stone said, far louder than he should have.

"Shhh," said Ceres. "You're right, but we need to think of something."

"My right hand fell asleep," Adler said. "I'm certain in a few minutes I'm gonna be getting the poking pins in it."

Then a couple of loud voices were heard to their right. Two men with heavy footsteps in the brush were walking past. Their voices were slurred and quick. Stone could feel Ceres tensing next to him, and he felt himself in the same state.

"They'd be boppin' ears," Stone heard one man say.

"Best 'er getter some," another said. The rest was hard to hear, as it was in a thick accent.

Both men entered the closed flaps of the front of the tent, both were shirtless with stomachs bulging from too many ales and meat, and thick sweat clung to their hairy arms and chests.

"Stone," Ceres whispered in a worried breath.

Stone felt helpless, and he wanted to tear the bindings clean from his wrists and shove those two heathens from the tent more than anything. But he couldn't move, and still felt foggy from the earlier blow to his head.

The two men continued to babble, not seeming to notice the three of them on the grassy floor of the tent. They were talking at one another while facing the other. But then, the one on the right with the tan shoulder-length hair said something that made both men suddenly shush.

The other man, slightly shorter and balding with graying hair pulled a pouch from his pocket, untying it and shaking a fine powder into the other man's extended hand. The bald man then poured some into his hand as well. Stone, Adler and Ceres watched in sheer confusion and fear of what was in the two mens' hands.

Both men stared at the gray powder in their hands with a hard stare.

"Three, two, one," they counted down together, and then raised their cupped hands up to their noses and inhaled deeply. Their inhale was labored and had an animalistic tone to it as their eyes were both bulging.

They soon had inhaled all the powder, and both licked their hands clean.

"We've got to get out of here," Stone said. "I'll go first, hopefully knock one down, and then…"

Both of the mens' gazes were laid heavily upon them. Their eyes were nearly as red as wild strawberries. They glared at the three of them with cocked heads, drool creeping out of the corner of the balding one's mouth. They looked at Stone first, who was at the center, and then they glowered at Ceres, eying her up and down with grizzly glances.

"Leave us alone," Stone said. "We're already your prisoners, let us get some sleep at least."

They both eyed Adler, and with a nudge from the tan-haired one, they both looked at each other and smiled. To all their horror, both of the men rushed at Adler, with the bald one fidgeting with the bag in his hand. The tan-haired one went around Adler's back, and held his head in place with his hands.

"Get away from him!" Ceres screamed.

"I'm gonna kill you," Stone yelled. "Let go of him!"

Adler tried to break free, but the sweaty man behind him held his head firmly and had shoved his strong hand over his mouth. The balding man poured some of the gray powder onto his hand, and while the tent erupted with yelling and screaming, he said, "It's all right, it's good fer ya." The balding man had a crazy stare in his eyes with an awkward grin.

"No!" cried Ceres. "Get that away from him. He did nothin' to you!"

It was then the man covered Adler's nose with the hand with the powder in it. Adler's eyes went wide as he tried to shake his head free.

"Breath in," the man behind him said in a mad, low tone. "Breath it in."

Stone fought to break free, and he scooted to his side and kicked the tan-haired man, who hardly seemed to notice, as he was so focused on Adler.

In all the commotion in the tent, Stone could tell Adler was having trouble breathing, as his mouth and nostrils were covered.

"He can't breathe!" Stone said as he kicked. "Let him go, let him go!"

Then the bald man took his hand back and Stone was devastated to see his hand was clean of the powder, yet the powder covered Adler's nose. The tan-haired man loosened his grip, and both men took a couple of steps back, watching and waiting for his reaction.

Adler looked to Stone and Ceres with sad eyes, with tears forming at their corners. "I don't feel very well. I feel like I'm going to vomit."

In his eyes, Stone could see his pupils were shrinking and beads of sweat formed on his forehead.

The two men grumbled something within themselves and then the tan-haired one bent over and picked Adler up, placing him over his shoulder—Adler hardly fought at all.

"No, no, no!" Stone yelled, fighting his bindings as Ceres cried in rage.

The tan-haired man carried Adler out of the tent quickly, and just before the balding man was about to exit, through his crooked teeth, he said clearly, "Dinna' worry, you'll have yer fun with us later." He then left through the tent flaps and was out of sight.

Stone yelled out, telling them to stop, for someone to stop

them, and for someone to help his friend, but he heard no response. Ceres was sobbing on his shoulder.

What do I do? I feel so helpless. I can't let them hurt Adler. This isn't happening. This is all just a nightmare. I'm still asleep from being unconscious. No, Stone... this isn't a dream. Adler's in trouble, and even with tied hands, you've got to help him.

He leaped to his feet, and started to run out of the tent, but quickly found a strong fist fly into the tent, cracking him in the chin and knocking him on his back. Another man entered the tent, his eyes held that same wild strawberry hue. He took a strong stride forward and kicked Stone in the side, knocking the wind from his lungs. Ceres was screaming. The soldier gave Stone another blasting kick, it seemed like for good measure.

Stone was gasping for air as the soldier knelt and tied his boots together, and then left the tent. There in the tent, Stone laid on his side, struggling to breath as his side was searing in pain, and his jaw felt stiff. Ceres sobbed, with her chin down on her chest.

"What do we do, Stone? What're we gonna do?"

It was then that Stone heard something fluttering on the back of the tent, some sort of big bug or something. He hardly noticed it or cared, until it was loud enough that it was clear it was on the bottom of the back flap. It started to crawl underneath the flap, and at first Stone, while slowly regaining his breath, thought it was a scarab crawling under, but he couldn't have been more wrong.

"Is that...?" he asked, sitting up as he watched it enter the candlelit tent.

Next to Ceres, the thing that was merely six inches long stood up, flapping angelic blue butterfly wings. Its body was that of a slender female woman's and it had violet hair that fell over her shoulders. Her face was pale and cute with slender lips.

"It can't be..." he whispered. "Is that the same one?"

Ceres nodded. "Yep. That's her all right. I remember that face like it was just yesterday…"

Chapter Twenty-Three

❦

Stone blinked, staring at the fairy as it fluttered its wings and hovered in front of Ceres' face, motioning with her tiny fairy arms for them to follow her.

"I can't," Ceres whispered, moving her shoulders around, showing she was stuck. "Even if I could, they're right outside the tent."

The fairy with the flowing purple hair only shook her head and continued waving her hands, ushering them out of the front of the tent. Stone was so entranced by the fairy, he forgot the pain in his jaw and ribs, and his elation grew even more by Mud's face that was fully in the tent from under the same flap the fairy had entered.

"Mud!" he whispered.

The fairy then flew out of the front flap of the candlelit tent, and out of view. That's when Mud wiggled his way into the tent.

"I'm happy to see you!" he said. The black-furred dog with the white spot over its eye dove its face and teeth to Ceres' back as it tore into the rope that bound her. "Adler's in trouble. We've got to go help him!"

Ceres was soon free as the fairy entered back into the tent, and Mud went to Stone's bound hands as Ceres brushed the loose rope from her wrists and untied Stone's ankles. They were both free and standing in the tent shortly after, and the fairy continued to beckon them to exit the tent through its entrance.

"Come on," Stone said to her as he clenched his fists—ready to fight.

"I suppose we don't have a choice," she said. "He's in trouble."

Stone barreled through the tent flaps, with Mud right behind. He was surprised to see the guard who'd attacked him was slunk on his side, snoring quietly in an awkward pose. Stone didn't linger long though by the sleeping guard. The fairy had already flown off a few yards, urging both of them to follow her. She was around the right side of the tent. Her violet hair shimmered in the flickering moonlight that wove its way through the thick, shadowy trees that loomed overhead. There were eight other tents pitched behind the one they were in. Only half had candlelight glowing within.

Stone and Ceres tread lightly through the brush and crackling, dry leaves under their boots as they followed the fairy. He was pleased she was leading them toward the tents, and not away. Adler was in one of those most likely, and one that had candles burning within, he thought. And the quicker they approached the lit tents, Stone soon realized which tent Adler was in by the muffled, thick-accented voices from within.

The drugged-up soldiers inside wouldn't be easy to defeat without weapons, Stone knew, but he wouldn't let them harm his friend, he was sure of that! They were soon in front of the tent, with its flaps shut tightly. Stone rushed to enter the tent but was surprised to find the fairy flying in front of his face, waving her arms wildly for him to stop, and to not enter the tent. From within he could hear Adler groaning, and motioned for the fairy to get out of his way with a wave of his hand.

"Wait," Ceres said to him with a firm hand on his shoulder. "Trust her, she hasn't strayed us wrong yet. See what she wants…"

Stone relaxed and took a small step back. "Fine. One minute," he whispered.

As if the fairy understood, she zipped into the tight folds of the tent, disappearing quickly, and Stone and Ceres both listened intently on the goings-on within. The two voices continued their babbling, which Stone thought was good, because that meant they hadn't seen the fairy enter. Stone and Ceres were as quiet as barn mice as they listened, with their ears nearly pressed flat against the canvas tent. Seconds later, the voices waned and faded, followed by two thumps on the grass floor. Stone didn't wait for a signal from the fairy. Instead, he pulled the flaps open wide and was stunned to see the two bare-chested bastards laying face-first in the grass. Adler was tied down with his chest on the single table in the room, with his shirt removed but his pants still on and buckled. His eyes shot around the room sporadically like a birds'.

"Are they dead?" Ceres entered in the tent, untying Adler's bindings.

"I wish," Stone said, cracking his knuckles, standing over the two of them. "Only sleeping."

"How'd she do that?" asked Ceres after removing the rope from his wrists and helping him to his feet. He staggered so much she had to heave his arm around her neck. "Magic? Some sort o' fairy dust?"

"Not sure, but I'm sure glad she came when she did."

"We have to leave this place." Ceres led them out of the tent.

"I wonder how asleep they really are," Stone said, as he was about to leave the tent, but then turned around and kicked the tan-haired soldier in the teeth, and then stomped on the bald one's groan. Ceres opened her mouth to try to get him to stop, but then changed her mind and watched in glee.

"Wassa—?" Adler murmured. "Wise-a?"

"Shhh," whispered Ceres. "You're drugged up on somethin', we're gonna get ya outta here."

They began to walk back westward, toward the tent they were in, but then again, the fairy fluttered her wings in front of Ceres. She waved her arms once again for them not to go that way. Instead, she pointed at the ground for her to hold her ground and stay there.

"We have to go," Ceres said. "That way." She pointed farther into the trees to the west. But the fairy waved her hands no, and then quickly flew over to Stone, surprisingly asking him to follow her back to the tents. Ceres seemed concerned with that, but Stone, now trusting the fairy's wishes, quickly followed.

This time, the purple-haired fairy with blue wings led him to one of the tents without lights on. It was the one at the very back of the group, and Stone did his best to remain silent as he trailed behind her. A fairy's wings flap silently, but a man's boots aren't so magical.

Once there, she waved for him to stay put, which he did, and moments later she ushered him to enter the tent. A few minutes passed, as Ceres waited on the outskirts of the encampment nervously, still helping Adler to stand. Stone emerged from the dark entrance of the tent with their three swords and sheaths nestled under his right arm with a wide grin on his face. Under his left arm were three bows of dark wood, and on his back were three full quivers of arrows. A small payment for the trouble they'd been put through by the wicked soldiers. Stone honestly wished all of the soldiers would leave the same beaten manner as the two drugged ones in the tent back there, but his consolation would be their freedom. He didn't complain too much.

They left the area of forest the tents were in together with the fairy leading the way, and Mud following behind. The Everwood wasn't dense in the area they were in, so traveling wasn't terribly difficult, but helping Adler along was. Once the tents were out of view behind them, they found a creek bed, which they decided to take, so as not to leave footprints for the soldiers to follow if they tried.

"North, still?" Ceres asked, while Stone was helping Adler find his footing in the ankle-deep water. "We did tell the soldiers we were heading there…"

"Those soldiers can a' lick me' cowpie crusted boots," Adler blundered his way through the words, trailing off in some other mumbled insults.

"If we don't go to Hedgehorn," Stone said. "Where else is there to go?"

"We could go through the forest like we discussed, I'm not as familiar with the western side of the Everwood as Adler, but I know Tibrín, Verren and Salsonere are somewhere out there. Verren is farther north, but the others may be somewhere along the way.

"As good as some soap and warm water sound," said Stone, "being free of those twats back there feels far better. Through the forest we go then."

Walking through the creek for the better part of the evening, Stone's legs grew tired as the drug slowly wore off on Adler, and he was able to walk himself. Ceres explained what had happened to him once he sobered up, even though a splitting headache lingered afterward.

The warm light of the sun emerged through the trees as the orchestral sound of loud chirping birds awoke in the forest. Stone's eyelids were heavy then as the sun's rays warmed his face and arms. The fairy that had been leading them then turned and hovered in front of them. With tiny, outstretched arms, it told them to stop, then motioned to the ground at their feet, and then with its head resting on its two hands pressed together to the side of its face, seemed to tell them that it was OK for them to sleep in the place. Stone trusted the fairy enough then with their safety to gladly take her up on her invitation.

Each of them removed their boots to dry and nestled down to a patch of grass. Mud yawned loudly, tucking snuggly up into a ball, they were all soundly asleep soon. Stone trusted the fairy and Mud would wake them if need be, and even a half-hour of shuteye would be better than none at all—as every part of his being yearned for rest.

STONE AWOKE to the glowing hue of a golden sun that filled the forest with a warmth that beckoned him to rise from the morning dew that beaded on the grass beneath him. He sat up, sending his arms out wide as he let out a deep yawn. He wiped the sleepiness from his eyes with the backs of his hands, hearing Adler stir at his side. Ceres was already up, standing with one of the bows in her hand. It was pulled back taught as she aimed at a thick tree ten yards off.

He heard the snap of the bowstring as she let it go, and the arrow stuck into the old tree with a *thunk*. She pulled out another arrow from the quiver and pulled it back in the bowstring. To Stone's side, Mud was looking up at him with his dark eyes, and his tail was wagging from side to side.

"You must be hungry," he said, patting the dog on the head.

Something occurred to him then, *where is the fairy?*

He looked around for her pale body, her flowing purple hair or her blue wings, but didn't see her anywhere. Ceres let the bowstring fall back slowly, letting the arrow aim harmlessly at her side, she seemed to notice Stone's glances.

"She flew away in the night," she said.

"Hmph." He sighed. "Would've liked to have said goodbye and thank her."

"I'm not so sure you won't see her again." Ceres pulled the arrow back once more, and let it fly at the tree again—it landed just a foot above the other. "I started calling her Ghost by the way."

"Ghost?" Stone asked. "Why ghost?"

"Well, I thought she may be Marilyn's ghost for a second, after she helped us like she did. But then I thought Ghost sounded better."

Adler sat up with a heavy moan, holding his head with both hands.

"How you feelin'?" Ceres asked.

"Like a tree fell landed on my head," he groaned.

"We're lucky all you escaped with was a headache," Ceres said. "Whatever powder they made you take fogged you up good."

"Should've killed the dirty bastards," he said.

"I gave them both a nice beating before we left," Stone said. "Kicked one of them square in the jewels."

Adler seemed to have a sense of relief when Stone said that with a wry smile.

"How did we…" Adler said, getting slowly to his feet with the aid of Stone. "How did we escape? I don't remember too well."

"Ghost," Ceres said. "The same fairy that led me to uncover Stone, helped us last night. It came to us in the tent, and then Mud freed us from the ropes. She has some magic that puts people to sleep."

"I—I do remember faintly blue wings that glowed brightly in the dark forest…"

"That's her," Ceres said.

"Who sent her?" Adler asked. "Why's she helping us?"

"That'll be a mystery for a while, I fear," Stone said.

"Could it be that the Mystics sent her?" Adler asked.

"It's possible," he replied. "But I don't think so... Marilyn would've mentioned that I figure. And Ghost helped Ceres rescue me before Marilyn found us. I think the Mystics sensed me once I emerged from that grave."

"Another mystery, great..." Adler sighed.

"What other mystery are you talking about?" Stone asked.

Adler flicked him in the forehead. "You! Hollow head."

Ceres chuckled as she went over and collected the two arrows.

"We should get moving," she said. "We need to find food."

"Which way are we headin'?" Adler asked.

"Through the woods," Stone said. "We'll find shelter somewhere west."

THE DENSE WOOD took them the better part of a week to traverse. There was a wide river they had to cross that Stone had to carry Mud through, it was waist-deep and nearly swept Ceres away. The days were humid and warm during the afternoons, and cool and crisp during the nights. There was one, long, miserable night with heavy rains that soaked every inch of them, and there was one night where the owls were so loud, they awoke abruptly each time they hooted

Aside from Adler's knowledge of what berries were safe to eat, they were fortunate enough to eat some meat each night by a warm fire. The arrows proved to be far more advantageous than Stone had expected, and with Ceres' gift of aim, even a couple of rabbits could satiate them for a night under the stars. Stone and Adler both had beards coming in, as it was long enough on Stone's neck that it itched constantly. Ceres was about to go mad from the constant insect bites on her scalp, and she talked about how she dreamt of soap constantly, and that she'd never take it for granted again.

As the forest trees thinned; growing sparser as the sunlight appeared more and more overhead, they knew they were reaching the outskirts of the Everwood on the ninth day. They emerged from the forest like three hardened travelers. Each of them was covered in dirt, their clothes were torn from thick brush and thorns, and each had a determined look in their eyes.

The three of them stood side by side, the Orphan Drifters Trio they called themselves, gazing out over the wide plains that lay on the western edge of the forest. A warm breeze whipped over the vast fields of grass, letting them roll on like an ocean's waves. Pillowy, white clouds hung in the sky like pulled cotton, while the sun rested behind one of them.

"The Plains of Argoth," Adler said. "I'm happy to finally lay my eyes upon you once more."

"Where to?" Stone asked. To the west and north was nothing but grass, and to the south he thought he saw the tips of mountains peeking up over the horizon.

"I'm figuring we're a little south from where we entered the forest," Adler said. "Salsonere should be northwest from here, and Tibrín is due west, but hundreds of miles off."

"Salsonere it is," Ceres said, scratching her blond hair. "A warm bath takes precedent over saving the world… sorry."

PART V
THE GUILD

Chapter Twenty-Four

Two days into their walk, they'd found the road that led to the city of Salsonere, as was so stated on the wooden sign with the name of the town burned into it. Stone's feet ached and his head felt as though flames were burning through his scalp. The three of them walked side by side, eating with one another each measly meal they found, and tried to get as much sleep as they could muster.

The plains had grown chill at night, but the soft grass proved much nicer than a hard forest floor. Adler had guessed that they'd arrive at the city within the next few days, and tried to convince them to enjoy their journey, at least that's what his old master used to tell him. A hawk flew overhead in the blue afternoon sky, and Mud ran off chasing a chipmunk. They'd only seen a handful of travelers on the road, and all were on horseback, one even pulled a heavy, creaking wagon behind it with a white, cloth top.

The white-tailed hawk dove then, disappearing into the tall, swaying grass, and once it emerged again, a long black snake writhed in its sharp talons. Just as the three of them saw that, Mud burst through the grass and back onto the trail, he was barking wildly, and his eyes were focused behind them.

Just as Stone turned to look, Ceres' hand gripped his wrist tightly—and then he saw it. The dragon was high in the sky, letting out a thunderous roar as it flapped its white wings out wide. Its long neck was glowing, brimming with fire inside of it. Long red horns curled back, behind its head as it showed it menacing teeth and its curling tongue wriggled on the outsides of its mouth.

"Into the grass!" Adler said, holding Ceres' hand—pulling her behind him, and Stone with her. Once in the grass they watched through the whipping grass blades in the breeze. The dragon was flying in a large arc, like a vulture waiting for some injured animal to die.

"Did it see us?" Stone scratched his pant leg.

"Not sure," Ceres said, brushing her hair back behind her left ear.

Mud stayed on the path, barking still, and running at the dragon. Stone thought that perhaps he was trying to lead the dragon away from them, but he thought after that Mud just had a thing for trying to scare away dragons.

Ceres then took down her bow and fixed an arrow in the bowstring.

"You think that's gonna stop it?" Adler asked.

"What's your plan?" she asked. "Stick it with the pointy end of your sword? I'll keep me' distance thank you very much."

Stone and Adler both had their bows in their hands.

Mud was out of sight soon, as he wound around the road barking at the beast, still circling high up near the thin clouds. It was then that Stone heard the roar he'd wish he'd never have to hear again. It was that same explosive boom followed by a sound like crackling glass.

"That's what the dragon was hunting…" Stone said as the

massive dark dragon and rider flew up from the plains. It was twice the size of the great dragon above that growled back. Stone wanted desperately for the dragon to be able to kill the Nefarian, but he'd heard not a single dragon had survived a fight with one of the riders. He'd already seen one decapitated by the dark beasts, and he didn't wish to see another.

The dark dragon's long black neck pointed straight up as its wings flapped, blowing great swaths of winds to flatten the grasses below. Everything in the plains seemed to scuttle away. Every sound around them died away to mere squeaks compared to the great roar of the mighty, invasive beast. Stone held that same notion.

"Let's move," he said, the others nodded in affirmation.

With their bows still held tightly in their hands they moved quickly away in the tall grass just off the road while the two dragons exploded in a terrifying fight. Stone looked over his shoulder to see the two dragons bite and claw each other, winding around each other as the white dragon blew great plumes of dragonfire on the Neferian, who continued to unleash crippling tears into the white dragon's wings and neck.

The rider of the dark dragon straddled the seat upon the dragon's back, sitting firmly atop as though strong magic fixed him upon its back. It didn't pull the reins back that were affixed to the smaller horns on the sides of the dark dragon's head. The rider held a silver sword in his hand, ready to dive into the white dragon if the chance arose.

Stone and his friends moved farther and farther away from the battle as the cries of the white dragon behind continued to grow. Stone looked behind him in horror that the Neferian was biting furiously on the white dragon's neck, causing blood to drip down both of the bodies. And Stone knew that if the Neferian killed the white dragon, it may search for another victim.

"Keep going," Ceres said, pulling Stone after her, causing

his gaze to move back to the grass. "We've got to get as much land between it and us as we can before the dragon gets killed." She seemed to see something in Stone's eyes. "And be certain —it's going to die."

It was almost as if Ceres caused the dragon's death by a cry that coursed through the air like thunder, as Stone looked back one more time to see the Neferian let out a burst of fire into the white dragon's head that incinerated the dragon's scales right off, leaving a blackened and red burnt head that fell limply to its side. The dark dragon, still with thick smoke bellowing out of both sides of its toothy mouth, snapped its strong jaws onto the white dragon's neck just underneath the head and with a jerking motion, popped the dragon's head off.

The Neferian loosened its grip of the body of the white dragon, letting it fall all the way back down toward the grassy ground below. As the dark dragon flapped its monstrous, black wings it lifted its neck upward, and with a chewing motion, let the white dragon's head fall down its long neck with a strong swallow. The rider then sheathed its sword with a sort of satisfaction that was almost like picking your teeth with a sharp needle after a big meal.

Stone gasped at the horrible sight of such a mighty beast, beautiful in its own destructive way, being slaughtered like that. He never thought there would be any way for one of those riders to be defeated, especially when seated upon such a winged nightmare.

The Neferian, now far away back in the blue sky, let out another ghastly roar like thundering breaking glass, and to Stone's surprise, it quickly dove back to the plains, right to where the white dragon's body fell. The white dragon's body was out of view because of the distance and the rolling grass fields that hid it, and the dark dragon elegantly fell out of sight, which was not only a relief to Stone, but also made him think that the dark dragon was feasting on the carcass of the dead dragon.

It was then that he worried about Mud who'd run after the two dragons, and as he cared for the fearless dog, his first impulse was to run after him and fight the dragon off, but Adler seemed to notice this quick impulse, as Adler said, "Don't even think about it."

"What?"

"I like him too," Adler said, shaking his head, "but I'm not letting you go back there. He can take care of himself. And he's quick and excellent at hiding. He'll be all right, he'll find us later."

Adler's words calmed him, but there was still that fear in him that something bad was going to happen to his best friend then.

"Keep going," Ceres said, with a wave of her hand. "Let's go."

They continued walking through the grass for another half an hour, but then after not hearing the dark dragon's roar that whole time, moved back to the road, even though they'd eyed the obscuring grass, ready to leap into it again at a moment's notice.

Each of them scratched their heads as the itchiness had not only not faded, but seemed to be intensifying, especially under the warm sun's rays. Stone still worried about his friend who still hadn't returned yet, but he was beginning to share Ceres' passion for a bath in warm water with frothy animal fat soap.

☙❧

THAT NIGHT, on the side of the road, and after a warm fire burned that Adler had built, a pair of skewered rabbits rotated over the licks of fire. The two skewers crackled and smoldered as the aroma of lean meat wafted through the camp. Stone watched as if in a trance as he turned the meat slowly. Ceres had killed both of them with her sharp-tipped arrows just before the beginning of the red-skied sunset.

Then, under the pinpricked star-filled night sky, Stone looked at Ceres, whose eyelids were nearly closed as she looked into the fire. With her boots off to dry next to the fire, her pale feet stretched their small toes to bask in its golden glow. Adler stared past the fire, almost as if glowering in a pensive gaze.

"Hey," Stone said to him, startling Ceres back to consciousness, "you all right?"

Adler stirred back to his usual, colorful self, wiping the paleness from his face. "Yeah, why you ask?"

"Seemed like you had something on your mind." Stone rotated the skewers. "Want to talk about anything?"

Adler raised an eyebrow at him but didn't answer.

"I mean…" Stone said, feeling a brisk breeze flow past the whiskers on his chin. "We've only all known each other a short time now, but we've been through a lot. I'm just saying if there's something you need to talk about, I'm here to listen."

A confused look crossed Adler's face, and Stone took that as a sign he didn't want to talk about anything, as Ceres only watched both of them curiously, slightly scratching her head.

"I'm fine," Adler said in a serious tone, as if he simply wanted to end that conversation—which it did. But it left a lingering feeling in Stone that Adler's personality was a strong one. He was brave and proving more and more to be a good friend, and loved to joke with them, but he—and Ceres—didn't care to share too much about their personal stories. Stone supposed if he remembered more of this past—if he even had one! —he didn't know if he'd want to talk about it if it was less than full of fond memories. So, he dropped his question to his friend.

"You just looked a little off is all," Stone said. "Nothing to talk about. You think this is done?" He pulled the rabbit from the fire and held it out for Ceres to check. She squeezed it with two fingers, and clear juices ran out of it as the drops fell onto the fire with hisses.

She nodded. Just as Stone put the first piece of pink, fleshy meat into his mouth, Mud appeared from the southern part of the road, walking at a steady speed at them. But then he ran to them as if the aroma of the meat had made its way to the mutt's nostrils.

"Mud!" Stone petted the dog's head as he ran up to him, but Mud didn't look at him, instead staring at the skewered meat. "Sit." Mud sat, and then Stone handed him some of the leg meat, as Mud's tail wagged wildly.

Chapter Twenty-Five

※

The road to the city of Salsonere grew more occupied and robust the closer they got. Sweet families, squabbling merchants, and fatigued soldiers strode the roads as they turned from bumpy dirt and rock to a semi-smooth cobblestone once the city came into view. Stone was quite impressed by his first impression of the city.

It was later in the afternoon that day, as the sun hung a quarter of the way above the horizon until it would find its resting place that night. Salsonere's walls were high, made of large, rectangular stones that piled up into tall, blocky battlements with arrow slits shaped like thin crescent moons. The keep at its center was erected upon a large hill at its center. He was so fascinated by the raised castle and its dozens of silver pyres that he almost didn't notice the dark-water moat that surrounded Salsonere's walls.

The drawbridge was lowered, and the other travelers were waiting in a long line to enter the castle. The three of them got in line and Mud sat at Stone's side, itching his ear. Stone and the others tried not to itch, as the guards may not want to admit some flea-ridden, dirty orphans in their city. They stood in line, covered in filth—although they had done their best to wash off their skin and clothes in a cool creek the day before— and Ceres was fidgeting with her hands so much Stone thought she'd gotten a case of the shakes. Stone watched her as she bobbed up and down on the tips of her toes, staring past the line of people and peering into the inside of the city.

Once they made their way to the gate of Salsonere, the guards seemed to pay no mind to the three of them, and Stone thought that their quick wash had given them enough of a descent appearance that they'd be getting through without even a question. A few guards with worn looks glanced at them but their gaunt gazes went to the many behind them. It was the woman who was sitting behind them, picking her teeth that removed the wooden pick from her yellowing teeth and pointed at Mud with it.

"Aye, no dogs in here," she mumbled. "That mutt'll carry the plague in 'ere!" She prodded one of the soldiers on the back of his armored shoulder. "You gonna let 'em just stroll in 'ere with…"

By the time the soldier had finished rolling his eyes at her nudge, and looked for Mud, the dog was already well off into the city after a quick rush through the crowds in front of the three of them. Stone smirked. "What dog you talking about?" He gave the woman a cold gaze, which caused her to stick her slimy tongue out at them, which Stone returned.

"Hey," the soldier said as he pressed his hand into Stone's chest. "Don't be causing no ruckus here. We don't take kindly to vagabonds causing trouble. You'll find yourself in a nice, cold cellar behind lock and key, you follow?"

Stone calmly pushed the soldier's hand away from him. "Yeah, I follow."

He pushed through and the Orphan Drifters Trio found themselves in the crowded, yet elegant city of Salsonere. From the outside the city looked like an old fortress, but from within its walls, the cobblestone and stone-lain roads had been recently washed, and almost had a sheen to them. Most of the buildings inside of it were made of layers of thin, rocky, round stones that were quite beautiful, resembling something like the rocks in a water-trickling cave to him.

White linens blew in the breeze from clotheslines, pinned up on the second stories of the dwellings. Long banners flapped from high masts that lined the market courtyard before them, and the people talked in casual tones as they walked by. It wasn't a loud cacophony of sounds and voices like Atlius, instead in Salsonere, it was a more refined crowd of passersby. Stone imagined that the soldier was correct about them being stern upon ruffians there, so he decided he'd play calm, assuming no one dared to attack them—because then he'd have to defend himself.

Stone looked back at Ceres whose gaze was shooting around as if she'd just been told there was a pile of coins hidden somewhere free to the first to find them—a chest full to the brim of tandors, where even one coin was enough to buy a steed. But instead she sought eagerly an inn.

It didn't take her long to find one, right down the market square on the right side, basking in the glow of the sun on its stone front and red-linen awning. The sign outside said The Scarlet Matron Tavern.

"That the place?" Adler asked, scratching his head and light beard at the same time.

Stone looked at Ceres as she was already off through the crowd. He shrugged with a grin. "Any place is the place. Am I right?"

They followed her, and past the square that smelled of strong, sweetened coffee and musty-burning candles that smelled of oak—they entered the inn. It was dim with a pair of windows at the entrance that were covered in thick, ornamental tapestries. The inside of the inn wafted heavily with tobacco smoke, intertwined with the smoldering fire on its right side. A handful of round tables were scattered around the room, seated with lively short fellows smoking pipes and pouring frothy ales into their bearded mouths; it was quite soothing to Stone. It was a welcoming feeling, something like coming home must feel like.

Ceres was already talking to the innkeeper by the time they got there.

"Cool ales?" Adler asked them with a warm twinkle in his eyes.

"Later," Ceres said. She quickly tossed him a key. "You're the room on the right… together. I'm down the hall to the left. I'll catch up with ya later." She was soon up the stairs and out of sight.

Stone smiled, sitting at the barstool, scratching his head—but then stopped, as to not worry anyone there that they'd infest any pillows or blankets.

"Two ales," Adler said, sitting then with a wide grin.

"Ugh," Stone spat. "Two ales for you perhaps. Wine for me, if ya' will." The innkeeper nodded.

"It's been so long since Atlius," Adler said. "At least it feels that way… I'd nearly forgotten. But I'll gladly have two. One for me and one for you!"

They both soon had their drinks in hand, and downed them together, watching each other, as if to see who would be the first to put them down.

"Another!" they both said, even though Adler seemed to forget he still had a full ale on the countertop, which they both seemed to notice at the same time, giving a hearty laugh with the other. Indeed, it felt brilliant to be off the road.

The two shared cheers and many drinks through their glee of making it to where they were then. Exhaustion gripped their minds and bones, and exhilaration was in their hearts, but both of them knew—even though they may not have wanted to talk about it then—that they still had a hard road to travel to Endo —to the Mystics in the mountains.

"To Marilyn," Stone said as he raised a glass through foggy eyes.

"To Marilyn," Adler said as they clinked glasses, and both drank.

"I should've—" Stone said in a grave tone.

"Eh, eh, eh" Alder waved his finger. "None of that here, not right now. There's nothing we can do about it now, even if we both hold that regret the rest of our lives. I like to think she'd want us to just enjoy this moment, because they're turning out to be pretty rare since I met you." He winked.

"Yeah, she'd probably be happy we've made it this far. You know, Adler. I can't say I'm not curious what we're going to find up in those mountains. What'll those Mystics have to say to us, to me? What's this Corvaire going to be like?"

"I hope he's like she was," Adler said with a sip, letting the mug fall heavily on the dark wood countertop. "And honestly…" He laughed then. "I hope we even get all the way there. It's a long ways…"

"We'll get there," Stone said with a stern determination in his voice. "We promised her. We'll get there."

An hour passed and Stone and Adler agreed they should probably make it up to their room. Since Ceres hadn't come down, she was probably *still* in the bath, or laying in a warm bed. They both flipped a coin to see who'd get to bathe first, and it was Stone. He thought about letting Adler go first anyway, but the itching in his head was about to drive him mad, even with all the wine in his stomach.

It's hard to describe that first bath you've taken in far too long a stretch. The steam that wafted up from the wooden washtub caused his eyes to water. It was excruciatingly difficult for him to wait until there was enough water in it for him to submerge himself into. But once there was enough, and as he was stripped bare in the small, steamy room adjacent to theirs, he dipped his toes into the hot liquid.

A deep sigh of relief went from his lips as his skin tingled in the encompassing warmth. He dipped his head beneath the surface, letting his long black hair fall over his shoulders. The fatty soap slathered in between his fingers, and it smelled faintly of lavender. He drove the soap into his scalp with vigor, and he let his head sink again to wash away its foam. He did this four or five times, and then he lay in the water with his head back, with that flood of exhaustion washing over him again.

He stared at the glowing candlelight that lined the door from the other side. The steam rolled up from the waters, dancing slowly in its glow. It was then that those same thoughts rolled through his head again. *Where did I come from? Do I have parents? Was I even born?* He tried to shrug them off, but his mind persisted. *Why do the Mystics think I have something to do that could help? What if they're wrong?*

"Stop it, Stone... just enjoy this." He took a deep breath, closed his eyes and lay back.

Stone... I still don't even know my own name... but then again... maybe this will be the only name I ever have. What if I don't find answers to my past or who I am? What if this is how I'm going to have to live the rest of my life?

He took another deep sigh.

If this is all I'm ever going to know, then I'll just have taken care of the ones I care about. If they're the only family I have, then they're the only family I have. But that doesn't mean I'm going to stop looking...

Chapter Twenty-Six

※※※

The following afternoon the three of them walked back down the marketplace. Each of them carried a warm tea they'd taken with them from the tavern. The sun was bright and warm overhead, hanging in the blue sky with fluffy white clouds floating by. The people of the market browsed elegantly, strolling casually down the lines of vendors' wares, speaking with one another in sincere tones, and there was no lack of soldiers walking down the square as well. With their bad luck with soldiers already in their short time together, Stone felt uneasy around them.

Something caught Ceres' eye as she made a sharp turn and went straight to a kind-eyed old man sitting cross-legged behind an array of sweets filling cotton bags. There were fifteen types to choose from. Her mossy eyes lit up as she closely inspected each one. There were round chocolates, a deep-purple colored taffy, and long sticks of assorted nuts covered in honey and salt.

As she looked through the sweets, Stone looked at his friends and felt warm from how refreshed each of them seemed. Adler even was grinning while looking around the market with his fists on his hips with his chest puffed out. Ceres gently took the delicacies from the bags and placed them neatly on her hand as the man behind the bags made a mental tally. Stone took another sip of the tea, that had lost its steam but still warmed him with its fruity taste.

"Three Quorts," the man said to Ceres. She rummaged through her purse and laid the three-polished silver coins in his leathery hand.

"Which ones first?" Stone asked.

She answered by popping a chocolate in her mouth as it gushed, and she closed her eyes, feigning a great grin.

Something familiar caught his eye then as Mud creeped up the backside of a dried meat vendor's table. "That dog…" He shook his head.

Less than an hour later, they decided to sit on a wide staircase that led down from the entrance of the keep, the staircase that covered the hill it was erected upon. They'd walked the main roads of the city, seeing more of the inhabitants, and many more soldiers. They were halfway up the stairs with seemingly hundreds of them, looking down upon the city as two more soldiers walked down past them.

"You ever think of that fairy?" Adler asked. "What'd you call her? Ghost?"

"Yes," Ceres said, popping a taffy in her mouth. "I think about her a lot. If I ever see her again, I don't think I'll have a moment's hesitation if she wants me to do something."

"Someone is looking out for us," Stone said. "I'd be dead back in that coffin if it wasn't for her."

"There's just something about it," Adler said, running his finger around the lip of the empty teacup in his hand. "Why is someone, whoever it is, looking out for us. And honestly, who can talk to a fairy and tell them to help us? It all seems so surreal."

"Whatever or whoever it is," Stone said. "I'm grateful."

They sat there for a few moments while Ceres chewed her taffy, and Mud began to run up the stairs to them. Mud made his way up quickly and sat on the stair by Stone's side.

"How long you think we should stay," Ceres said after a big swallow. "We still have a ways to go before we reach the mountains by the sea. I could stay here the better part of a year, that was one of the very best baths I've ever had last night."

"I second that," Adler said.

"I say…" Stone said. "I think most of the week; give us enough time to get our minds ready, gear up, and make sure we don't have to live off squirrels in the forest anymore. Let's leave that sort of traveling behind us."

"I second that," Adler said again.

"So?" Ceres said. "Four more days? Then leave at the morning light of our fifth day here?"

Adler and Stone nodded.

"What should we do the rest of today?" Stone asked. "I feel like I could sleep the entire day away in the tavern. It would be good to get caught up on rest. It's been a long road to get here."

"Sounds good to me," Ceres said, eating another sweet.

"There is one thing I should do today before we go back," Adler said. "It's just down the road. I'll go alone."

"No, that's OK," Ceres said. "We'll go with. I'd like to see more of this place."

"You don't have to," Adler said. "You can walk around, and I'll find you later at the inn."

Stone and Ceres looked at each other with raised eyebrows.

"We'd like to stick together," Stone said. "Is there something that you *need* to do alone?"

"No." Adler shook his head. "It's not like that. I just don't think you'll be interested, and where I'm going, you may not be welcome."

"Well, now I'm interested!" Ceres said.

Adler shrugged, stood up, and dusted off the backside of his pants. "Fine, follow me."

They walked down the long stair, curving off to the right, and then after twenty minutes of walking, Adler suddenly took a sharp turn down a narrow alley. The sun had arced down enough in the blue sky to cause a cool shade, making the alleyway resemble a low corridor in an old castle. Just as quickly as they had turned into the alley, Stone could already feel the leering eyes upon them. Halfway down, there were three men with dark demeanors glaring their way.

"It's all right," Adler said. "Just keep behind me."

"Adler, what is this place?" Ceres asked in a quiet voice.

"It's the local assassin's guild."

"Oh," she replied while Stone and she exchanged surprised glances.

A burly man crossed his arms covered in tan-leather gauntlets that squealed as he stood before Adler. The man's dark eyes glared down at him but didn't speak a word.

"The rains smell quite dry, and the winds look wet, wouldn't you say?" Adler said. Stone thought that was a quite peculiar thing to say to a stranger. But he was shocked then when the burly man with a bushy beard stepped aside, letting Adler past—but he still gave Stone and Ceres a cold stare.

"Adler Caulderon, apprentice to Armonde D'Amere. These here are two of me' mates," he said to the gaunt-looking old man sitting next to an aged-wooden door. The man had a thin, scraggly beard, and nodded to him as the third man went and unlocked the door, letting Adler in—Stone and Ceres followed. Stone had to duck slightly to enter into the dark room with dim torches lit around a square room with four long tables, and rows of weapon racks on each side of the room. A single door was upon each of the walls—with no windows.

There were two to four men and women at each table, many with drinks in their hands, and others playing a game of chess or speaking in soft, low voices to one another. Adler led them to sit at a section of empty tables by the door.

"What are we doing here?" Ceres asked, looking around. "Not the best-looking lot of folk here…"

"Well," Adler said. "They are killers, what'd ya expect?"

A thin woman in a yellow apron appeared behind Stone, he felt as if she'd rushed out of thin air.

"Somethin' to sip on?" she asked in a cheery voice.

"Glass o' water fer me," Ceres said, returning in an uplifting voice.

"Same for me," Adler said, tapping his fingers on the table. "He'll have a dry wine over there."

The woman was off quickly.

"What makes you think I didn't want water too?" Stone asked.

Adler brushed him off with a wave.

Another woman approached them slowly from down at the other end of the tables. She sat in front of Adler, with Ceres sitting next to her, who scooted slightly away.

The woman with the yellow apron placed their drinks in front of them.

"Greetings, Adler Caulderon," the woman sitting before them said.

"Hello," Adler said. "You the head of this guild?"

The woman had long brown hair that was pulled back to the crown of her head in a small bun, torchlight shined off her tan, clean skin, and her eyes were a light blue. She wore a leather vest studded with bronze rivets.

"Yes, name's Hydrangea, sounds like you've been through much to reach here."

"Very much so," Adler said, looking into the woman's eyes.

"You've got quite the reward placed upon your head back in Atlius," she said, then looked around at each of them. "All of you, actually."

"How could you know that?" Ceres asked with her eyes wide.

"We know much in the guild," Hydrangea said. "I also know that a group of soldiers from one of those dim-witted warring kings isn't too pleased to have seen you go in the night. In fact..." She leaned in. "Some o' them were saying you used a bit of dark magic to escape."

"That's not what happened," Adler said, shaking his head. "But I sure was glad we were able to make it here without becoming some king's prisoners."

Hydrangea nodded and smirked. "So, what brings ya here?" she asked.

"We've fallen on some ill luck but must make it to the mountains in the west, to a place where a there's a sharp, tall rock in the water with a white stripe painted down it. We've been asked to go there, and time isn't on our side. Any suggestions on a speedy trip? Or what roads lead there quickest?"

"All depends on how much coin ya got," she said flatly. "Horse is always the best, but they're costly and I don't have none to spare now."

"We can't afford horses," he said.

She leaned back with her arms over her vest and rubbed her chin as she looked up at a glowing torch. "Give me a few minutes," she said as she lifted her legs over the long bench, making her way out the door at the rear of the room. Many eyes were upon the three of them, even if they weren't looking *directly* at them; Stone could feel their stares.

"You're still a member of the assassins?" Stone asked him.

"Yes, I'm still an apprentice. It's a good thing to check in with the guilds when you get to new cites. They like to know who is visiting, staying, or even just passing through. Even though—unless you're one of the renowned for stealth—they probably know where you are anyway."

"I can believe that," Ceres said.

Hydrangea emerged from the rear door and sat again with them. She let out a subtle sigh.

"We were saddened to hear of the passing of Armonde," she said. "He was an impressive fighter, outstanding assassin, and good friend."

"Yes," Adler said with a sad tone. "Yes, he was."

She laid a rolled parchment on the table that was tied in a thin twine. All three of their gazes fell upon the scroll.

"Before his passing," she said, untying the twine. "He fulfilled a contract but wasn't able to collect the reward for earnings. Seeing as how he had no next of kin, spouse or parents left, its within my power to grant you half of that reward—but only half if a true heir emerges."

"That's more than I deserve," Adler said. "I wasn't looking for coin when I came in here."

"It's not much," she said. "But it might be enough to get an aged steed or a mule or two to carry bags."

She pulled out a heavy purse of coins and counted it out on the table for them. Stone wondered what the reward was for... *Who'd this assassin kill for us to get these bloody coins?*

To Stone's surprise, she counted out three twints, ten tabers, and two quorts. *That's seventy and a half tabers! And that's only half the reward. It must pay to be a killer...*

"We thank you," Adler said. "We'll put this to good use in our travels.

"We remember Armonde well," she said. "May his soul find its way well to the Golden Realm."

Adler nodded. "I hope it does as well."

"I'd take the Old Mire Trail due west; it'll take you to the rock you seek. If you fall on more misfortune, you can veer south to Tibrín to gather supplies and rest. But if you stick to the trail on foot, you should get there in a few weeks' time."

Adler took the coins from the middle of the table and laid them in his own purse.

"Now if you'll sign here," she said, unrolling the scroll and giving him a pre-inked-dipped quill. He signed it elegantly in curvy letters.

"Good travels, Adler Caulderon," she said. "Same to you, Ceres Rand, and the nameless one called Stone."

Stone's bottom jaw nearly dropped open.

"May you find what you seek," she said as she stood up from the bench again, Adler stood too, as they bowed to one another. Hydrangea went back to her table at the other side of the room and sat next to a square-shouldered bloke. They soon were back out into the shady alley, heading back to the main road.

"You nearly got a full tandor from your old master's reward," Stone said to Adler. "That's a lot."

"That's actually not that much for what we do," he said. "It must've have been a contract for some adulterer, or low-profile thief. But we need it."

"Did you expect to get something like that when we went in there?" Ceres asked.

"No. The most I thought we might get is some food and drink, and some instruction on obstacles on the road, but it seems like a straight shot, and she didn't mention any ambush points. We could most definitely get one horse with what she gave us. If only we had enough for two more... we'd cut our travel time down drastically—and save us from some nice blisters..."

Chapter Twenty-Seven

After they'd left the assassin's guild, the three of them spent the remainder of the day toying around the city, having another belly-stuffing meal and sharing spirited conversations. It was a joyous evening that was capped off with a gentle nudge—or more insistent—push from the barkeep of the tavern that they be off on their way. The last moment that Stone remembered was him and Adler bowing low to Ceres, as she curtsied to them at last before they were all off to lay in their soft beds.

The following morning, Stone woke to a splintering headache and dry tongue.

"Argh," he moaned as he sat up in bed to the early morning sun's rays blasting through the window, filling the room and blinding his sensitive eyes. "Ugh… I shouldn't have drunk ale. I knew that was gonna be the end of me…" He lay back in bed heavily, casting a sheet over his head. "Why'd I let him talk me into it… It always ends up this way!"

"Keep it down over there," Adler said with a groan from the other bed. "I'm doin' my own mental complaining over here…"

That's when Ceres erupted through the door with a boisterous grunt.

"Hope you boys are covered! We've got a grand ole day today, so let's get goin'. The sun is up, the sky is, well... a bit overcast... but..."

"Ceres," Adler groaned, "all due respect intended... walk back out the door, shut it gently behind you please, and come back in a few hours with a little less spirit."

"Absolutely not!" She clapped her hands loudly in front of her with a wide smile. "You're all getting up now. This is a big day!" She then paced back and forth humming an unfamiliar song to Stone, and then snapped back to attention in front of them. Stone felt she was waiting for an invitation or some form of question for her to continue.

"Why is it a big day?" he asked, with his head still under the sheets.

"I'm so glad ya asked. Today is the day we get us some steeds to make our journey one that is gonna change the course of our journey. We leave in what, three days' time? Two? Today's as good a day as any to get our quest back on the right path again. No more wet boots from here on out!"

"Why isn't the door closed yet?" Adler groaned, sitting up in his bed promptly and glaring menacingly at her. "And why are you still on this side of it?" He drove his head back into the pillow.

"Don't know what's gotten up his trousers..." she said. "Certainly, wasn't no girl from his temperament."

"Out!" Adler said.

Stone laughed and groaned under his blanket.

"Fine," Ceres said turning away from them. "I'm going to the market, but I'm comin' back in three hours. Hear me? You've got three hours to turn back from mowing cows to normal people again. Three hours!"

She was quickly out of the door. It closed with a crack that caused Stone's head to ache sharply.

"That girl's gonna kill me," Adler said.

"Hasn't killed us yet…"

※

True to her word, Ceres poked her head back into their room at promptly three hours afterward. Both the boys were asleep, but they both awoke to the slow creak of the door being opened. Stone's headache had subsided, but he wasn't sure about Adler.

"Sleepy boys waking up?" Ceres said like a mother to her children.

"We're not babies," Stone said, sitting up with a yawn.

"You sure about that? You sure act like some sometimes. C'mon, get up. We've things to do!"

Adler sat up and laid his feet to the side of his bed.

"Little grumpy man feelin' better now?" Ceres said in an exaggerated, belittling tone. "Or you need another day to feel better?"

"I'm gettin' up," he moaned. "Better to be on our way than to have you keep speakin' to me like that. You know you could drive a philosopher to the brink of looniness with the way you're talking now. A king would have you lashed for it."

"Are you comparing yourself to a king?"

He sighed. "Let's just get this over with. You're going to drive me to an early grave."

Stone laughed. "If I didn't know any better, I'd wager you two were an old married couple."

"What?" Ceres scoffed, shaking her blond hair from side to side. "The thought of that sends me to an early grave!"

An hour later, they were all outside the city walls to a pasture on the eastern edge of the city. It was a cloudy, gray day. The trees around the pasture swayed and cracked in the wind. The sun hid behind the clouds, as the horses neighed and grazed on the tall grass. The pasture was surrounded by a simple fence of old, weathered wood, which made Stone wonder how such brittle wood could keep in so many horses? He counted thirty, and that was without the ones in the stables.

Ceres was leading their pack to the interior of the pasture, toward the family at the center of a round ring of fences that was the inner circle of the pasture, as they were riding a single black horse on the inside of the fence. Stone took that moment to glance again back at Salsonere, and the keep that rested upon the hill with the long staircase that led down to the city. He also marveled at the unique crescent moon shaped arrow slits in the towers along the wall.

"Howdy," the man inside the pasture said to them, as the young woman riding the black horse slowed, as she looked at the three of them approaching.

"Hello, sir," Ceres said, with her hair and shirt rustling in the cool winds.

"What brings ya here? Interested in a steed of your own? Something fast? Something strong?"

"A little of both perhaps," she said.

"Well, we've got all that you'll need here," he said, his nose was red and bulbous, with thick gray eyebrows that draped over his narrow, yet kind, eyes.

"We're looking to do some good time on the road," she said. "We're heading to the Sacred Sea, you understand."

"Yes, yes," he said. "I've got just the thing… or things? How many you looking fer'? I see three o' you, if my eyes don't deceive me."

"Yes, three horses," Ceres said without hesitation.

Stone instantly snapped to attention, looking at her, as she stood in front of him, looking at the narrow-eyed man. But then he looked at Adler who seemed to have the same expression on his face. Adler walked up to her, with Stone following.

"Ceres..." is all Adler was able to say.

"I've got this," she said. "Let me handle this." She glared deep at both of them. "I've got this."

"Three is it," the man said, as the rest of his family looked at the three of them at the edge of the circular fence.

How is it that the three of us, as young as we are, can afford three horses?

"Just give me a few moments to gather a line up," he said, "and we can get ourselves a deal put together. But first... you do have the coin on ya'?"

Ceres nodded.

"Good, good, that's might fine!" he said as he snickered off excitedly toward the stables.

Ten minutes later that were standing before a line of five horses. Each of them looked elegant, powerful and majestic. Three were a tan brown, one was white, and one black. And they all had silky manes that trickled down their powerful necks.

"Well," Ceres said. "Pick one."

Stone was astonished. *How have we gotten here?*

Adler started to contest her. "Ceres... we don't..."

"Yes, we do," she said. "Pick one. Each of you. Oh, but I call the white one. Her name's Angelix."

"Actually, her name is..." the old man said.

"Her name is Angelix," Ceres said firmly.

Stone didn't hesitate. "I'll take the black one. His name's... uh... his name's..."

"I guess I'm taking one of the brown ones then," Adler said.

"His name's Grave, after me first name of course..." Stone said.

"I'll take the second one from the left," Adler said. "I'll name him... Hedron, after my favorite star."

"Grand!" the old man with the narrow eyes and bushy eyebrows said. "Excellent names. Excellent indeed. You gonna be needin' saddles and reins I take it?"

Ceres nodded.

"All comes together to be three tandors, and fifty tabers," he said.

"My good man," Ceres said with a deep voice. Stone smirked. "We've three come in to buy three fine horses, and hopefully well-crafted leather saddles on a dreary afternoon. We've been on the road long, and it's a hard road to be certain. I'd surely appreciate a finer deal than that." She looked over at Stone and Adler and gave a sly wink.

Twenty minutes later, each of them was sitting atop the strong steeds, as they made their way back to the drawbridge of the castle, they wore dazzling smiles on their faces, and Ceres' purse was only three tandors and fifteen tabers lighter.

"All right," Adler said as they were halfway back to the city, there was a playful tone in his voice. "Out with it."

"What?" Ceres said, quite playfully. "I don't know what you mean."

"The coin," Stone said. "I didn't want to pry, but that's what Adler's asking about, of course."

"What coin?" she asked not so playfully. "Don't know what you're talking about. We have three horses to get to where we're going now. What does it matter? You want to walk?"

"No," Stone said. "No, I really don't. We'd just like to know how we got them."

"I think I know," Adler said. "I'd just like to hear you say it."

"Don't know what ya mean," she said with a cold glare. "Why don't you tell me what it is you think I should confess to ya? Out with it, Adler!"

"I hate to accuse you of anything," he said. "I care for you. We both do. But if you're really calling me out, then I'll just say it outright. Is that what you want? Well, here it goes... I think you're selling. There. Now you have it. I think you're out slingin' things to people that shouldn't be sold. Am I wrong?"

Ceres burst out into laughter so loudly that her horse paused, and even seemed to look back at her.

"Ceres?" Stone asked, scratching the side of his head.

She only continued to laugh.

Finally, Adler asked, "What's so funny?"

"I fucking stole it," Ceres struggled to say through her laughing.

"What?" Stone asked, still amazingly confused.

"You thought I was selling, what, opioids? Snortables? Smokeables? I scored big off a lifted purse I snagged in the market. I had no idea how much was in there. You should be thanking me!"

"You stole someone's coin?" Stone asked, he was astonished and barely moved as his steed had paused as he looked blankly at his laughing friend.

"Yeah, what? Are you gonna be that surprised? I'm a thief. That's what I do." She looked at Adler. "You're an assassin. You kill people. Don't tell me you're gonna judge me. This is my thing."

"I, uh..." Adler said, trying to find the words.

"What if that person needs that coin?" Stone asked. "What if they've got plenty of children to feed?"

"Did you see that market?" she asked. "I lifted a purse that I thought would be full of tabers, but there were twints in there. So many beautiful twints!"

"I don't know if I should be proud or disgusted of you," Adler said. "But I damn sure am happy to be upon this horse!"

"Me too," Stone said, as they approached the front gate of the city. "I..."

"Shut your mouths about this around others," she said. "Can't have strange ears hearing about this. I'd like to keep me' head on me' shoulders please."

They passed back through the crowded gate, and no one seemed to give them a second glance. They must've appeared to be completely different people atop the horses. They must have seemed to have some sort of prestige of clout.

They made their way back to the tavern, feeding the horses with hay purchased from the bar. The air was crisp, and the winds were brisk, and it smelled of onset rain. Stone's hair rustled on his back, and Ceres stroked Angelix's neck.

"Why didn't you tell us?" Stone asked. "Is this a normal thing that you do?"

"Why? Because thieves don't go around telling people they're thieves. People don't trust ya! You honestly should be a little honored that I told ya. It means that I sort of… like you two. Now can we stop about all this talk? And, well—we're back. That was easy, wasn't it?"

They went back into their beds early that night, ready to awaken with the rising sun the next day. The horses were tied to the front of the building and gave Stone a warm comfort for the trek ahead. He thought it would an easier journey now, but when he awoke from a horrible sound that night while he was deeply asleep in bed, the terrible realization came back… that he couldn't hide forever from the monsters that lived in his world.

Chapter Twenty-Eight

※※※

Stone shot up in bed, seeing the brilliantly lit sky outside the windows, past the thick drapes. It was a fiery white light, almost like lightning, but twice as intense. He fumbled putting his pants on and stumbled over them as he ran to the door for his sword. "Adler," he said.

"I'm up, everyone in the city heard that."

Ceres sprang through the door. "We're leaving... right now!"

The other two didn't dispute her claim. Stone and Adler gathered their things—as scant as they were—and ran down the stair to see the tavern's keeper pacing from side to side.

"I never thought it would happen here... not here!" he stammered.

"Get to safety," Stone told him, but deep down he knew there was nowhere safe to hide from *them*. You'd have to be six feet under to be safe from that fire.

To the east they heard the screech... terrifying and overwhelming. That sound now resounded in Stone's stomach, correlated with the feeling of complete helplessness against such a dark dragon.

They ran out of the tavern doors, undoing the horses' reins from the wooden rod that rested above the long, dark trough of cool rainwater.

"Gotcha!" came a familiar, grunted voice as a strong, hairy arm wrapped itself tightly around Stone's neck. His hands went up to grab the arm as he saw the shock in his friends' eyes, and he saw another man do the same to Adler. A third had a sword tip nestled into Ceres' back.

"No magic or tricks are gonna save ya this time from what we've got planned fer ya'," one of the men said. "We gotcha!"

Stone couldn't believe they'd gone this far to find them. It was those same two powder-snorting soldiers from the woods, along with another man from their troop.

"Are you mad?" Ceres yelled. "The city is under attack. We're all gonna die if we stay here."

"Nuh-uh," the bald soldier said. "This here is more important than that rider in the sky."

"You made us look like pansies," the tan-haired soldier said. "We got orders to take ya back, and that's what we aim to do!" The soldier's eyes were wild, and his teeth gritted behind that slight grin.

Stone's hand had already moved to his sword at his hip, and attempted to draw it out, but the soldier's other hand behind him cupped his wrist, holding it in place. The third soldier raised his sword's tip to the back of Ceres' neck.

"And you've got us horses," the bald soldier said from behind Adler.

There's no way we're going back. And there's no way they're going to let us leave if they've followed us this far. There's only one way out... fight. But I can't let the others get hurt.

"Face me," Stone said to all of them. "Right here. Face me to a duel, and let's settle this like men."

The three soldiers looked at one another curiously.

"Nah," the bald one said, spitting at the ground. "We'll just take ya. Now, we're gonna bind yer hands, and if ya try anything, girly here gets skewered. We're not all that interested in her anyways…"

Adler looked at Stone for the answer, and Stone's mind raced. *Sure would be a good time for Ghost to show up.*

"Argh!" the guard behind Ceres groaned as the dog's teeth chomped down on his forearm holding the sword. Ceres didn't wait, she ran forward, and with her two fingers moving fast, and as another roar of the unseen Neferian erupted in the sky, she poked the bald soldier square in the eyes. He too, let out a frustrated groan of pain.

Stone felt a surge through his muscles, and he pulled his sword with all his might, and with both hands from its sheath. The arm around his neck squeezed harder, but once the tan-haired soldier saw Stone's sword flashing in the white light above, he released him, stepping back. Adler had quickly turned, and as the soldier rubbed his eyes, he kicked him right in the baby-maker.

Mud continued to tear at the man's arm as he screamed in pain, but Stone saw he was hitting Mud's neck with his free arm. A rage tore through Stone, as Ceres pulled down her bow and released an arrow into the tan-haired soldier behind Stone, piercing his chest. As Adler had jumped onto the bald soldier and was waylaying blow after blow on him, Stone ran at the third guard.

The guard who had held his sword at Ceres didn't have a chance, as his sword was still gripped in Mud's control, and with Stone's newly found sword skills, that rage sent his sword flying, lopping the man's arm completely off. The soldier let out a harrowing groan, and Stone quickly sent in the killing blow in his chest.

"Filthy pig," Ceres spat.

Adler breathed laboriously as he punched the bald man repeatedly. Stone glowered at the tan-haired man who lay on his back, holding the arrow's shaft that protruded from his chest.

He could then see the dark dragon, high in the sky—its white fire bellowing out of its toothy mouth, with the rider holding steadily on its back. In was in a vicious fight with two smaller dragons.

"You made a grave mistake following us," Stone said in a low voice as he walked toward the downed guard. "You made an even worse mistake messing with us in the first place. No one hurts my friends. No one!"

"Please," the tan-haired man said with a spat of blood trickling down the side of his mouth. "Please. We were just doing our duty; we are soldiers of…"

Stone sent his blade into his chest.

"I don't care where you're from," Stone said. "I don't care who your king is." He pulled the blade from the dead man's chest. "No one messes with my friends."

The soldier beneath Adler lay unconscious; his face completely bludgeoned and covered in blood. Adler stood, his chest heaving, and Stone had never seen him look so powerful. *Perhaps he could be a great assassin one day…*

The dragons continued to fight the dark dragon in the sky, each of them roaring and screeching with an array of that white Neferian's fire with the glowing orange and gold fire of the other two.

Ceres turned to them. "We should be on our way. There's naught we can do. There's nothing anyone can do against those beasts."

"What about him?" Stone asked, looking down at the bloody, yet still alive soldier.

"I know," Adler said, wiping his knuckles on the man's cloak, and then pulling a pouch from the man's pack on his hip. He opened the bald man's mouth and poured all of the powder from the pouch into it. "We'll see if he remembers anything after this, if he survives that much of that poison."

Stone honestly felt that the man deserved to die, but he trusted Adler, and Adler knew how powerful that powder was. He hoped the man, if he lived, would forget his own name and past—that would at least be some sort of vengeance.

Ceres mounted Angelix, Adler mounted Hedron, and Stone got onto Grave's back.

Is this what life is to be? Kill or be killed? I don't enjoy it. I enjoy nothing about it, but I must admit... I don't feel the same sort of remorse I would have pictured I'd have felt. They deserved it.

Their horses' hooves clicked heavily, and quickly upon the cobblestone roads. The flickering of torches whooshed as they rode. Stone didn't know if he'd ridden a horse this fast before and was bumping on his saddle wildly as they rode toward Salsonere's western edge, and as far as they could get away from the crazed dragons behind. The horses increased their speed dramatically, and they soon found they were at one of the side exits of the city.

There was no lack of panic, mind you, as they zipped past. Scores of people pleaded for their help, so that they may sit on the horses with them, to be taken out to safety. Even with as much ferocity at the dragons' battle raged with, the city itself seemed mostly unscathed by the dragons' fire. They seemed to be more preoccupied with each other than with burning Salsonere to its foundation. Stone hoped that when the Neferian won—which he assumed it certainly would—that it would just fly back off into the night sky.

Then, there they were, riding off into the plains on the city's border. The winds were cool and brisk, and Ceres, who was at the lead, kicked Angelix on the sides. There was no reason to slow, as the horses were strong and quick; they seemed to enjoy the run.

The cries of the city died down as they moved farther and

farther away—as well as the chaotic battle overhead, and eventually they slowed to a trot. The three rode side by side as Mud rushed up from behind to catch up. They looked at each and looked out at the lands before them.

"We've made it this far," Adler said, with his eyebrow length tan hair blowing in the breeze. His light blue eyes were gleaming with glee in the moonlight, while his fists were still stained with dried blood.

"I can't believe they tracked us all the way from the forest," Stone said. "They must've been threatened pretty hard to have come this far after us."

"If only they would've just stayed back down there," Ceres said. "We wouldn't have had to do what we did. But what choice did we have? And after what they did back in the forest to us… The Worforgon is better off without 'em. That much we know to be true!"

"Indeed," Stone said, with a pause. "There is one thing I've been wondering about the dark dragon back there…"

"White fire," Ceres said.

"Yeah!" said Stone.

"Before, the dark dragons had black fire—like smoke."

"Does that mean that they blow different types of fire?" Adler asked as Mud had finally caught up to them and walked next to Grave.

"Perhaps," Stone said. "Hopefully we don't see many more to compare them all, but we'll have to keep it in mind. Maybe we can ask the Mystics up in the mountain when we finally meet them."

"I get the feeling we're going to have a lot of things to talk about when we get there," said Adler. "What did Marilyn call them? The one's who use magic?"

"The Majestic Wilds," Stone said in a serious tone. "We're going to meet them there. She also called them the Old Mothers."

"I just hope they teach me a spell or two," Ceres said. "If we're gonna keep being attacked like this, I sure wouldn't mind having some card up me' sleeve—something they wouldn't be expecting."

"As long as we stick together," Stone said. "I think we'll be all right."

Adler grinned. "A lucky fairy doesn't hurt to have around either too much every once in a while."

"Or how about a street dog that knows just the right time to bite," Stone said. "Or when to bark at a bloomin' dragon!"

"Aye," Adler said. "We've had some luck, can't deny that."

They rode together that night, staring up at the starry sky. Each of them wondered what lay ahead on the road before them. What sort of adventure lived in the mountains to the west? Who was this Corvaire they were told to meet? But mostly they were just fleeting thoughts. They were tired, exhausted, and yearned only for a good night's rest—but there would be no bed that night, nor many nights on the road.

They built a small fire, which Mud cuddled up to closely. And as they fell asleep one by one that night, Stone was the last one up. His eyelids weighed down as he gazed into the trance-like fire. He thought of how far they'd gone together, and wondered… how much farther they would travel alongside one another…

PART VI
THE OLIVE TREE

Chapter Twenty-Nine

✿

Five weeks later.

The air had chilled, the mountains behind had led them to a long stretch of fields again, and Stone's rear was chapped and callused. The horses had grown lean, walking along the Old Mire Trail for so many days. The three had gotten to know their horses, and their horses to them. They then had bonds that made them truly care for their newly-named horses, and every night by a warm fire—well, at least most nights had one—Stone lay back on Grave as he slept. Mud too, who was their lookout with his keen senses, slept soundly each night from the long travel. He was known though to let out high-pitched yelps in his sleep occasionally, with his feet moving slightly. Stone liked to believe he was dreaming of running after hares.

Even with the horses carrying them, the road had not been easy, for the distance from Atlius, or even just Salsonere to the Sacred Sea was long and hard. Only two days west of

Salsonere was the murky bog that was made no better to traverse by the three days of rain that ensued. After that grueling, and quite pungent mess, they were soon upon the foothills of the Worgon Mountain range. The Worgons were known for their winding paths up and through the tree-filled hills. The path was narrow, and the horses slowed as they walked upon the edges of high cliffs with one side falling off to a certain death. At some points they climbed down off their horses to discuss if the steeds could even make it around narrow sections, always taking the chance, and luckily each time they made it, even if Hedron lost his footing a couple of times, making each of their hearts sink.

The Old Mire Trail wasn't so much a straight path either, especially in the bog, the trail was so weathered and sunken that they'd thought they'd strayed from it and lost it a few dozen times, only to find that when they found dry dirt again, there was indeed a trail, even it if was a ways off in either direction. The trail split and forked in the mountains, with them always taking the widest path, and keeping them doubting they'd found their way as they came to such treacherous cliff paths. But they eventually made it through.

And that doesn't even recall the packs of bandits that rummaged around the trail, attempting to pick off stray wagons or lone travelers. Adler and Ceres both had proven to be adept at spotting these packs—who really weren't all that good at covering their tracks in the first place. Stone wanted to attack each of them; keep them from attacking any innocent people on the road, but the others convinced him that they'd just warn those that went through, and even though their trust in soldiers was slightly above non-existent, they made it a point to point out where each pack was, and how many were in each camp.

Now, they'd convinced Stone not to *attack* the camps—but that didn't mean they left them completely intact... Stone felt as if he was a bit clumsy when it came to the whole sneaking around part… but Adler and Ceres were quite stealthy when needed. She found that the packs of bandits mostly slept during the day, with only one lookout, and that lookout was most of the time smashed on some strong liquor. And the others were in a deep state of sleep that would take two shields colliding to wake.

She'd walk in with a single blanket and walk out with a hefty handful of weapons: swords, daggers, clubs, each of which would end up in a cold stream miles away or tossed down into some deep crevasse. Stone liked to picture their angry faces when they tried to figure out who was keen enough, and quiet enough, to *steal* from a bunch of *bandits!*

They'd also heard the cries of the Neferian three times in those weeks, but thanks to the Golden Realm, they never saw one. Their cries could be heard for miles, and they always made sure to head in the opposite direction of their murderous screams.

By the time they got their first inhale with the saltiness of seawater, Stone and Adler both had scraggly beards. Stone's black beard was the scraggly one, with a thin mustache and its patchiness at the sides of his face. Adler's brown beard was quite full for his age. While Stone hadn't tanned at all in the many days of sunlight, still leaving his pale skin gleaming like a pearl under his tan hood, Adler's skin had darkened quite a bit, and Ceres' freckly skin had turned a pinkish-red hue. Her straight blond hair was lightened to a light golden tone, and her green eyes had gone from mossy to a vibrant lily pad green.

At that moment, with the sky lit a vibrant streaking of auburn oranges and reds in the sunset sky, the three of them were looking down from a high, grassy hill down upon the western sea. Their weathered faces glared down upon it with a feeling of fulfilled determination, and a longing to know what lay in those mountains just before the shores. They were still miles off, but they'd be down upon those salty waters the next day. Mud wagged his tail vigorously at the sight.

That night, sitting around a fire, with Stone's back to Grave, they felt the cool ocean winds blow up the plains and into their camp. It made Stone wonder; what exactly they'd find up there in those mountains. What old knowledge secretly lived up there? They weren't far away from the truth of that question. After all, Marilyn had given her life so that they would make it this far, and they'd gone through many trials to make it this far. The next day, they'd begin the climb.

※

Mounting their horses the following morning, they strode down the high hill, with crisp winds blowing into their faces. Stone's hood flew to his back, and his long hair blew behind him. They'd let the horses graze for an hour once the sun's rays woke them. They drank from a creek just off to the south, and Stone and his friends ate some berries they'd collected and heated the last of a pound of rabbit from the day before.

"Well, it's somewhere down there," Adler said, with the sunlight glowing upon each of them.

The clouds above the sea were streaking in an angelic, yellow hue. They were still miles off, but the anticipation was brimming in each of them.

"Remember what Marilyn said to us," Ceres said. "Find that point where a rock like a shark's fin with a white line meets the mountains and the sea. Climb the mountain there and find an olive tree where there shouldn't be one and climb there. Find Corvaire and learn to use a sword. I hope she's all right with me just learning the bow, but I'm sure she woulda' been pleased with you, Stone."

Adler nodded.

"Things would've been a lot different if she was still here,"

Stone said. "I remember the first time we saw her, aside from me just glancing at her up on the rooftop across from the inn. She was so strong; there when we were at our weakest…"

"I wonder if the Mystics know of her fate?" Adler asked.

"That's a good question," Stone asked. "I don't really care to be the one to break such sad news… but if we must…"

Hours later the grassy plains made way to gritty, sandy shores. Each of them got down from their steeds and walked up to the water. Ceres got naked quickly and got in the dark waters.

"Great Grindleword it's freezing in here!"

Stone wasn't sure if he'd ever seen a naked woman before, so he looked up at the sky embarrassed. Adler removed his tunic, shirt, boots and pants, running toward the water, and then dove into an incoming wave.

"Come on in, the waters grand!" he yelled up to Stone.

Do I know how to swim?

He disrobed and walked slowly into the water as Ceres was far enough out then that she was treading water while the waves bobbed her up and down with the warm sun overhead. Adler was shoulder-deep in the water waiting for Stone.

"C'mon ya big brute, don't be such a thimble-head, ain't nothing out here gonna hurt ya'!"

"How can you really say that?" Stone said, nearly waist-deep with his pale, strong arms up at his sides. "How do you know what's out there?"

"Ah, nothing that ain't scared of us!"

"Did you call me a thimble-head?"

They swam together in the water of the Sacred Sea out where Ceres was, and Stone found that he indeed did know how to swim.

"You see it?" Stone asked. "The rock with the white stripe?"

Each of them looked around but didn't say anything.

"It's supposed to be where the mountains meet the sea," Ceres said. "And there's the foothills of the Liolen Mountains, that's were Endo should be. But I don't see the rock…"

"Let's get back to shore," Adler said. "We'll take the horses south, see if we can see anything."

After they were dried off from the sun's heat and clothed again, they were back on the horses doing as Adler suggested. The Liolens were getting closer into view, with their high caps looming overhead.

"We're going to climb those?" Stone asked, scratching the beard hairs on his neck.

"They're higher than I remember," Adler said. "But I haven't been here since I was a young lad."

"Were you here with your parents?" Stone asked.

Adler nodded, but didn't give any other details.

Then, Stone saw it. As they carved around a small ridge it appeared like a giant fin bursting through the water, aimed at the shoreline, and a cracked, white painted line was down the front of its sharp edge. It must have been fifteen feet out of the water.

"We must not have recognized it from the side without seeing the white stripe," Stone said. "We're here." He looked up at the cliffs ahead of them.

"Ain't no way the horses are making it up there," Adler said. "And its gonna take longer than a few days to find Endo and make it back…"

"You saying we leave the horses…?" Stone asked with wide eyes.

"Not saying leave them," Adler said. "But we aren't tethering them up either. We'll just leave it up to them if they stay or go."

"I hope they stay," Ceres said, leaning down onto Angelix's mane. "I don't want to say goodbye."

"I wonder when we make our way back down from the

Mystics' city," Stone said. "Where will our next destination be? Will they give us a direction to go? Or will there just be more mysteries?"

"I don't know," Adler said. "But first things first. We've got to climb."

Chapter Thirty

※

Waves crashed high upon the shark fin rock with the white stripe down its front edge. They burst upon its side and then the mists seemed to dissolve into the air. The sea air blew through them, sending Stone's ponytail whipping to the side as he had a hand raised over his eyes to look up at the mountain before them, bright with the light of the sun upon it. Somewhere up there was the city of Endo—and they hoped they would be able to find it easily.

Ceres had her forehead pressed against Angelix's, and she had her hands on the side of the horse's head. She then kissed her between the eyes.

"I think we'll see each other again," Ceres said and smiled. "But if you need to go off and have some freedom and adventures, I understand, girl. I'm the same way."

Adler simply petted Hedron's neck. "Bye, friend."

Stone walked over to his horse, the one that had grueled through a murky swamp and sharp mountains to get him to this point. The horse neighed to him, nuzzling his chest.

"Me too, pal. Me too."

"Ready?" Adler asked them then, as they gave a long stare

at the tall mountain that stood taller than all the others on the range of the Lionel's that went south from there.

Unusual that a mountain would do that... they normally grow as the range goes on.

"That's a real climb." Ceres scratched her neck.

"Did you expect it to be a hike?" Adler asked.

"Not a hike," she said, "but not a mountain like this. How in the Dark Realm is there a civilization up there?"

"How'd Marilyn make it up and down this?" Stone asked.

"I was just thinking the same thing," Adler said. "She was pretty incredible. Maybe she had a spell to fly up there."

"Or she just did it the old-fashioned way..." Ceres said, walking toward the mountain.

"Ready?" Adler asked again.

Stone nodded. "Look for the olive tree where there should be none, and then head up," he murmured to himself.

They walked up the rocky foothills to the base of the mountain. The small rocks moved around under their boots, making it a wobbly trek up toward the boulders that encircled it. They'd accumulated an array of things in the weeks it took them to get there, so their packs were quite full. Each of them also had the same bows and quivers from the forest soldiers, their swords, the light armor they'd acquired from an abandoned hut and some bandits that awoke to find they didn't have them anymore...

Step after step they walked up, and Stone was finding that he was having issues catching his breath with the growing elevation and the heavy pack upon his back.

"Need to stop already?" Adler gawked with a wry grin. "You can wait down here if you'd like." He winked. "We'll let you know how it goes!"

"Screw off," Stone replied, taking a deep breath and pressing forward.

They were then at the large boulders, that they crept

through and over to get to the mountain itself. Stone was acclimating better then, but they all paused to take a breath and look out at the sea below and out to the plains they'd taken to get there. They could see the hill they stayed upon the night before, as they looked at the mountain they were next to then. Looking around, they noticed that they were beginning to lose daylight too. It had taken them much longer to get to the rocky base of the mountain than they'd expected.

"I guess we're used to horse-time traveling," Adler said.

"It's going to be a cold night up here if we don't find some wood before night falls," Stone said. "I'll start looking now."

"I'll go with," Ceres said.

"Well," Adler said with a stark tone in his voice. "I'm not gonna just sit around here by myself. I'll look too."

It took some patience and ingenuity, but they found enough dried timber to keep a small fire going that night. But as the darkness fell, and the near-full moon floated over them, the fire did little to help them keep warm from the roaring sea winds. Stone shivered from a cold breeze, and Ceres shook so fiercely she nearly shook off the rock she sat upon. Three hours into the night, and they had to move their entire campsite to the back of a large boulder, which helped them escape the cold—but only a little.

"Great start to the climb," Adler said.

"We've haven't done any climbing yet," Ceres said, with her teeth chattering. Stone wrapped an arm around her, and this time she didn't push him away.

It was a long night to say the least.

The next morning, Stone awoke to the sound of thin feet flapping on the rock he slept on. He shooed away the seagulls, and as he pushed himself up from the rock, he felt the warm goo slink between his fingers.

"Ugh," he sighed, wiping the bird poo off of it. "Looking to be a grand day!"

Ceres woke up next and stretched her arms out wide with a yawn.

"I don't want to wake up," she moaned. "I could sleep for a week…"

Adler snored soundly next to them.

"I think he feels the same," Stone said, still wiping his hand free of the stinky goo.

A half hour later they were all back on their feet and moving more and more up the mountain. It was a lot of hopping up rocks and squeezing between them until they got to the beautiful base of the mountain. They'd called it the 'easy part.' When they got there, it was easy to find paths that wound around the mountain, which they'd also named, 'the rocky beast.'

They decided to take the widest path, old and weathered with thousands of feet that had trampled it over the ages, perhaps millions, Stone wondered

"How long do you think they've been up there?" Stone asked. "Strange place to create a city… raise a family."

"I've been thinking the same thing," Ceres said. "Did they start up there? Or go to hide? Why would anyone think to live up in such a desolate, hard to find place unless you were going to escape from something."

Adler scratched his beard. "I've been too busy climbing to think about it."

"We really haven't done any climbing yet," Ceres said. "More like vertical walking and boulder jumping."

Stone laughed, holding his stomach.

It wasn't long before they reached that real climbing though. They were still upon the same path, but it became important to find each step carefully as the path behind them was growing steep and treacherous if any of them mis-stepped and were to fall backward.

The farther they inched their way up the mountain, the

sorer their fingers went, the more their calves and knees ached, and the farther they got away from the safety of the ground far below. By that point, the horses had either gone away, or were too small for them to spot clearly from that height.

They'd stopped to take a breather after hours of grueling moving up steep, narrow paths or hopping up boulders to continue their climb. The path split into forks at points, and they always decided to take the road that led up higher, directly toward the mountain's peak. Yet, there was no olive tree to assist in their mount, so they only took the more difficult route each time.

Stone wondered if they'd taken a wrong turn, or if the olive tree was still somewhere far up ahead, and the peak of the mountain still looked like a distant climb, but he was determined. They'd made it that far; they were going to go all the way!

As they were about to make their way back up after the short break, Stone spotted something reflective sticking out of Adler's side, leather bag. It seemed unusual, and he hadn't noticed it before.

"What's that?"

"What's what?" Adler responded, closing the flap casually to the bag.

Stone cocked his head to the side as Ceres continued forth at the lead, as the two paused, yet Adler turned and walked on.

"In your bag, I haven't seen it before."

"Don't worry about it," Adler said, climbing on. They were on a winding, rocky path with small pebbles that moved beneath their feet.

"Just tell me what it is, will ya?"

Adler sighed, pausing in his climb. "It's a surprise, can we leave it at that?"

"A surprise? What do you mean, for who?"

Adler turned with a blank stare on his face, and wide-eyed

as if speaking to a child, replied, "Do you know what a surprise means? Or is that something you don't know about from before you rose from the dead?"

A surprise for me? Stone tried to suppress his excitement, but he didn't know if he'd ever received a surprise before. He shrugged and continued walking.

The day grew long, and it was long into the dusk that the whipping winds turned chill once more, leaving them to get a fire going on a rocky outcrop on the northern side of the mountain. This time though, they collected the wood as they climbed. Ceres huddled under her hood, Adler lay on his side staring at the fire, and Stone sat up cross-legged in his long-sleeved shirt petting Mud as he slept next to him. All they had to eat that night was stale bread and smoke-dried meat.

They drifted off to sleep that night, or the best sleep that they could get, for the next morning, they were in for a stark reminder of the difficulty that climbing a mountain could be. In the early morning hours, as the sun was hidden by thick, gray clouds that hung ominously above, a biting rain turned to a near-icy sleet. Even with their hoods over their heads, holding the cloth above them to keep the stinging rain away, it did little to help the freezing conditions. The rocks at their feet were growing slicker and slicker, and fighting their way up felt like a near-impossible feat.

"Over there," Ceres yelled, pointing up and the to the left—off the path. They both looked up and saw a slight overhang a few dozen yards off. She went off, carefully climbing up and over large, knee-high rocks off the path. The boys followed. Fighting off the cold—even though they were sopping wet and nearly frozen—Mud included, they made their way to the overhang, and once underneath finally found their reprieve from the storm. It was a five- or so-foot wide stone over them and helped to keep the winds away as well. To Stone's surprise though, there was a cave underneath the rock, and they were staring into it. Even Mud seemed fascinated by it as he sniffed the warm air coming up from it, and he started to go down into it.

"Mud, wait," Stone said. "We don't know what's down there. C'mon back here, boy."

The dog turned to look at Stone, but then went down into the dark cave anyway as Adler and Ceres gave quick laughs.

"Nice listenin' dog ya got there," she said, then shook the wetness from her hair.

"Mud," Stone said. "Argh, where've you gone off to? Mud!"

He walked into the cave, which he had to duck slightly to get into, but the cave soon grew dark with the overcast sky doing no help to show him the way down.

"Stone, stop," Ceres said, rubbing her bare arms after she'd taken over her long-sleeved, woven shirt. "The dogs got senses ya' don't. Don't go down in there, he'll be fine. Just goin' to sniff around and…"

Mud's bark rang out in the cave like a ripple in a pond. Over and over the dog barked wildly, and then the clear sounds of a skirmish by the dog's barks turning to a low growl.

"I've got to go down there," Stone said with his hands out wide as he began to creep down farther into the darkness.

"Stone! Stop!" Adler yelled, quickly going after him as the scuffle echoed through the tunnel.

Stone refused to stop though, even drawing his sword as he had to feel each step carefully with his boots to find sure footing. But then… all of the sudden, the scuffling stopped.

"Mud! Mud! Come here, boy. I can't see you, come back up here you hear?" but Stone heard nothing—just dead silence from below. "Boy?"

Stone stared down into the cave, waiting nervously as his heart pounded in his chest.

"Boy?" but all Stone heard was silence. Ceres and Adler

were nervously waiting and watching too. Ceres didn't seem to care for the dog that much, but she was as silent as a whisper to a deaf, old man as she watched, motionlessly.

A scamper of claws on rock slowly crept up the cave then, as Stone held his sword in his right hand, ready to enact vengeance if need be whatever sought to harm his friend. He quickly found out it was his friend though as he ran back into the light.

"Boy!" Stone said as he knelt, letting his sword fall to the rocks and wrapping his arms around Mud's neck. He was so exhilarated he hadn't seen what the dog had in his mouth as he ran up…

They decided to camp out under that overhang that night, scavenging for enough wood to create a fire that would last the night, if by only a low smolder. The winds and rains hadn't let up throughout the day, and one day to dry their clothes—hoping for fairer weather the next day would prove to raise their spirits.

The plan was to get the fire roaring to a nice temperature to roast the treat Mud had brought up to them from down in the depths of the mountain. It was a mangy creature… something that looked like an overgrown squirrel that mated with an ugly beaver. But they were sure done with near moldy bread and the last morsels of that dried meat. This was fresh, and as it cooked next to the fire, each of them had saliva gushing in their mouths, and Mud wagged his tail wildly.

As they bit into the meat, that when fully cooked was nearly as round as a frying pan, wide smiles grew on their faces, and the rains even seemed to let up for the first time in the whole day. It was the welcoming warmth that warms the soul—rejuvenating the body and welcoming a sound sleep. Each of them gave Mud their appreciation in the form of rubbing his muzzle, petting, and kisses on the top of his head.

Even if the dog stunk, they each had to admit that they did too!

As the skies cleared that dreary night, and Stone lay on his back looking up to the sky filled with countless, beaming stars, he imagined what each of those tiny lights were. Were they the remains of the spirits of their ancestors looking down upon them? Were they the souls of future spirits waiting to come down and fill a new life upon conception? Or were they futures of every person in the world watching them, waiting to come down and fulfill a destiny? Maybe they were the powers of the god Crysinthian held up over them to protect them?

All he knew for certain was that it was a pretty night to look up at the stars with a full belly with friends, wondering what else was out there? What powers-that-be existed in the world that they didn't yet know about. He smiled at the thought of meeting the Mystics, and what knowledge they held, and what sort of welcoming they'd receive once they got to the top of the mountain.

Chapter Thirty-One

The following afternoon, the sun felt warm on their skin, the blue sky was brimming with splendid vibrancy, with only whispers of clouds remaining from the day prior. Yet, the air was thick from the wetness left behind. Sweat was heavy upon Stone's brow, and Mud panted quickly, as they made their way higher with each step. The pack upon his back felt twenty pounds heavier than it did before.

Not only were they struggling with the thick, humid air and the altitude... but the path they were on seemed to have splintered off it every twenty minutes now. Making the right choice up the mountain was beginning to be a confounding one—and they'd already questioned their decision to take the widest of the trails.

Ceres paused at the lead, looking around. She wiped her brow with her shirt and put her hand flat over her brow to look out over the horizon. Adler and Stone did the same, while Adler took down a bit of water.

"See anything?" Stone asked, as Adler poured water for Mud into a small, clay dish.

"Yeah," she said, raising Stone's spirits, but then they quickly fell. "See that dead tree over there? We've been here before. Somehow, we've gone in a grand loop. We're just a smidge higher."

"How's that possible?" Stone asked, looking down at the tree, which he did indeed recognize. He thought he saw something else out of the corner of his eye, and quickly looked farther up the mountain, as what looked like a rock's shadow moved. He looked down at Mud who was lapping up water, who wasn't concerned for anything but that crisp liquid in his mouth. Stone looked back up, but there was nothing there.

"Screw the paths!" Adler said. "Let's just climb straight up. Can't go in a circle going over the mountain."

"We just need to find the tree," Stone said. "It's got to be around here somewhere. It's not as if we're on the wrong mountain, right?"

"Olive trees aren't known for their size," Ceres said. "It could be hip height, not so much a tree as a shrub…"

"Let's face it," Adler said. "We're lost, let's just take a different path and see where we end up. Could it be worse than ending up here again? I mean… It's not as if climbing upward is gonna send us farther down, and Endo's up, right? Let's just try another path. Let's take that one over there. That one looks good."

"Fine," Ceres said, seemingly frustrated and at her wits-end. "You want to lead? Go ahead, but we end up back here don't be complainin' about 'we weren't taking the right way.' You lead, and you're responsible fer' it!"

Instantly Adler went to apologizing, "I wasn't blaming you!" His hands were out wide, and he looked sheepish. "We agreed on it together, I was just…"

She turned abruptly, heading toward him with her eyebrows angrily down and her eyes darkened. Her finger was pointed squarely at him. "Go on then, you get us there!"

Stone shrugged, wanting to stay out of the way of Ceres' anger.

"Let's just keep on the same way we've been going," Adler said, ushering for her to lead with a gesturing with his hands and a slight bow. "Maybe we just missed our turn."

She groaned low, but walked past him, back up the path. They followed after, but Stone and Mud trailed her, with Adler slinking back to the rear.

At that part of the mountain, there were huge spikes of rock that protruded from it, making visibility poor going up. The trail they were on wove in and out of the great rocks, but it did make it difficult to tell where they were going, but at least they were heading upwards almost all of the time. Looking back down the mountain and into the valley below, they knew they'd gone far, but the olive tree would be the final sign that they had gone the right way, and wouldn't eventually have to tread back down to find the correct path.

The day was growing long, and they'd reached another point where climbing up knee-high and hip-high rocks made Stone's legs feel as if they were about to burn off. Even Mud, with all his jumping, laid down and panted often in the shade.

"Let's take a quick breather," Stone said after Ceres helped him up a boulder with her hand. *She never seems to tire!*

"Fine," she said, as Mud leaped up the rock and laid down. "Stone sat heavily with his back to the next rock to climb, trying to catch his breath. Ceres helped Adler up onto the flat, gray rock. Adler quickly sat too, while she stood, scanning the area while blocking out the sun from her eyes with her hood pulled over her head.

"See anything?" Stone asked, while sitting with his arms on his knees, wiping the cool sweat from his forehead.

"We're making progress," she said. "Definitely getting higher. The air is thinner here."

Moments later they were back on their way, aching and

pushing their way higher and higher. Yes, the air was thinning, but that wasn't Stone's concern, that was more the blisters on his feet in his boots and the scrapes on his fingers from climbing. Another time he thought he saw a shadow move, but it proved to just be a tree blowing in the breeze. It did occur to him that he should pay attention to his instinct about shadows, so he kept the sword on his hip ready to draw at any moment.

Suddenly, they turned around a massive stone, that stood ten feet high, and Stone let out a great breath of relief. There it finally was, poking out through the stone like a thin needle in a large, outstretched sheet of fabric. The olive tree. They walked up to its side as Adler clapped his hands in excitement. The tree was no shrub, as Ceres had mentioned—this tree was high-reaching, and looked ancient with its curling branches, twisted, knobby trunk and lusciously vibrant green leaves. Mud sniffed it and relived himself on the gray-brown trunk.

Adler reached up to grab olives from the branches.

"Perhaps we shouldn't," Stone said, putting his hand up, motioning to him to stop. "There may be something special about this tree to the Mystics?"

"Marilyn didn't say anything about that, did she?"

"No," Stone said, but lowering his hand, he felt a sort of... presence from it... "Can you feel that? It feels like it is... alive, or something like that... like it has a soul?"

"A soul?" Ceres asked.

"You don't feel it?" he asked.

Adler put his hand on its trunk, listening for something like a heartbeat. "Nope," he said.

"Let's just find the path and be on our way," Stone said. "It may be close now."

Adler shrugged, "Fine. Olives look under-ripe anyway. I don't see no path though…"

They all looked around, looking for the path Marilyn said would take them up to the city of the Mystics, and Stone found what seemed like the faintest of trails... more like a mouse's path than a person's.

"No way that's it," Ceres said. "That can't be the path to a city with people."

"I don't see anything else," Stone said. "Do you? Worst case is we have to turn back around?"

"Let's try," Ceres said. "Night's gonna fall, and we'll need to take up shelter if we don't get there soon. Let's see where this snake-trail leads."

"Snakes?" Adler gasped. "Did you see one?"

"Not yet," Ceres said. "Maybe we'll find one in the tall grass up there though." She winked at him and started up the path.

Adler looked unsure if to follow.

"There's no snake," Stone said. "I'll let you know if I see one, so you don't have to get close." He then followed Ceres with Mud. Adler gulped but then hesitantly went after them.

The thin path went straight up a long-inclined hill with dying, yellowish grass nearly up to their knees. It was a strange sight that high up on the mountain as the olive tree fell beneath and behind them. It was difficult to follow as the grass did a devilishly good job of concealing it. Ceres had to use her sword to brush the grass out of the way as to find it.

They were a few hundred yards up when Stone saw that shadow move out of the corner of his eye, and this time, he knew it was something. He picked up his pace to walk next to Ceres, whispering in her ear, "There's something out there."

She whispered back, "You sure? What is it?"

"Don't know, but I've been seeing it the last couple of days."

"This isn't a good place to stand and fight," Ceres said. "Is the shadow up or down?"

He motioned with his head, up.

She groaned. "If we can get behind one of those stones ahead, use it as a shield, maybe we can…"

The brief plan was in vain though as a shadowy figure stepped out from one of the rocks ahead. It appeared to be a broad-shouldered man, tall in stature with his shoulder-length hair blowing in the wind. His hand rested upon his sword; still sheathed.

"Who are you, why have you come to this mountain?" the figure called down in a powerful, yet restrained voice. His stance was wide and as the shadow faded and they could slowly make out his features, his face was stern, and he was ready to draw his sword at a seconds notice.

"We've come to speak with the Mystics," Stone called up. "We were told to come to this mountain and take the path up from the olive tree." He paused, then asked, "Are you one of them?"

"No."

Three of them looked at each other, trying to figure out what to make of the figure's response, and what to do next. Stone looked at Mud, who seemed to have the same question. He wasn't barking, that must be something…?

"Sir," Stone said. "We must be on our way; we made a promise that we would make it to Endo. We are going to continue up this path. Please don't get in our way. We've come far, from the city of Atlius we've traveled to get here, and there is no way in the Dark Realm we are turning back now."

"A promise? A promise from whom?"

"Her name was Marilyn, she found us, and told me that I had to come here. It has something to do with the Neferian… but I don't know what…"

"Marilyn?" the man asked as he took a step forward. "What of her? If she beckoned you to venture here, where is she, then?"

"He doesn't know…" Adler whispered.

"She fell," Stone said, as Ceres bowed her head. "She gave her life so that I could make it here. My name is Stone, and I'm the one she thought arose from the dead to fulfill some part of a prophecy the Mystics have."

"Should we be telling him all this?" Ceres asked him.

"He knows Marilyn," Stone said. "For now. That's enough for me…"

The man then looked up at the sky as his hair continued to blow in the wind, taking a moment to think.

"Marilyn the Conjurer has fallen?" he said to himself. "This indeed is a bad omen." He groaned. "After me." He turned and walked up the path for them to follow.

Stone walked after him, and the others followed.

They didn't have to walk long to find that this was the right place. For once they stepped through a thin break in an otherwise long stretch of vertical stone, they saw it. They finally laid their eyes upon the city of the Mystics on the Mountain… they'd reached the city of Endo.

Chapter Thirty-Two

Stone led the way through the gap in the long stone wall. It was more than three feet thick as they squeezed through. What lay on the other side was breathtaking.

It was a round clearing, a grassy outcrop hundreds of yards wide. The man who'd appeared from the shadow stood at the side of the opening into the clearing; he smelled of musky pipe smoke as Stone walked by. In the clearing goats and cows grazed. A great black steer with wide horns poked his head up from the grass to look at the visitors.

There were old, clean, buildings of white stone, each with two stories and glass windows on each of their four sides. Their roofs were made of a reflective black, round tile, and each of the doors to the buildings were a sea-like blue. There were twelve of these buildings that Stone counted, and at their center was as beautiful a structure as he'd ever seen in his short life.

Its architecture looked to be developed after the mountain itself with the olive tree that led up to the city. It was a brilliant, vivid carved white marble with streaks of grays and blacks that ran down it like streaks trickling water from a cool rain. It stood forty feet high, with a wide base like a mountain, but with curving, knobby roots like the tree. There was no glass upon it, and it looked as old as time from its unique design, yet it looked freshly carved.

"This is a magical place," Stone said in awe.

The marble structure at the center had long, branch-like protrusions erupting out of it like a leafless tree, as the winding, carved veins of a tree would all the way up into the strong branches. From each branch hung flickering, golden lights that shimmered like fireflies.

As each of them had stepped out into the clearing just as the last light of the sun shown over the surrounding stone wall, a golden glow hung majestically in the air. They marveled at the beauty, and serenity of such a place. *How could a place like this exist this high up in the mountains, and how was such a piece of marble ever found up here?*

"Welcome to Endo Valair," the man said. "City of the Old Mothers."

"This is the city of The Majestic Wilds?" Ceres asked, her mouth nearly hung open in splendid awe.

The man nodded.

"We must speak with the Mystics," Stone said. "Marilyn said they would help clarify the prophecy to us. We have so many questions…"

"Well," the man said, pulling a black, curved pipe from his pocket and stuffing dried tobacco leaves into it. "You've come to a place where answers are as easily found as the stars in a clear sky, yet as difficult as a white herring in the sea."

"This is gonna be more riddles, isn't it?" Adler whispered to Stone.

"Shh."

"You'll have to wait until morning, however, to get the answers you seek," the man said.

"What? Why?" Stone asked.

"The mothers are asleep."

Stone felt baffled and taken aback. "What? Well, can we gently wake them? We've come far."

"We don't wake the mothers," the man said. "You're welcome to rest in one of the homes if you wish for the night, or you may sleep back out on the mountain if you choose. The mothers may wake at first light."

"May?" Ceres asked with a perked eyebrow.

"The mothers are very old," the man said. "Sometimes they may rest for days, sometimes weeks. You'll have to wait and see when they awake."

"Weeks?" Stone said, "we can't wait that long. We've got to speak with them now."

The man glowered into Stone's eyes, and then lit his pipe with a flick of flint and steel.

"You'll wait, or you can leave."

Stone felt unable to do anything to argue with the man, who casually, yet powerfully puffed on his pipe.

"But if Marilyn sent you here, and with how far you've come to get here," the man said. "I think it wise for you to stay. There is plenty of cheese and wine here after all…"

"Wine?" Adler asked in a high pitch.

At least it's not blasted ale…

"Here," he said. "I'll lead you to a place you can rest until they awaken."

They followed him to a white building on the other side of the marble monument at the center. Stone let his fingertips glide along the smooth, yet intricately textured base. He couldn't help but feel a similar presence to the olive tree lower down upon the mountain. *It's almost as if the mountain itself has a soul…*

"Here," the man said after he exhaled a plume of smoke. He was standing at the blue front door of the building. "You'll find most everything you need inside. Over there is the supply house, he pointed at an identical structure three buildings to the left. Take whatever you need, but don't be greedy. There's spring water for drinking or washing up at the north end. Over there is the weaponry if you need a whetstone or need your leathers oiled."

Stone had so many questions for the man: *how old is this place, where did the marble come from, how long have The Majestic Wilds been here?* But he decided to look around and let the place sink in. After all, it seemed they'd have the night to figure some things out, and take a night to rest.

"What are your names? And from where do you hail?" he asked, his shadowy, hazel eyes staring at them.

"Stone, like I said. I supposed I was born in the Ruins of Aderogon."

"Me' names Ceres Rand. I hail originally from the north. A town called Briewater on the coast."

"I'm Adler Caulderon from the south—city of Valeren, though I don't remember it much."

"Ah," the man said. "You were Armonde D'Amere's apprentice."

Adler nodded after cocking his head in confusion. "I was."

"How'd you know that?" Ceres asked.

"I'm familiar with the guild," the man said, stroking his short, black beard after another deep inhale off his pipe. Stone just then noticed the curled, bone-like earrings on the man.

"And you knew of his mentor's passing?" Ceres asked. "How'd you hear that all the way up here? In fact, how do you get anything up here?"

"We have our ways," he said. "Now, if you need anything, I'm sure you'll find it." He turned to leave, but then paused, looked back at them with those same shadowy eyes. "Do not enter the marble tree. Do not wake the mothers."

"What would happen if we woke them up on accident?" Adler asked, half-kidding with a grin.

"What would happen if I threw you off the side of the mountain?" the man responded quickly, without returning a grin. "Don't enter it, you are welcome to make yourselves at home to the rest of the city." He turned and began to make his way toward the entrance to the city once more.

"Sir," Stone said loudly. "What's your name? We're looking for a person named Corvaire here too."

He paused, gazing deeply at Stone. "I'm Corvaire."

Stone was taken aback. "Marilyn said for us to specifically search for you here."

"And you've found me," he said as he turned and continued walking, as he slipped back into the crevasse in the wall and was quickly back out of the city.

"Cheery fellow," Adler said.

"Why do ya' always need to make a joke outta everything?" Ceres said. "He's just a serious fella. Quite the opposite of you." She opened the door to enter into the white building. "You could learn loads from him I can already tell."

"She makes me sound like a fool, a jester," he said to Stone.

"Well… he is easily twice your age, and quite a bit more handsome too. Maybe Ceres saw that too but didn't want to ruin your cheery mood." Stone winked and slipped into the dark interior of the building that Ceres had already lit the candles in."

"I'm just trying to lighten the mood, geesh," Adler said to himself as he entered. Mud slipped in behind him. "She's always taking everything so seriously…"

❧

Hours later, in the warm, welcoming interior of the building, a waist-high fireplace burned brightly with many dry logs. The nostalgic smell of crackling fire filled the room as Stone and Ceres sat side by side in a pair of creaking wood rocking chairs. Candles still burned on the mantelpiece that had scant cobwebs clinging to old-leather books. Wooden cabinets and large, wicker baskets lined the walls, and a small kitchen was in a room adjacent to the one they were in.

Adler and Mud were off to the spring to bathe. Ceres had already returned and dried from her time in the fresh, mountain water. Stone would be off next. They'd collected stone-ground crackers, firm, orange cheese and a dry red wine from the building Corvaire told them about. They brought back pails of spring water, and their dry feet rested upon a soft rug with intricate blue and gold dyes flowing down it.

Stone took a sip of wine, swallowing it with a soothing sigh.

"We've made it," he said. "But I can't feel as if we're wasting time sitting here. I still have so many answers."

"Be patient," she said, gulping water from a clay mug. "Enjoy it while we can. We won't be here forever, I'm sure."

"He said it could be weeks. Weeks!"

"It won't be."

"How do you know," he asked.

"I don't. But I'd rather be in here, eating and drinking by a hot fire without the bloomin' wind. I know that much."

"Corvaire," he said. "What do you think of him?"

"Mysterious, quiet, and mysterious. What's not to like?" she laughed.

"I'm serious, Marilyn sent us to him. We even told him that, and I feel as if he wouldn't have even told us who he was if I hadn't asked. It's as if he didn't even care…"

"He cared when we mentioned Marilyn for the first time, hardly even hesitated to bring us here. Ya ever stop to think that maybe he wants to see what the mothers say first, before holding our hands, and teaching all the magic he knows?"

"I know you're kidding," Stone said. "But, do you think he knows magic too? I still have dreams about that spell that

Marilyn did that burned all of those soldiers back in Serenity's Pub. I know the word but would never repeat it unless…"

"*Excindier!*" she shouted, letting her voice echo in the room, and sent Stone nearly toppling over out of his chair. Yet nothing happened, the fire remained in the fireplace and at the tops of the candles.

"Great Grindleword, Ceres!"

"What?" she said with laugh. "I don't know magic. It's just a word."

"But how'd you know that? How'd you know it wouldn't burn us alive."

Ceres looked away. "Because I tried it already… I wanted to see if it would work."

"What?" he asked.

"While you two slept at night, a few times I snuck away and tried it. I thought if I could get it to work, then it would help us get to where we were going quicker, and in less danger."

"You could've hurt yourself." He got back up into the chair. "You know what that spell is capable of. You could've died, or at the least burned the forest down."

"But I didn't, did I?" she spat. "It didn't happen. So, it's fine. Want to drop the lecture now?"

He shut his mouth.

They sat there for a few minutes, and Stone sulkily drank his wine.

"Do you even know what Great Grindleword means?" she asked.

He hesitated to answer, "No. Just heard you say it."

"Grindleword was a great wizard long ago. Don't know if he really lived or if it's just a tale, but he was the first wizard to learn to speak to the moon. Me' ma used to tell me that he could use the moon to look down on all us and protect us when we needed protectin' so we could sleep at night. His staff was pure silver and had a jewel at its top that held moonlight into its gem-cut blue crystal. She tol' me if you say his name three times before you drift off to sleep, he'll watch over and protect ya."

"Do you do it still?" he asked. "You still say his name before bed."

"No," she said quickly. "Not every night. Only when I feel I need to, and I don't say it—I whisper it."

"You gonna do it tonight?" he asked.

She shrugged, taking the wine from Stone's hand and drinking it, and then handing it back. "Don't think so. You think I need ta'?"

"I feel fairly safe here," he said. "I trust Marilyn wouldn't send us to a dangerous place all this way's away. I think we can rest tonight."

"Me too," she said. "Me too. I think I kinda like this place…"

Chapter Thirty-Three

It was a chill, overcast day on the mountain the following day. A gloomy haze rolled into Endo, filling the space between the twelve white buildings and the marble tree at their center. The stream at the far side of the city was almost visible through the thick fog.

Stone had woken alone while the others slept. He'd gone and brewed some tea in the supply building and was sitting on the wet grass, cross-legged in front of the marble tree. He looked up at it, marveling at the way its creator had chiseled away at it with such defining features that it may have well just been a tree that was turned to marble through some sort of wizardry or witchcraft. He wondered if it was Grindleword who'd done it?

But more than taking the time to bask in the exquisite beauty of it, he was waiting semi-patiently for the Old Mothers to awaken. After all, he'd come far and wanted some answers. He sipped his tea with the cup cradled in both hands thinking about all the knowledge that the marble tree held inside it. He thought also about Corvaire—all the things he knew but was evasive enough to keep those secrets to himself so far.

After a while, he grew uncomfortable with his pants getting as wet as they were, and the Old Mothers were still inside sleeping. Mud had come up to him and was itching his muzzle on Stone's thigh too, so he got up and ran with Mud out in the fields.

Adler and Ceres both walked over to them out in the field, and Stone hoped they'd come with news that the mothers had awoken, but they didn't.

"They're still asleep then?" Stone asked.

"Suppose so," Ceres said. "Hadn't heard or seen anythin'. I reckon Corvaire would've told us."

"What do we do?" Stone asked. "It's gonna be hard to sit on our hands while we wait. I can hardly sit still."

It was then they noticed Corvaire walking toward them with smooth strides through the gray fog, which seemed to be fading away as the sun peaked out slightly through the clouds. A rush surged through Stone. *The mothers, the mothers must be awake!*

The three waited eagerly as he approached through the grass. His black, wavy hair rustled on his neck as he approached. He wore a tan vest tied over a white cotton shirt that ended just above his elbows. A long sword was sheathed in a black leather scabbard at his side. The hilt of the sword was a dark brown leather with an ivory sphere on its bottom.

"Walk with me," he said in a gruff tone as he stood before them. He turned and they followed. He walked them near the stream that flowed out of a gap in the mountain and flowed out another crevasse. Corvaire led them to a pattern of rocks just to the left of where the crevasse was, as a pack of goats scampered out of the way as they neighed. He climbed up the rocks that stuck out of the wall by only a few inches each. They didn't hesitate though; each of them followed him as he silently climbed. The wall was only fifteen feet or so tall, so they ascended it quickly to a breathtaking sight.

Upon the wall that was six feet thick and wrapped around the city, they found themselves looking down upon the coastline where the shark fin rock was nearly a speck from that height. The Sacred Sea flowed on to the horizon with its sparkling deep-blue water. The hills and valleys on the other side went on with blowing fields of green grass. The sun had shown itself through the parting clouds and the top of the mountain loomed behind them. They could see nearly everything, including the snaking pathways up the face of the mountain and the olive tree blowing in the breeze. A cool, crisp wind blew through, which Stone had to lean into as they were strong this high up.

"Beautiful," Ceres said, with her blond hair whipping behind her.

Corvaire stood stoically next to them, his strong jaw showing as his own hair danced behind his face. Stone wondered why he'd brought them there, only for a good view of the lands?

Then the rock beneath their feet shook and each of them huddled down toward it. A powerful bellow came out from within the mountain, like an earthquake. It was getting louder, as if some sort of force was burrowing up from within the core of the mountain up toward them. Then it erupted like a blasting volcano.

It burst from the mountain's face only thirty feet under them. Its head was wide with hulking, long muscles glimmering beneath teal-colored scales that reflected almost like mirrors in the sunlight. A single white, brittle horn wrapped backward on each side of its head. It roared so loudly they each had to cover their ears as smoke smoldered out of both sides of its mouth. A red stripe coursed down its spine, lined with rows of spikes the same color as its horns. It was massive, as Stone couldn't believe his eyes—none of the dragons he'd seen so far were nearly as big as this beast. Its wings, while outstretched, seemed to be as big as the city itself.

"Grimdore," Corvaire yelled out, with his voice wanting to echo out in the open air, but being drowned out by the shattering roar of the mighty dragon that was turning in its flight back toward the mountain. Its eyes were a fiery red with yellow, sharp pupils. Stone felt an overwhelming fear filling his heart. It was flying right at them, smoke still flowing out of its toothy maw.

Stone nearly fell over the backside of the wall as it landed next to them, perched up on the wall with its front and rear legs clamping onto it with strong claws that were the length of curved swords. Stone's eyes watered from the hot breath from the dragon as it lowered its head—more than the size of a full-grown man—down to inspect them. Its breath smelled like a forge on a sweltering, dry-heat day.

"This is her," Corvaire said, walking past the three of them and laying his hand on the tip of the dragon's snout. "She's been the protector of this place for a long, long time."

"Grimdore is a her?" Adler asked. "Can I touch her too? I've never been this close to one. I feel as if I should be a bit more scared than I am, but can I?"

"If she'll let ya without biting your hand off," Corvaire laughed, showing the first sign that he had any inkling of humor in his bones. Adler withdrew his outstretched hand. While he did that, Ceres marched over and laid her hand on the dragon's scaly snout, next to Corvaire's, who was slowly stroking it as it let out a deep growl, hopefully of satisfaction.

"She's enormous," Stone said, finally standing up. "I've never seen one as big as her."

"Don't insult her," Adler said, still shaken from the threat.

"You've probably never seen one as old as her either," Corvaire said as the dragon lifted its head back and itched the back of its wing with a gnawing of her teeth. "I know what you're going to ask, so I'll just go ahead and answer it… no, she's never fought one of the Neferian riders. But if she had to, I bet she'd send them off to rot out in the plains or at the bottom of the ocean."

Stone admitted to himself that he was indeed thinking that question to himself.

"Is she as old as the Old Mothers?" Ceres asked.

"Hard to believe anything is as old as them," he answered, scratching his beard. "That'd be a splendid question to ask them yourself."

"The Old Mothers," Stone said. "Have they awoken today?"

Corvaire groaned. "No."

Stone nodded, looking down at the sea crashing into the rocky coves below.

Just then, Grimdore expanded her wings out wide, basking them all in their shadow, and flapped mightily, sending plumes of hard, whooshing winds down on them.

"Get down," Adler said as the other two followed his advice. Corvaire remained standing with his strong arms at his sides and a wide stance with his right leg out front.

With one last great flap of its teal wings with scattered black scales it leaped from the wall, shaking it and leaving the last sounds of the scratches left from its claws. It glided down and away easily, like a falcon flying down from a tree looking for its next meal, and Stone was sure glad it wasn't going to be them.

"Ha," Adler laughed. "This place is full of surprises, ain't it. You've got a giant dragon here too? Absolutely incredible."

"Corvaire," Ceres asked. "Would you mind answerin' me a question…" He nodded. "How old is this place? Who built it? How did it get to be up in this nestled area?"

He took his pipe out, and while filling it with dried tobacco leaves, smiled and said, "That's actually three questions, my dear."

"Oh, sorry, I'll…"

"It's fine," he said as he lit the pipe and smoked. "Endo is short for Endo Valair, named for the first of the Old Mother's father. He was a wise man whose daughter learned the ways of an old magic long ago. She still lives to this day, while he passed long ago—thousands of years ago in fact. She and the other two built this place so long ago they don't remember how long it's been. Feel free to ask them though, maybe they'll remember for ya'."

"How did they get that great marble stone carved?" Stone asked. "Did they do it themselves?"

"I'm not sure they'd want me telling you that part. Best to save that for later. It is a shining good story though."

"What about Grimdore?" Ceres asked. "How'd they get a dragon like that as a pet?"

"A pet?" he said with both eyebrows raised. "She is *no* pet. She is part of the family here. And of course, the only way to get a dragon to stay with you, is to raise it from birth. I imagine they found her orphaned or something similar. Hadn't thought to ask them."

"How long have you been here?" Stone asked. "Were you raised here?"

"No," he said, turning out to look at the sea, puffing on his pipe. "I'm from the west, me and my sister both came here when the Neferian came." His head slunk as he let out a deep sigh.

"Marilyn," Stone said softly. "She was your sister, wasn't she?"

He nodded with his eyes closed.

"I'm so sorry," Ceres said, with her hand covering her lips.

Corvaire cleared his throat and took another puff.

"Yes," he said. "I'll need you to tell me everything that

happened when we meet with the mothers, they'll want to know too."

"She did save us," Stone said. "A few times actually. She was strong. We still think about her every day."

"Aye," he said. "She was strong—stronger than I. She'll be missed sorely. Well, I've got to be off, got some things that I need to tend to. The mothers may wake tomorrow, and there's much to do."

"We can help," Ceres said with her arms out. "We've got nothing to do here but relax and eat."

"You should be doing that," he said. "At least for the next couple of days. You've earned that. If they don't wake in the next few days, I'll put you to work, but until then; eat, drink, and enjoy your time. For after you have your talk with The Wild Majestics, your lives will never be the same."

Chapter Thirty-Four

※※※

After Corvaire had taken them to the top of the wall and led them back down into the city, the three of them—along with Mud, who'd been hounding Stone since Atlius—gathered a bit of food and sat by the mountain spring. They marveled at the wondrous dragon they'd just been introduced to and were allowed to sit next too. They couldn't deny they felt a warm sense of safety they hadn't felt in all too long.

Ceres was razzing Adler about being afraid of Grimdore, while Stone clutched at his sides at the sheer, splendid humor in it all. While Adler blushed and bit his tongue trying to hold back his defensiveness of why anyone should be afraid of a dragon that size—he decided to bring out the surprise he'd mentioned to Stone earlier on their climb up the mountain.

"Here," he said, rummaging through the purse on his hip. "I was gonna save this for an important—spectacular— moment, but I now see that we're not going to have that time, now as everything is just a joke to you! How's one not to be hesitant at the thought of one losing their hand to that beast up there? I was just acting in my own best interest…"

Stone just about toppled over where he sat while Ceres giggled, and Mud licked his paws.

"If that's the way it's gonna be then..." he said as he pulled his hand back from his purse as the winds howled overhead, blowing over the walls of Endo.

"No, no," Stone said, pushing past his laughter. "We want to see. We want to, honestly. Let's see please."

Adler glowered at him. "I feel that the surprise is ruined now, and I brought this all this way." From within the purse he pulled out a vial of clear liquid. He held it up to the sky, letting its contents roll back and forth as he tilted it.

"What is it?" Ceres asked, eying the peculiarly viscous liquid.

"It's called Antholily," he said, looking at it as well as he held it overhead.

"What in the bloody devil is that?" Ceres asked, twisting away with her eyebrow raised.

"It's a serum that, well... makes you act more genuine, more like yourself."

"But we already are ourselves..." Stone said, just as confused as Ceres.

"Trust me," Adler said, holding it out for them to grab and inspect. "I've taken it before. I know we are each ourselves. But this is more of a... time enhancer. Antholily gives you a sort of introspection at yourself, and it's a great waste of time while we wait. None for Mud though, tends to give animals a nasty spell o' the squirts."

"Why would we take this?" Stone inspected the vial.

"Don't have to," Adler said. "I just thought it'd be a bit o' fun. Got it from the guild in Salsonere. Good to do on your own with strangers, and even better to do with good friends. Don't have to. Just thought it might be a fun time before we go in to meet the mothers."

"What's it do?" Ceres asked, taking the vial next. "I don't want to be pent up on somethin' I don't need to be on…"

"It's more relaxing than anything…" Adler said. "I've only done it once, with my mentor, and it's difficult to describe… it's a kind of *other* feeling."

"I trust you," Stone said, itching his shoulder. "But I just don't know about this before meeting with the mothers."

"This is the prime time to do it," Adler said with his hands out. "We don't know when they're going to wake. We have a gigantic, blooming dragon protecting us… not to mention Marilyn's brother! After this, when are we going to feel this safe?"

"How do I do it?" Stone asked, as Ceres had a bewildered expression on her face with her eyes glaring at him. "What? He's right. When are we ever gonna feel this safe again? Not like I'm gonna suffer any memory loss!"

Adler erupted in a burst of laughter, and after wiping a tear from his eye, he grabbed the vial and took a teaspoon's worth of the liquid in his mouth, swallowing it down with a refreshing gulp. Then he passed it to Stone.

Stone took it, looking at it inquisitively once again. And after careful inspection, said, "If you say it's safe…" and took it up to his lips, trying to take down just as much as Adler did, but accidentally taking much more. He coughed, pulling it from his lips, holding it out to Ceres.

"Nope, nope, absolutely nope."

"What're you afraid of?" Stone asked. "At the least we'll have a bit of fun before we go off into those forsaken forests and roads. If you don't want to, that's fine, but remember those insects biting at your scalp…?"

She took the vial and drank twice as much as Stone had.

"There, happy?"

Stone and Adler glanced at each other in disbelief, and then a roar of laughter followed.

"What now?" Stone asked.

"Now, my dear fellow, we sit, enjoy the grass and stars, and we wait."

They continued in a lively conversation for the following hour, talking about all manner of life and stars and creatures and dragons and moons and mountains. There was hardly a break in it all.

Time went by so quickly that the moon and stars had replaced the bright sky before even a shiver ran down any of their backs. Stone didn't feel weak of will either, he felt such a loving connection to the other two that everything in that moment warmed his soul. He didn't quite remember all of what they'd talked about, but his spirit snapped back into the moment when Adler asked this question, "You ever think about what life would be like if we hadn't lost them… our parents?"

That was the first real pause in the conversation, and Ceres took a deep sigh. "Every minute of every day."

"Me too," Adler said with his head down. "Me too…"

"I remember my mother's face," she said, rubbing her cheek. "I can remember it… every freckle, her long eyelashes, and her eyes. Oh god, I miss her beautiful eyes." The others sat back and listened in silence. "My greatest fear…" She teared up. "My biggest fear is forgetting what she looks like. I don't want to not have that memory. I want to remember what her eyes looked like."

A weird flash of something familiar floated into Stone's mind, but he couldn't make out what.

"For me it was me' pa," Adler said. "He was so confident, so warm to my ma', he was everything I wanted to end up being. He taught me so much before he was taken away… and a hell of a fighter he was too with a sword!"

"My father," she said, with a bright liveliness coming to her eyes like an angelic shimmer, "he was so wise and gentle. I can still remember what it felt like to have him wrap his arms around me, and the feeling of him kissing my forehead before I dove off to a peaceful slumber." She began to cry. "I can still smell him, he smelled like vanilla tobacco. Every time I went off to school, I remember smellin' like that after he hugged me as I left. One day I was walking past the waterfalls of Hope's Rung Falls and a traveler walked by me. I looked back three times just to make sure it wasn't me' da."

"My mother," Adler said, looking up at the night sky, blazing with trails of endless stars and a bright moon with a halo-ish aura. "I never realized how much she was my everything. I still real at night for all the nights I told her 'no,' or all the times I acted as if I was asleep when all she wanted to do was say 'hello my son' when she got home. I'd give anything for just another second with her; another smile, another kiss on the cheek, and another, 'tomorrow will be better son, just go to sleep, and everything will be better when the sun comes up and decides to make it a good one!' I think about her all the time. All the time."

Another flash ripped through Stone's mind, as if it passed to quickly to see, but he felt a warm exhilaration burning from inside.

"Stone?" Ceres asked, leaning in toward him and putting her soft hand on his shoulder. "You're sweating, you all right?"

He was glaring into the stream, not really hearing what she'd asked. He felt as if he was gazing into a reflection of himself, he hadn't seen in a lifetime. He recognized his face's reflection, but he looked much younger, as if he was looking into the past.

"Stone?" Adler asked, only sounding like a mute fog to Stone.

A pair of eyes glowed from beneath the water at him from behind his own. Instead of his own gray eyes, there were a pair of dark green eyes the color of a cold forest leaf staring back at him. He leaned in with a trance-like allure, he watched the eyes glaring back at him behind his own reflection. Stone watched as the green eyes turned from their normal color, slowly turning to a mute blue, and then as they widened, they turned to a dazzling, bright blue with a great aura emanating from them.

"Stone?" Ceres asked.

Stone was completely fixated upon the eyes, and hadn't noticed that his reflection had turned from his own of a younger age, to that of a man who was many years his elder, with crow's feet tucked away at the corners of his eyes, and gray hair replacing the pulled-back, black widow's peak hair of his own.

"Stone, everything all right?" Adler asked, but his words were foggy to Stone.

Then the reflection's mouth moved, while his eyes glowed that majestic blue hue. Stone leaned in to hear. Behind the reflection, thousands of stars glistened behind. Stone was completely hovering over the stream's edge then, looking down at the older man, about to speak, and Stone was overwhelmingly entranced in the words that were about to come out of the reflection's mouth.

"What? What do you want to tell me? I'm listening. I'm listening."

But as the reflection's mouth moved, another voice grew from within the city, and as it grew the reflection before Stone slowly faded back to his own.

"No, no! Tell me. Speak to me. Tell me what you wanted to say. I need to know. I need to know!"

"Stone," Ceres said softly as she wrapped her arms around his neck gently. "It's all right. There's no one there. It's just you."

"No, he was there. He was there! I saw him. He looked like me and wanted to tell me something. He's gone though. He's gone…"

"Corvaire..." Adler said in a surprised voice. "What're you doing here?"

Corvaire took a moment to look around at them—his eyes were inquisitive and leering.

"You took a bit of Antholily, didn't you? I can see it a mile away. Well, I can't fault you, but I can say with extreme certainty that you picked the worst time to take it."

"What do ya' mean?" Ceres asked. "This is the perfect time. "We've made it here, all is well, we're protected by Grimdore and you. Why would this be a bad time to take in all that there is to love in life?"

"The Wild Majestics... They've awoken... and they want to speak with you. Right this moment."

PART VII
THE MAJESTIC WILDS

Chapter Thirty-Five

❦

Those same dark green eyes glowed in his mind as Corvaire led them back to the heart of Endo. The city had burst to life during the midnight sky. A flurry of dazzling torches burned brightly around the marble tree, and to Stone's astonishment there were dozens of people sitting around the tree. Looming high over it Grimdore lay past the circling structures, with her red and yellow eyes glowing like a snake's eyes from the reflecting torchlight.

"This is it," Adler said with wild eyes as he looked back at Stone. "This is what we came here for."

All of the things that Stone wanted to talk to the mothers about flowed through his head like a river running with wild rapids, jumbling themselves in the chaotic mix of excitement and anxiousness.

There they are, just up ahead. Will they be able to tell me who I am?

The three of them, led by Corvaire headed toward the marble tower, glowing in magnificent light, now looking like a divine statue, found themselves being stared at by the dozens of people surrounding the tree. They were all dressed in white clothes, whether it was dresses or vests, most were older than Stone, although there were at least two kids littler than him. None of them said a word, and soon all of their eyes were focused back upon the tree—or at least in front of it.

Two roaring torches burned brightly on each side of the opening of the marble tree, and Corvaire beckoned for them to sit side by side in front of the tree, and with all the dozens behind them. Mud laid behind Stone. They all sat next to each other, cross-legged with only the sounds of the burning fires, the whistling of the star-chilled winds, and the chattering of crickets filling the space between them. Stone's knees bobbed nervously as those dark green eyes still burned into his mind. They were so vivid, so crystal-like in their stare upon him. Their gaze was so foggy; faded, yet so familiar.

"Welcome, friends of Marilyn the Conjurer," a woman with frazzled hair said to the side of the chestnut-colored wooden door at the front of the marble tree. "You have the honor of attending the presence of The Majestic Wilds, protectors of these lands, and seers of truth." The woman's gaze upon them was instructional yet warmed with glee. "They've insisted an audience with you. But before you see them, you must know that you will answer every question they beckon with the truth. This is only for formality. They will know if you are telling the truth before the words even leave your lips. If you dishonor them with lies or deceit, you will be asked to leave the mountain of Elderon for as long as you live."

She didn't ask if they understood, and Stone knew this was a supreme honor and privilege to be a witness to. The woman moved aside with a steathful grace and the door creaked open, moving outward leaving the three of them, and as Stone looked over at him; Corvaire with gleaming eyes.

Out of the dimly lit interior of the tree, three maidens walked out. Ceres gasped. From what Stone expected to be appropriately aged women for being many lifetimes old, the Old Majestics walked out looking no older, and showing no more age than scarless, mid-thirty-year-old woman. One was a dazzling blond with rose-red lips, one ashen-haired with blue eyes that could pierce the sky itself, and one with no hair, and with eyes as deep and black as charcoal.

The woman at the side then proclaimed, "All praise The Wild Majestics; mothers, protectors, and seers of all things."

All the dozens bowed at the sight of the mothers as they looked out upon the crowd, but the bald mother's eyes were fixed upon Stone. He tried to look away, but her gaze was entrancing—it was enthralling. It was like looking into the all-knowing sky and space, but wanting to know all the answers in the beauty of the dark sky.

"Please be seated," the woman at the side of the tent said.

Everyone sat, including Corvaire, and even Mud laid back as if ready to go off to chasing rabbits in his slumber.

"Welcome," the bald mother said. "I am Seretha Valair, first of the Mystics, and honorer of these lands."

"I am Vere Drenar," the blond mother said. "Welcome." She gave them a heartfelt, yet aged smile.

"Gardin Herenstead, the last of the wilds," the third mother said with a slight bow of her head, but more like a slight dip of the chin, all the while looking at Stone.

"We know who you are," Mother Seretha said, looking at Ceres. "We know who you are, and we know of your master and his fate." She was looking at Adler as he appeared a bit nervous. "But we don't quite know who you are."

Stone's heard sank. *They don't know who I am. They don't have the answers I need to know…*

"You're familiar," she said, "like the whisper of a ghost, but without leaving the warmth of a soul left after a bitter, dark departure."

Her dark eyes were entrancing, but Stone felt a looming strength and power behind them that made it hard to look away, but he felt weak looking into them.

"I don't know who I am yet, either, wise mother," he said. "I was hoping to get some of those answers here this eve."

Grimdore groaned from behind their building, rustling as she tried to drift off to sleep, letting her tail flap onto the ground, making it shake for a quick second.

"Marilyn sent you to us," Mother Vere said, as the mothers sat on their knees, looking nearly eye-level into the three of the them. "We've heard that she's no longer with us. She even perished defending you and your honor. We wish to hear about what happened. We'd like to hear it now."

"She did die protecting us—protecting me," Stone said. "There's no greater regret in this short life I've experienced than not being able to save her, as she saved us. She found me after Ceres had liberated me from certain death, being buried in that grave."

"Tell us everything," mother Gardin bade.

For the next hour, Stone and his friends gave every detail they asked for, every second of memory they had with their fallen protector. Every time the mothers asked for more description, the three of them gave it the best they could.

"So, she cast Searing Flesh upon those soldiers?" Gardin asked. "That must have been dire, and quite a violent end to behold of men."

"Yes," Ceres said. "It was quite a gruesome sight to witness."

"And then she fell?" Vere asked.

They all nodded, gloomily.

"And now you are here," Seretha said, with her arms out in front of her, and then raised up to the sky. "You've come far to see us, and for us to see you. Are you ready to hear what we see of you? What we see *in* you?"

"Yes," the three of them said, then Ceres, who was sitting in the middle, reached out and grabbed both of her friends' hands.

"Are you sure?" Gardin asked. "Once you've heard what we have to tell, there is no second life that will come to you of ignorance or bliss. You should know once you have an eye for the true future, it's difficult—nay, impossible—to veer away from your destiny. And destiny always remains one thing —promised."

Each of them nodded, holding each other's hands tightly. "We're ready to hear our fates," Stone said.

"We've lived here for many ages," Seretha said, with her dark eyes gloomy. "We've seen many things; many wars; many victories of men, and many losses. Many lives have come and passed while we've watched over all we could." She leaned in with a startling wink at them. "We've known of your coming for an age..." She leaned back. "But we hoped we'd never have need to find you. But that time we never wished for is upon us, and too many lives have already been lost. You're the key to stopping the Runtue."

The three of them looked at each other with puzzling expressions.

"The Runtue," Vere said, emphasizing the word with puckered lips. "The ones who've come to burn everything."

"You mean the Neferian?" Stone asked, still quite baffled.

"Oh!" Seretha said, slapping her legs in disgust while looking out to the night sky. "That's just a word the kings came up with to make them seem eviler than any other creature. No, they're the Runtue people who've now learned to ride dragons. Well... not so much dragons... we really don't understand how that's come to pass, yet."

"Why are they here?" Ceres asked.

"We don't know yet why they've come," Gardin said. "But

we've known of them all along, and we've known of the prophecy of defeating them for just as long."

Under the marble tree with its tiny, glittering lights hovering around the ends of the leafless branches, Seretha began the tale of the Runtue.

"Many ages ago, you see—" she began, with her dark eyes looking off as if remembering a dream, as it was so long ago. "The Runtue were us. They lived here, worked our soil, drank with us, broke bread with us. But wars can and do show you the worst of us. It was a grueling war. We didn't have bows, arrows, and catapults like we do now. By Crysinthian's holy word, there were hardly any city walls to stop a strong attack. It was sword to sword, spear to spear, fist to fist."

"The Runtue revolted?" Adler asked.

"Revolted?" Seretha said, snapping to meet his gaze. "Another word the kings would teach you. The winning party always gets to choose who created treason. It was the Runtue against the rest of the kings. King Arken was their savior. He wasn't even a king before that, but he was once he led them into battle for the first time. He was actually quite an impressive man all those ages ago. He was articulate, quite charming and able to inspire great swaths of men. We even knew him when he was that man. It's unfortunate how things turn out as time spins its grinding wheel."

"What happened to him?" Stone asked. "We've seen him. He's only got one eye and looks like a madman."

"The kings decided to take both of his eyes," Vere said. "Didn't know he had one again. That's interesting."

"The kings not only took his sight," Gardin said, with her eyes wide. "They took his hands, and his legs below the hip."

"But they didn't kill him?" Ceres said. "That's so cruel. Why not just kill him?"

"That's not how they did things back then," Gardin said. "Death to a soldier was the divine reward for your fight, for your duty. Those that ruled back then decided to send him and all his surviving followers out onto the Obsidian Sea on their own nearly destroyed ships. There was little chance they'd find land, but that was their only chance. For if they ever returned, they were told they'd live lives far worse than the grasp of death could ever do to them."

"Worse than death?" Adler asked.

"They were told if they ever returned," Vere said with saddened eyes, reflecting the torchlight, as Stone noticed Corvaire drop his head. "They'd be thrown into cells and treated like cattle. They'd never see the light of day, but they'd be forced to breed. Every son would be taken to the slave yards for the remainder of their miserable lives, and the girls would be…" She looked down in disgust.

"… Killed at birth," Seretha said. "That's how twisted those kings were back then… War creates the worst in men… and especially in already rotten kings."

"But…" Vere said, brushing her long blond hair over her shoulder with a flick of her neck, "… to all's astonishment, after months upon those boats… they found land. The Runtue had a new home."

"They made it past the storms?" Ceres asked. "Past the Aderon? How's that possible? Nearly every ship out to sea still can't survive that storm's fury."

"They made it," Seretha said. "And somehow they've survived all these thousands of years there. We don't know much that can be told of their new land, its far beyond our magics, and the distance of our gaze."

"How's he lived this long?" Stone asked. "How have you lived this long? If ya' don't mind my asking?"

The three Wild Majestics looked at one another with a bewildered gaze. They sat there, all young-looking women, each with fine skin, rosy cheeks, but there was something different about them that Stone saw in that moment—something out of the ordinary—like staring at an orange leaf twirling while floating down a stream and noticing the beauty in it for the first time. There was an old wisdom in them, far more than a couple of wrinkly-eyed fellows sitting around a table talking of politics. These women—they *knew* things. They'd *seen* things in their long lives. These women—they *decided* things that changes lives, and possibly even the present.

"Only the people in this city know this," Seretha said, looking around at the enamored eyes of those sitting around them. "We would never divulge our wisdom in this way, except that Marilyn found you after we sent her to find you…"

Stone was too nervous to ask about how they knew to send her out after him, so he sat quietly.

"To you, we may seem old," Gardin said.

"A lifetime to you is but a dream to us," Vere said.

"We are like you, and so *un*like you," said Seretha. "We'd never know we were the way we were if we hadn't found it out the difficult way. We are of the Lilitha."

There was a long pause in the conversation as the winds whistled through, the glowing firefly-lights of the marble tree above glowed, and the three mothers sat before them looking at Stone and his friends. He looked up to Corvaire then, who only nodded back.

"The what, sorry?" Adler asked.

"The Lilitha," Ceres said letting go of his hand in a sign of annoyance. "Haven't you heard of them?"

He shook his head.

"You?" she asked Stone, who also shrugged.

"My mother used to sing about them, you don't know this tune?" she hummed a sweet, yet forced melodic tune with a high pitch, which she rattled off a little too quickly to sound elegant.

"No," Adler said, "sorry, don't recall it."

"I've heard it," Corvaire said, breaking his silence. "Ever since I was a lad."

Then Ceres, growing impatient, rattled off the end of the song:

To those who yearn for cute ole' age,
　Ye' bones with crack with fiery rage,

When the winds of time come rushing through,
　We must remember our respects are due,

The ageless ones of lifetimes passed,
　That still draw breath with magics cast,

The Lilitha breathe easy through countless score,
　And thanks to thee, guardians of lore!

"That's pretty," said Stone, enjoying her song, even if her pitch was slightly off—she wasn't trying to create a masterpiece, but it was sweet.

"I like that one!" Gardin said with a smile. "You'll have to sing the rest of that to us some other time. And you can sing it like you are trying to entertain next time too." She winked.

"Yes," Seretha said. "We found when we reached our current age of appearance that we were to grow no older, our bodies would change no further, but our minds continued to acquire all sorts of knowing, and our magic grew deep into us. We are of the Lilitha, known as The Old Mothers or Wild Majestics to you. There is only one trio of us in our generations. When we die, at some point another one of us while spawn, grow and learn. We learn so that we may save life, and at this moment, there is so much more life being lost than born. It has to end. That's why we sent Marilyn to find you, Stone… you may be the key."

"I don't know if I am. But I will try…"

Chapter Thirty-Six

"Marilyn said the prophecy about him was vague though," Ceres said. "It said something about when the King of Dark Dragons comes, the dead with aid in his end?"

"It's something like that yes," Seretha said. "But dead isn't the correct word. The prophecy is in our native tongue, and the word Marilyn used to describe 'dead' is *mordina*, more like 'raised from the afterlife.'"

"Was I dead?" Stone leaned in to hear their answers. His heart pounded as they all three looked at each other and bowed their heads slightly to him. His head was beginning to clear from the Antholily by that point.

"Yes," Seretha said. "You were in the lands of the Dead Kings."

"Do you know how I died?" Stone asked. "Do you know how my family died or who they were?"

"We cannot know things in the past that our eyes and minds were not upon," Vere said, stroking her blond hair in front of her chest. "And we don't recognize you. There have been many wars in the last few generations, many lost, and even with our lucid memories, we don't know who you are or where you came from."

Stone's head sank. *Again, no answers...*

"However," Gardin said with a finger raised. "That doesn't mean there is no answer for you to find. Maybe you shouldn't be looking so much to your past, but perhaps to your present."

"What do you mean?" Stone asked.

"The most glaring of all glarings," she said with wide, blue eyes like crystals. "My boy, you've come back from the afterlife. We've *never* seen that in all our years. I believe your answer lies somewhere in there. When and if you find out how that came to be, and for what reason, then perhaps you'll be able to find the answers you seek."

"Where do I even start to find that answer?" Stone said with his hands on his thighs as he sat. "I thought you'd possibly have an answer for me here."

"The answer we give," Seretha said in a dark tone, "is what we've already mentioned to you about why Marilyn sought you out."

"You mean...?" Ceres said in a low tone.

"The Dark King Arken?" said Stone.

The three mothers nodded again.

"It will not be a quick road, or an easy road," Vere said. "You must be cautious. One sighting of him is enough for him to burn away anything that could be buried and resurrected. You'll have to keep to the shadows and find out what you must in order to one day defeat Shadowborn."

"Sounds easy enough." Adler snickered, and he received a sharp elbow in the arm from Ceres and a scowl.

"How do I do that?" Stone asked. "I have no idea how to find the answers or way forward to killing him."

"I'll be clear," Seretha said. "There's nothing about you being the one to *kill* him, it only eludes to you perhaps being the one to *find* how to kill him. There is a great distinction there."

"And..." Gardin said. "We're not going to send you off alone, and without some of our old wisdom."

Stone and his friends looked at one another in surprise.

"By the time you leave Endo Valair off on your quest, you will have at the least, the most basic knowledge of our magics, and you'll have some of the most finely crafted weapons you could dream of. They'll be specially crafted for you, and you'll have a mighty guide with you."

"Who?" Ceres asked.

"I will accompany you," said Corvaire with his arms out and his fists on his hips. "Until this quest is complete, or death's grip finds me by age or dragonfire. I will follow where you need me."

"Knight Drâon Corvaire is one of the best fighters in ages," Seretha said. "He and his sister are of the line of Darakon. They've been legendary warriors almost as long ago as we drew our first breaths."

"You're of the lineage of Darakon?" Adler asked with his eyebrows raised and his shoulders tensed. "Marilyn was too?"

Corvaire closed his eyes and nodded.

"I can't believe I'm sitting next to a Darakon," said Adler. "The guild will never believe this. They haven't heard anything about your family for... fifty years!"

Corvaire smiled. "I'll take you where you need to go to find the answers you seek. But let's not toss around that name everywhere we go, eh?" He winked at Stone. "Too many drunkard charlatans wanting to prove their muster. Takes a lot of me' free time away having to swat away flies everywhere I go."

Stone smirked, and Adler quieted his excitement.

"We'll learn magic?" Ceres then asked; now with herself brimming with enthusiasm as her knees bobbed.

"If we're able to pass some knowledge to you," Gardin said. "And you prove worthy of wielding such power, then yes, we will teach you some of our ways."

Ceres slapped her knees with a great grin upon her freckled face, and with her green eyes beaming with glee.

Adler groaned.

"How did Marilyn learn her magic?" Stone asked. "Was she born with it like you?"

"No," Vere said. "We've taught her and Corvaire some of the spells we thought would be most useful."

Stone looked up at Corvaire. "How long did it take?"

Corvaire looked up at the stars and scratched his chin. Then he looked back down at Stone's waiting gaze. "Ten years?"

"Years?" Stone gasped.

"You will not be in this city for ten years, Stone," Seretha said with a wave of her hand as her bald head reflected the torchlight. "You are much more urgently needed out there. I fear we do not have the answers here that you need to find the way to defeat Arken. We will teach you what we can, in as short of a time as we can."

"Is there anything else you can tell us about him?" Ceres asked. "You said you don't know how he survived all these years, but do you know anything else?"

The three mothers looked at one another. "He and his people are far different than what they were when they lived upon these lands with us. They've changed into something else. Even the dragons they ride are creatures we've naught seen ever in our skies. There's something out on the Neferian Isle that they found that created what they are now."

"And…" Vere said. "King Arken… used to be a friend to us…"

Stone gasped.

"He was a different soul back then," Seretha said softly. "Back when he had a soul."

"Yes," Gardin said. "Thousands of years ago he came here and ate and drank with us. He was a kind and loving man back then."

"Do you think he would remember you now?" asked Ceres.

"I do not know the answer to that question," Seretha said. "I only know that he had blood and ash on his mind. He seeks to undo all the wrongs he was dealt all those ages ago. There is a newfound power in him that we sense—a power whose roots we cannot find. It's as if he's become a divine being."

"Like a powerful sorcerer that has found the gift of invulnerability," Vere said with narrow eyes.

"But there must be a way to defeat him," Gardin said. "*You* need to find that way while we continue our search here."

Corvaire interjected there, "And there's no way those cross-eyed kings are going to stop him while they're quarreling with one another over a bit of land or pride."

"The dragons too," added Ceres. "The dragons who fight the Neferian, they're all dying. We can't let them keep dying while trying to help us."

The three mothers nodded in agreement.

"Yes," Seretha said. "The blood of the dragons is on our hands."

"What do you mean?" Stone asked.

"We called the dragons from the lands of the Arr," Vere said. "A vast desert land to the northeast. Years ago, the dragons returned to the sands. And now we've called them to our aid, for if King Arken succeeds in burning all things living in these lands, he may go off to all other lands in his bloodlust. The dragons are the most powerful creatures in existence, and they always have been. There's still hope they'll be able to find a way to kill the dark dragons, but until then… yes, their blood is on our hands."

Stone's head felt foggy from all the things they'd been telling him. There was so much coming at him, and all the while, after all these things that'd been said, he still had to remember that the mother's key to it all—the answer to saving the lands—was *him*.

"I've never seen anything as violent as a Neferian killing a dragon," Ceres said with a deep sadness in her eyes. "It's a horrible, horrible thing to witness."

"Agreed," Stone said. "I'll try to find a way to stop Arken. Yet, I haven't the faintest idea of where to start looking."

"We'll keep you here with us," Seretha said. "That is, until the light of the next full, blood moon."

"That is no more than a little over six weeks from this night," Vere said.

Stone looked around him then, surrounded by the followers of the mothers who sat behind him with their eyes fixed upon the Old Majestics. Torches burned brightly under the dark star-filled sky with a crescent moon hanging low from the east. *We've only got six weeks? That's not enough time…*

"We will teach you as best we can all the knowledge, you'll need for the road ahead," Gardin said. "We have our best armorers in Verren crafting you weapons of legend already."

A warm smile crossed Adler's face.

"The divine knowledge of even our ancestors before us will help to send haste to the answers we hope you find," Seretha said. "For the Worforgon is vast, and not all roads are straight."

"Yeah," said Adler. "We saw that on the way here."

"We suspect though," Vere said slowly. "There may be something to the Ruins of Aderogon, the place where Ceres unearthed you."

Stone's head cocked.

"The ruins?" Ceres asked. "There's nothing there."

"We know," Gardin said. "We've had many comb over them. But there's something important about Stone being buried and resurrected there. There's something very special about that. But we can't see what... at least... not yet."

"If there's something there," Stone said. "We'll find it."

"Yes, we will," Ceres said in a strong voice.

"We promise you, we will do our best," Adler said.

"One more thing," Seretha said. "You three must stick together. The three of you found each other for a reason. Destiny has woven your fates, intertwined your paths. Stay together, for Stone will need your strengths on this long road."

"Ceres Rand of Briewater," Vere said, making Ceres stir on the ground. "Over the weeks we will share with you stories of your family's past if you wish. We'll share with you tales of your grandparents and their grandparents before them. You are stronger than you know, you just need to remember your parents' passing wasn't your fault." Ceres whimpered and began to cry. "You were young. There's nothing you could've done to stop it. You must only grow now and protect the ones you love—because now you are strong enough to."

Ceres clasped her hands over her face and wept. Stone draped his arm over her back. "I'm sorry, Ceres, I didn't know."

"Adler Caulderon of Valeren," Gardin said. "Remain vigilant. Your training will prove useful even if you feel your lessons weren't complete enough." He seemed startled by that statement as he seemed uncomfortable as he shifted where he sat. "Your destiny is not to belong to the guild. You are no more an assassin than those that sit next to you. You are a warrior. You are a soldier of righteousness. You won't slink in the shadows; you'll fight in silver-clad armor with a banner behind you someday. Your mentor deserved his fate."

"What?" Adler asked. "How could you know?"

"We know," Gardin said, glaring into him. "You must let your soul free, for there is much work to do. And focus is needed to help Stone. Remember that the past doesn't define us, for when we all meet Crysinthian at the gates of the Golden Realm, He will look at our greatest accomplishments, not our lowest defeats."

Adler looked like he wanted to say something, but then closed his eyes and bowed his head. "I understand. Thank you."

"Stone…" Seretha said, and was going to say something, but her head snapped back to Grimdore. Stone's gaze followed, and he saw the mighty dragon had perked her head up from her slumber and glared out at the northern sky.

Corvaire's sword rustled on his hip.

"What's happening?" Ceres asked softly.

Every single set of eyes in the city was looking to the dark northern sky.

"I don't know," Stone said back in the silence.

That's when he heard the roar off in the distance—that same terrible roar he'd never hoped to hear again…

Chapter Thirty-Seven

Grimdore spread her long, teal wings out wide as she turned to face the direction of the loud roar out in the distance. The thick muscles in her back tightened as the rows of spikes down her back protruded sharply out with the long red line rolling down her back. She turned to let her red eyes with the lively yellow slits scan the night sky for the source of the screech—but Stone already knew what it was...

As the teal dragon stood up on her hind legs, letting her long, powerful tail sway from side to side, Stone looked to the mothers, who had all slowly gotten to their feet to look up to the sky. Corvaire was walking toward them as Stone, his friends and everyone behind them were getting up.

"We've got to get you underground," Corvaire said while holding Seretha's arm and leading her away from the tree, toward the entrance of the city. The other citizens bustled out of the main courtyard urgently; scattering in different directions.

Grimdore growled heavily, letting a smoky fire brim in her long neck.

"Come!" Corvaire said, waving his hand to Stone, Ceres, and Adler. "Hurry now." He was leading Seretha, Vere, and Gardin away with him. "The others know what to do."

"Is it coming this way?" Ceres asked as she ran behind Stone, who was pulling her along by the wrist. Stone looked over his shoulder just in time to see Grimdore flapping her mighty wings. The teal dragon then let out a rippling screech that Stone could feel deep within his chest. He was holding Ceres' wrist with one hand, and the other unsheathed his sword, letting its steel shimmer in the light of the torches and the crescent moon.

After Grimdore had finished with that long screech and had lifted herself from the grassy ground and up into the air, the Neferian let out another roar that reminisced of shattering glass and exploding fire.

The Wild Majestics ran in front of Corvaire, as he led them toward the front entrance of the city. Their long dress tails flew behind them as they ran, and Stone wondered if this was the first time a Neferian had come close to Endo…

"It's getting closer!" Adler said from behind Stone and Ceres. "I can see the rider!"

Stone turned to see Grimdore hovering fifty feet about the marble tree. It grunted and snapped its jaws and its long tail hung low, marked with a long, tooth-like spike at the tip of her tail. Below her, in the dark sky, he could see the dark dragon gliding toward them, and he could see the rider perched upon its back. Something about the rider looked familiar to him, but it was so distant, he couldn't tell what gave him that feeling. The dragon was still doused in shadow, but the star and moon-light gave the beast an eerie, white glow on its curves and angles. He could already tell that the dark dragon was a monster far larger than Grimdore.

"We've got to get you all underground," Corvaire said urgently, with his wavy, black hair clinging to the back of his neck from nervous sweat. "Under the mountain!" The Neferian roared again, shattering the sky around them, while Grimdore continued her hovering over the city.

Stone and the mothers weren't even halfway to the city entrance by then, and he looked back to see the Neferian was flying at them at a terrifying speed.

"We're not going to make it," Adler huffed as they ran. Corvaire didn't respond.

Grimdore groaned from deep within her chest, letting out a large puff of black smoke lined with an orange, streaking fire. Stone could feel the intensity of the heat all the way back where they were from the dragon.

"Just out of the gate," Corvaire said, "and to the left. There's a secret door that leads deep into the mountain. You'll be safe in there."

"Nothing can keep us safe from that thing," Ceres said, "I've seen them fight. A mountain won't shield us if it's coming for the mothers."

"It may be coming for us," Adler said.

Another thunderous roar exploded from the Neferian as it was nearly upon the city, with its wings out wide and its head fully extended toward them. Its eyes were a hellish, beady yellow. Its crimson head was thick with strong muscles as it showed its sharp teeth. Upon its back the rider glowered down upon them, and Stone felt as if he was looking straight down at him. He wore a thick, gray armor that looked like rock; he wore a helmet with two upward curling horns that resembled an old oak. And once the rider was fully into view, Stone could see then that the rider had only one eye.

King Arken... its him... he's after The Wild Majestics!

"It's him," Stone said. "The Dark King. He's here..."

Corvaire stopped in his run yet ushering the mothers to continue toward the gate. He scanned the Neferian. "You sure?"

"Yes," Stone said, standing next to him with his sword drawn. Corvaire drew his own sword. "Go." He looked at Ceres who was standing next to him. She responded by shaking her head and drawing her own sword. Mud was next to him and barking loudly up at the approaching monster.

"It's almost here," Adler said as the two dragons exchanged roars. "We can't fight it. We should go with the others. It's going to kill us if we stay here."

"He's right," Corvaire said. "Follow the mothers. I'll stay here to keep it distracted."

"You'll die," Ceres said to him, with his hair whipping in the wind.

"Don't worry about me." He winked. "I've got a few tricks he won't expect if I need them. Now go! Quickly!"

"Come," Ceres said as she turned to run, grabbing Stone's hand. "You're not staying either!"

"It is him," Corvaire said grimly as he now saw the king upon the huge, dark dragon. "He's here..."

The Neferian crashed into Grimdore with a powerful blow of muscle, scales, teeth, and claws. Grimdore bit and pawed at the dark dragon as it toppled backward. But just as it looked as if the Neferian was going to land upon the fighting, teal dragon, the dark dragon shoved Grimdore aside. It was flying past the scampering teal dragon then, and it was heading toward the entrance of the city. It was flying toward the mothers.

"No!" Corvaire yelled as it flew over him. "Here! Come back here!"

"Run!" Stone yelled to the three women as they were nearing the break in the rocks that led out of the city.

Corvaire then held his sword up at the Neferian as it rushed over. "*Arachanor!*" he called out into the air. Grimdore fell onto her back with a ground-shaking crash. She quickly got to her feet and began to fly toward the dark dragon. Stone, who was running as fast as he could toward the mothers, watched as small pools of a silky, white thread cracked out of the ground before them. And as the Neferian was almost upon the entrance, and with a white fire crackling out of its mouth, and streams of smoke poured out of its nostrils, the white threads shot up at it, wrapping their thin threads over its wings, back and neck.

"It's Corvaire," Adler said. "He's using his magic!"

The Neferian thrashed its neck and wings, snapping some threads as more wrapped around him. King Arken himself slashed at the threads, cutting the ones upon the dark dragons back.

"They're like spiderwebs," Ceres said with a sense of hope in her voice. "Run mothers!"

Stone watched as the three mothers slipped into the crevasse as the enormous dragon roared overhead, fighting off the webbing, but just as he breathed a sigh of relief, all his hope of beating the king then extinguished as a white-hot dragonfire erupted from its mouth. It was a wide blast of surging heat that burned the hairs off his forearms even at that distance. He watched helplessly in terror as the flames ripped into the crevasse and completely enveloped the rock wall to the city.

"No..." Ceres gasped.

"Seretha!" Corvaire yelled, running toward the dragon.

Grimdore then landed on the Neferian's back with its weight sending it to the ground as the webs continued to shoot up from the ground, winding their way around its body. Grimdore's teeth bit at its arm and wing as it was perched upon the dark dragon's back. The Neferian's fire left a trail leading to the entrance of the city as grass burned and a wide, black stain of smoldered ground pointed to where the mothers had run.

Each of them ran at the dragon who, for the moment, was

fighting off the increasingly growing white threads, and trying to get off its chest so as to fight off the ferocious teal dragon.

"Come on, Grimdore," Stone said to himself. "You can do it…"

It was then that she blasted the dragon and rider with a punishing inferno of orange dragonfire. King Arken only looked up at the dragon as it spread its mouth wide as it erupted its fire upon him. Corvaire, Stone and the others ran past the violent fight, heading toward where the mothers had gone.

Grimdore's dragonfire, unfortunately had the unintended effect as the webbing upon the dark dragon's back singed and burned, freeing the great beast from its restraint. It whipped its head back and bit at her neck. It was then that King Arken left his saddle and dropped down to the ground. Stone looked back and saw his one, dark eye glaring at him.

As the two dragons fought, and the Dark King walked toward them slowly with a thick, white sword at his side, Corvaire and the others ran into the crevasse. And once they emerged on the other side, Corvaire stopped in his tracks, and Ceres clasped both hands over her mouth.

"Oh, no," she cried.

Stone looked between them and saw the charred remains of three blackened bodies, each burned away, stuck in their cowering positions like terrorized statues.

"He killed them," Adler said. "He killed them… he used to be their friend… why would he do this?"

"Because he is evil," Stone said, with his fist clenched tightly. "We're going to make him die for this."

Corvaire knelt and began a quiet prayer.

"They can't be gone," Ceres said, shaking her head. "The mothers can't die. They just can't!"

"Get under the mountain," Corvaire said to them as he

stood back up, looking back into the city. "Go now, there's no time!"

"No," Stone said firmly. "We'll end this now." He was glaring into the Dark King's one eye as he strode toward them, with the two dragons viciously fighting behind him with a mix of blinding white flame and dark orange fire. The dragons tore at each other savagely with tooth and claw, and Grimdore had long cuts down her ribcage and back. Thick trails of red blood coursed out of them as she continued her fight.

"I said, go!" Corvaire said again, giving a stern look at Stone. "You're the one who's supposed to figure out how to kill him. You're our best chance. You've got to get out of here before it's too late. Now, go!"

"I said no," Stone said, returning the stare. "I'm not running away anymore. We can kill him right here, right now, and we can end all of this."

"Stone…" Ceres said softly. "We can't kill him… we're going to die just like they did if we stay…"

"I don't care," Stone said while Mud barked at the approaching Dark King. "I'm not leaving. I'm going to kill him or die trying…"

Chapter Thirty-Eight

Scorching hot winds blew at them from the warring dragons, intertwined in a chaotic and violent mess of bites with thick jaw muscles and sharp teeth. The fires burned each other as they battled on the ground beyond the Dark King. Stone put his arms up in front of his face to hide it from the heat. Arken's leathery cape blew in front of him, whipping as it did so. And his one eye, that one dark eye leered at them as he strode heavy strides.

"There's still time," Corvaire said with a stern voice. Stone looked up at him and he had a focused intensity on his face. His hazel eyes held a wet glisten upon them in the heat and his dark hair, now wet with sweat flowed behind him. "Leave at once. Its madness to stand against the king."

"You'll die too," Adler said, holding his sword out in front of him. "We're not going to just let them die without trying to defend their honors."

"You do no honor if you don't draw breath," he responded.

"Stone," Ceres said, gently laying her hand on his forearm. "We'll be better prepared later, but we have'ta be alive ta' do it.

Corvaire's a knight, he's one of the Darakon, we aren't. Seretha and the others bade us to go out and find how ta' kill the king, but they wouldn't want us dying with them here."

"She's right," Adler said, "whether ya' can see it now or not. But deep down inside, past your anger, you know it's true."

"Go!" Corvaire yelled, startling Stone as Grimdore let out an ear-piercing screech from a bite to her neck. Stone took a step back, and Ceres pulled him to come with her toward the entrance into the mountain. But his eyes remained upon Corvaire as he'd been pulled back four steps. Corvaire held both his arms out wide, with his shining sword in his right hand. Bands of white smoke appeared from both hands, and they curled up his arms to his shoulders as they glowed a bright, warm hue.

"Another spell," Adler said. "See, he's got a plan to take care o' the king."

King Arken was only a few dozen paces from them then as the smoke blossomed on Corvaire's arms. He'd adjusted to a wide stance, and Stone stopped his pace backward.

"C'mon!" Ceres yelled through the loud, fighting dragons beyond the approaching king.

He watched as Corvaire let out a loud, groaning yell, sending his arms forward in a fantastic arc, and throwing the white curls of steam out at the king. They shot out like water cascading down a powerful waterfall, and they quickly exploded into the king with a wild fury. They whooshed around his tall body, tightening and squeezing. The puffy, cloudy steam had then turned to a sheet of white like ice on his body.

By the time the steam had all but vanished, the king was frozen in a sheet of hard ice that resembled marble. Corvaire breathed heavily, as the spell had seemed to take a lot out of him.

"Is he..." Stone said.

"Not dead," said Corvaire. "I've just stopped him. He should remain that way for a few hours—a day if we're…"

That statement proved to be so far from the truth that Ceres again began pulling Stone back as the marble figure of the king let out a cracking sound, and soon chips broke from it.

"It's not working," Adler said. "He's too strong…"

"Stone, I'm going to cut yer' legs off and drag you if you don't come right this instant!" she growled.

The layer of thin ice exploded off the king like a shattered mirror, and he stood there, with his one menacing eye glaring at them—his cape blew in the hot winds of the fires and his two-horned helmet shadowy in silhouette.

"What do you want?" Stone yelled at the king. "Why'd you have to kill them? Why do you have to kill anyone? What have they ever done to you? You were friends once! You're supposed to love your friends, not burn them to death!"

Corvaire and the others were surprised by his call out of the king, and that he had tried talking to him at all. Ceres' grip loosened, as she seemed to be interested in the king's next action.

In a sudden jerking motion, the king cocked his head slightly to the right. The Neferian dragon then let out a menacing groan of pain as Grimdore unleashed her own bite upon its chest.

"You…" the king said in a low growl. "You have no idea what you speak of…"

"They were as old as you, older even!" Stone said. "They said you were friends once, before the kings banished you. Those kings are dead now! Why punish the living? We did nothing to you!"

King Arken Shadowborn's eye fixed on him as he gave an angry glower.

"Your kings are innocent?" the king said, his voice rumbled like some powerful god. "You are innocent? Who is innocent? You believe your Wild Majestics were innocent? They were sick…" A dark liquid oozed from his mouth as he said that, with his mouth turned down, and disgust was on his breath. "They turned on me. What *friend* turns on another?"

"They didn't turn on you," Corvaire said. "You betrayed them. You made a promise to them that you broke. It was your fault your people got banished."

"My fault?" King Arken said, taking a lurking step forward, pointing at him.

"You made a promise," said Corvaire, taking a step forward of his own. "And you broke it."

The Dark King growled. "You know naught of what you speak. You only recant the lies of Seretha and the others. You're a puppet pulled by their strings. There's a history untold in these lands, hidden and twisted, but I'm going to bring back the truth, and all that live in these lies will burn. They'll all burn!"

"Not while we're still standing," Stone said, pulling his arm from Ceres' grasp. He held his sword out at the king and went to stand next to Corvaire.

Corvaire whispered to him, "If you're in this now, aim for the weak points: the eye, mouth, throat, and groin."

Adler then said, "Ah hell with it all," as he went to stand in line with them, with his own sword in hand.

"You go," Stone said to Ceres. "We don't all need to die this day."

She sighed with her head down. "Stubborn son of a bitch." She went and stood in line with them. "If I die because of you, I'm never gonna let you rest in peace."

"Fly away from this place," Corvaire shouted. "Fly back to your lands and be with your people. We don't need this war. No one is going to win, and so many are going to die. There's no dishonor in going back. This is all so senseless. The revenge you seek died ages ago. Your rage will not end here—it is too far within."

"You're wrong, Dakaran man," he groaned. "I will avenge my people here. And whoever does not kneel will feel what my rage holds. It's limitless, boundless, and exacting. While your lands burn, I'll return back to my lands, bringing my people here to live the way they should have all those years ago. No more pain, no more suffering, no more humiliation. The present will become what it always was meant to be. Truth will become law here. No more false kings. No more queen's snubbing those beneath them, no more idols. I will bring these lands into the future. But first, fires will burn, swords will shed blood, and these kings will squeal like livestock from terror."

"That will not happen," Corvaire said, through clinched teeth.

The Dark King gritted his own yellow teeth, with that same liquid oozing out of his mouth.

At the front entrance to the mystical city of Endo Valair, in the midst of a clear-skied, starry night, the protector of the city battled the Dark King's dragon. Incinerating fires spewed, dragon blood poured to the ground in pools, and a glow emanated from the violent battle. The Neferian's tail rushed through the air in a huge arc, smashing into two of the white structures around the marble tree, sending them crumbling down. As the dragons fought, and the mountain shook from the tremendous force of the two fighting dragons, a man with no memory of his past rushed at the Dark King with his sword in hand, letting out a loud battle cry as he did so. The three behind him ran after him, and toward the king.

Arken widened his stance, twisted the grip of his sword and readied his long, dark gray sword at his side.

"I can't believe we're doing this!" Adler yelled as they rushed at the king, which didn't take long until they were upon him.

"And you," Arken said with his mean eye glowering at Stone. "You're the one Seretha and the others said would be the one to defeat me? You're just a child, a scared little boy who doesn't even know his own past. What can you do against me, Stone? You have no power against me. You're going to die, praying to false gods to save you as you feel my sword's steel deep in your heart. There's nowhere you can hide from me. I'll hunt you down to the corners of these lands. I'll not rest until I've tasted your blood, and your heart is ripped from your chest."

Corvaire got to him first, but in a blinding flash of speed, the king sent his sword in a roaring arc at him, which luckily Corvaire was agile enough that he ducked and rolled underneath. But to even the king's surprise it seemed, his sword met another as Stone blocked his arcing swipe away. The king drew his sword back and sent it into another swipe, and Stone knew he couldn't match his strength, but from those first two blows it appeared he could at least match his speed.

"I'm not afraid of you," Stone yelled out. "If the mothers said I'm the one to kill you, then kill you I will!"

Adler and Ceres stood on the outside, waiting for their opportune moment to enter the fray—looking for a weak spot in the king's defenses where they could strike.

Stone and the king exchanges quick blows, with Stone moving like a fully seasoned, and decades-long trained swordsman. Arken growled in annoyance at Stone's agility, and Corvaire had regained his footing and was fighting the king from the backside. Arken let out a mighty roar, pushing both of them back to stand side by side as he moved back.

The fight had only been going on over a minute, and Stone's confidence was rising rapidly as the Dark King's eye glowed a vibrant red. All the while, Mud had been feverishly barking at the king.

"What's he doing?" Stone asked while deflecting one of his blows.

"Don't know," Corvaire said. "Keep fighting but be ready. He was once a moderately-talented wizard."

"*He* has magic?" Stone asked in disbelief.

"Of course, he does…" Adler grumbled.

The red eye of the king grew brighter and brighter until it became a beaming red glow on his hands, that ran up his sword, engulfing it in a white-hot glow like it had just been pulled from a forge. He let it reign down a mighty strike at them, which each of them moved to parry, but instead it slid through their hardened steel blades like a smooth, sharp glass through snow.

Corvaire and Stone were left holding swords that were half what they were, and they looked at each other in disbelief as the king held up his glowing, white-hot sword before them.

"Your souls will be sent off to the Dark Realm where they will burn for eternity," he growled. "No one in this life can defeat me. I'm immortal. I've suffered more than any man alive, and now, I'm going to show this world a taste of my pain."

"Grimdore!" Corvaire called out. "*Alies borun eradidore!*"

"What?" Stone gasped, as he watched the teal dragon blow a hot burst of raging fire upon the Nefarian, brushing him back enough to flap his wings.

"You'll not escape your fates," the king said, raising his sword again. What happened next sent a terrifying shudder through Stone's body. He was so fixated by the giant dragon flying toward them, and the king's hot sword about to attack them—he hadn't noticed what was happening behind the king.

"No!" Ceres yelled out.

From behind the king, a dozen men and women ran at him with swords and pitchforks in hand. They stabbed, sliced and poked his body, but nothing pierced his thick armor and skin.

Mud sank his teeth into his leg, trying to rip his flesh. He slowly turned in annoyance as he growled. He kicked one of the men so ferociously in the stomach it sent him flying back through the air, rolling violently end over end on the ground that he lay in a broken, motionless position.

"We're leaving," Corvaire said as the dragon landed next to them. "Up!"

"We've got to help them," Stone said, with beads of sweat running down his forehead.

"There's nothing we can do for them. Up!"

Ceres and Adler climbed up the wing of the dragon.

"Mud, come!" Adler yelled, causing the dog to run from fighting the king to climbing up the dragon's wing into his lap.

"There's got to be something," Stone said, worry heavy in his voice. "Use your magic. We can still fight!"

"There's no time," Corvaire said, urging him to get on Grimdore's back.

"I can still fight; I can still fight!"

"Stone," Ceres said as the king slaughtered the attacking men and women with his blazing sword.

"What?" he said back frantically.

"They're doing this for you," she said.

"No!"

The Neferian dragon had gotten to its feet and was flapping its mighty wings then.

Ceres looked deep into Stone's eyes with her mossy, green eyes filled with tears of worry.

"There's no time," she said. "And this isn't our day. We will have our day, but it's not now. Now I *need* you to get up on this bloomin' dragon!"

Stone sighed with a deep breath.

"We're not giving up," Adler said. "We're just gettin' ready to fight another day when we're more ready. Now, up!"

Stone reached out and grabbed his hand, who pulled him up, and Corvaire quickly mounted the dragon after.

Grimdore flapped her massive wings and her feet left the ground as the Neferian took to the air behind them, and the bloody cries of the citizens of Endo called out. Stone looked down at them as they lay in misery, and the Dark King's one red eye trailed their path through the air as his cape flapped in the winds.

"Fly like the winds!" Corvaire said to the dragon. "Fly as if the power of The Wild Majestics flowed through your veins and muscles. For if we die this night, there will be no stopping King Arken ever…"

Chapter Thirty-Nine

Upon the back of the great dragon and guardian of Endo Valair Stone clutched on tightly onto a thick, teal scale. He also held in Mud tightly to this side as the winds rushed past him as the mighty dragon flapped its wings. Stone felt a wetness on his hands and pulled one up to see him palm covered in thick, warm dragon blood. He looked up the long neck of the dragon and saw his friends all glaring down at Endo in disbelief and worry. Even Corvaire, who normally seemed collected, had misty eyes as he gazed down upon the city.

The massive Neferian dragon that was chasing them was closing the distance between them quickly with its wings nearly twice the size of the dragon they were upon. Its dozens of yellowing, sharp teeth showed as it snarled a wicked growl. White dragonfire brimmed from deep down within its chest. Grimdore had shown she was strong enough to withstand a blast of the dark dragon's fire, but none of them perched upon her back would last a split second when those fires came at them.

A deep worry rolled over Stone. Not for him. Not for

Grimdore, but for his friends and the people back there in the city that he'd left behind. The Neferian's fire raged from within its chest and neck as it rolled its neck back, and then opened it scaly mouth wide, ready to spew hellishly hot flames at them.

Grimdore turned abruptly in flight, shooting down to the right.

"Hold on!" said Corvaire as each of them ducked down onto her back, holding on tightly, and Stone gripped the scruff of Mud's neck, pulling the dog into him. The loud burst of the Neferian's hot fire blasted just to the side of them, and it nearly took the air from Stone's lungs from the unrelenting heat. Grimdore's flight was astonishing as Stone felt as if he was falling through the air, with the speed they were hurtling down with. The Neferian arced its head to pursue them, but Grimdore proved to be a superior flyer.

The dark dragon's breath seemed to wear out, and it inhaled—extinguishing the flames—but continued in its pursuit… until… Stone looked back to see its head cock back, and then with abrupt flaps of its wings, it started to fly back up to the mountain, leaving Grimdore escaping quickly back down the slopes.

"What happened?" asked Ceres, half-smiling, half-concerned, with her face flushed.

"It's going back to its master…" Adler said. "Crysinthian save whoever is left up there… it's a slaughter. They don't stand a chance…"

"Take us back up there," Stone said in the rushing winds. "Grimdore!"

"*Passa al terran dava*," Corvaire said to the dragon.

"No," Stone yelled. "We have to go back. We have to help all those people!"

"Stone," Adler said. "Don't you see? They're already gone… They did what they did for you. You have to survive. That's the whole point about us fleeing. You have to let it go!"

Stone felt an overwhelming rage and pain down in his stomach. His chest burned, the blood in his arms pumped heavily, and his eyes watered as he looked back up at the mountain and the dark dragon flying up there to kill. He hated that feeling. He hated that helpless feeling like he was trapped down in his own coffin and not being able to break free. He resented that he'd given in to his fate all the way back in the cold, lonely place. Feeling a regret that he wasn't stronger, that he wasn't good enough, that he wasn't able enough to kill that king back there—it was almost too much for him to bear in that moment.

"I swear upon everything I know and love in this world," he said. "Upon the lives of every innocent person that walks these lands, I'm going to kill that demon. I'm going to make him pay for what's he done, and all of the lives he's taken. You hear me Shadowborn? I'm coming for you!"

※

Twenty minutes later Grimdore attempted to land on a hill overlooking the plains before the mountain and sea. It was more of a crash than they'd have cared for. Each of them was flung off the mighty dragon's back as she collided with the ground as her back legs buckled from fatigue. She collapsed onto her chest and neck, shaking the ground and bumping Stone up her neck before being thrown into one of her back-horns which hit him in the arm and thigh, afterward he fell to the ground onto that same side with a *thump*. Mud landed on his feet of course—he always seemed to. Stone lay on his side in pain as the dog licked the side of his face.

"Everyone all right?" Ceres asked, getting up to her feet, looking at her friends and the dragon that was wheezing, trying to catch its breath. Stone stood and checked on his friends too, as Ceres seemed unscathed, Adler was holding the side of his face as a trickle of blood rolled down his cheek. Corvaire stood up with great strength, and went over to Grimdore's head, stroking it.

"*Al aimen herr reszo ahor Grimdore... reszo...*" he whispered to her.

Then they all heard the shattering roar of the Neferian at the top of the mountain. They could vaguely make out that Arken had mounted the dragon's back again, and to all of their horror, the dark dragon was breathing its white-hot flames down upon the city in great swaths.

Corvaire watched with his mouth agape, but then lowered his head, letting his hair cover his face.

"The city is burning," Stone said, shaking his head from side to side. I know what you told me was true Adler, but this is too much. He's killing everyone up there. He's erasing Endo from history."

"He'll pay for his crimes," Adler said. "There's nothing we can do now. We've got to get moving again."

Ceres went and ran her hands down the thick gashes on Grimdore's body.

"You need to rest, pretty thing," she said. "We're alive because of you. You just rest. We'll take care o' you now."

"She needs to get to the sea," Corvaire said. "She can rest a few minutes longer, but she'll have to take flight soon again."

"What?" asked Ceres with a high pitch.

"She's a sea dragon. The waters will heal her. But it will take time. We'll need to be off on our own. We've got to find cover before Arken comes down after us. Come now, we have to make it to some woods or a cave soon."

"She can't fly," Ceres said. "She's injured."

"Oh, young lady," Corvaire said. "This dragon sure can. You don't know her strength. She's going to be just fine. Give her ten minutes and then watch her take back to the skies.

She's not going to die this night. She'll live another thousand years if the winds are good to her."

"Yes, let's make haste for cover," Adler said, looking out onto the horizon back east as the earliest of the morning's rays began to poke up.

"Can you walk?" Corvaire asked Stone.

"Yes, yes, I'm fine."

Up on the mountain the dark dragon took long dives over the city, burning it down with great blasts of its white fire. Endo was then completely engulfed in a raging inferno.

The four of them and Mud ran off through the tall grass, as fields of it rolled in the early morning breeze. A red sun crept up from the vastness of the great plains, illuminating fiery clouds over it. After a lot of running, they indeed heard Grimdore roar to life with a loud screech that echoed through the lands, causing a startling silence. Every chattering insect, slithering snake and gnawing squirrel cowered in silence at the terrifying roar of the dragon.

Far up on the mountain, the dark dragon was circling the city that was still ablaze as Grimdore made her way out to sea. She'd taken a route a bit more to the north, and as they'd all turned to watch, she disappeared into the dark waves with a splash—and then she was gone.

Down at the bottom of a ravine, they'd spotted a small alcove with a rocky outcrop. Running down the grassy hill, they found there was a small cave with which they could huddle into and hide. Corvaire rushed them in and was the last one to enter as the sun had risen enough to light the green grass all around them in a warm, red haze.

They all collapsed in exhaustion. Stone rested on his knees to catch his breath, Adler sat with his back to the cave's rocky wall, and Ceres fell onto Stone's shoulder—gently sobbing. Corvaire let out a deep sigh as he stood with his back against the rock and finally sheathed his broken sword. Mud panted heavily with his head resting on the cool ground.

For twenty minutes they all stayed there, silently, yet letting out sobs every now and then for the fallen.

"What do we do now?" Stone asked finally, looking up specifically to Corvaire.

"Sleep," he said in a soft voice. "This isn't going to be a short journey. There's many things that need to happen for us to find our path forward."

"What do you mean?" Adler asked, scratching his head.

"The Wild Majestics have been murdered," Corvaire said, looking out to the swaying grass glowing in red sunlight. "Word of their passing will spread quickly, and the search for the new mothers is going to happen soon."

"What?" Ceres asked. "New mothers?"

"With all the ill tidings happening in these lands," he said. "New mothers should be awakening shortly. The balance of life will cause it to happen… it could be any day now."

"Who will be looking for them?" Stone asked. "Who even knows of their existence?"

"The problem with such power that the mothers wield is that others will seek to take it for their own."

"The kings?" Ceres asked. "The kings are going to look for the new mothers and make them soldiers for them?"

"More than kings seek power here," said Corvaire with keen eyes. "Many will be looking for these woman, but we'll have to find them first."

"We?" Adler asked with his arms out. "Couldn't they be anywhere? Where would we even start looking?"

"I have my ways…" Corvaire said.

"Magic?" Ceres asked with wide eyes.

"No," he said with a rare grin. "I cheat…"

"You cheat?" Adler asked. "What does that mean?"

"You'll see…"

There was a long moment of silence and contemplation.

"Corvaire," Stone whispered. "Seretha and the others mentioned weapons and magic… Is that all gone with their passing?"

"A bit o' magic sure wouldn't hurt in finding the mothers," Ceres said with her head tilted to the side.

"Oh, you just want magic just to have magic…" Adler mocked.

"Shut it! Or when I do learn magic, I'll turn you into a blood-suckin' bat!"

"Your weapons are being forged," Corvaire said. "We'll need to get them. While we're heading that way, I'll see if any of you are capable of wielding magic. Not everyone can, and you're all reaching the age where you'd be past the age anyway. I can't promise you anything. But if it's there in you, I'll do my best."

Ceres gleamed at that statement with a wide smile, her hands in her lap as she bounced up and down.

"How are we going to figure out a way to kill Arken?" Stone said, sending a deep gloom upon them once more.

"Stone, young man," Corvaire said with a dark gaze. "That's for you to figure out for us. It's up to you to find a way to kill him, for every life in these lands depends on it…"

The End

Continued in Book II:
The Majestic Wilds

Author's Notes

Well, I don't think any of them saw that coming... And after all that time that Ceres wanted to learn magic...

With this first book I wanted to tell the tale of three souls meeting each other by fate or chance.

Stone, with no lack of bravery is stuck with the reality that he may never know where he came from, or if he ever had a family.

Ceres, impulsive, stubborn and somewhat arrogant at the beginning finally starts to give in to acceptance of the boys, and of Mud.

Adler, I like to have fun with because he can be a pretty off the cuff sort of kid, but also knowledgeable about the lands from his former master.

Mud's just a badass mofo. That dog ain't scared o' nothin!

Telling this story, I really wanted to throw them, especially Stone, into the middle of two wars going on. The lands are in chaos, while the cities themselves are just trying to keep a sort of order while the Neferian battle other dragons out there. The civil wars are still a bit of a mystery. Expect to get to know more about what's really going on in the next few books.

AUTHOR'S NOTES

Loosely, I'm thinking this will be a five-book series, but who knows how the story unfolds. I didn't plan on killing all of the Mystics, in the first book, but the search is on for the new ones!

Peace and love, C.K.

Continue Reading

The Story Continues in
The Majestic Wilds.

About the Author

Having grown up in the suburbs of Kansas, but never having seen a full tornado or a yellow brick road, I have been told more than my fair share of times while traveling, 'You're not in Kansas anymore.' I just respond, 'Never heard that one,' with a smile.

In the 'burbs' though, I found my passion for reading fantasy stories early. Reading books with elves, orcs and monsters took my young imagination to different worlds I wanted to live in.

Now, I create my own worlds. Not so much in the elves and orc vein, but more in the heroes versus dragons one-- there's a difference, right?

Yes, I grew up with The Lord of the Rings and tons of RA Salvatore books on my shelves, along with some cookbooks, comics, and a lot of video games too.

Other passions of mine are coffee, good beer, and hanging around the gym.

To find out more and learn about what I'm working on next please visit CKRieke.com.

C.K. Rieke is pronounced C.K. 'Ricky'.

Go to CKRieke.com and sign-up to join the Reader's Group for some free stuff and to get updated on new books!

www.CKRieke.com

Printed in Great Britain
by Amazon